CW00433610

Copyright © 2022 Jane

Published by The Peapod Press

ISBN: 9798359950305
Cover photo © 2022 Jane Phillips
Cover design © 2022 Amy Phillips
First edition 2022

This is a work of fiction. Names, characters, places and events are products of the author's imagination. Any resemblance to actual persons, living or dead, is purely coincidental.

In memory of
Mary
my big sister and very best friend

Acknowledgements

Don't ever let anyone tell you that writing a book is quick or easy or a solitary endeavour! This book started life at City University. Since then, with the help of numerous friends, it has been through so many iterations that it has been transformed. At City, Bill Ryan and Laura Wilson were dual inspirations and Claire McGowan gave me 'Moira'. My City friends, Vicki Bradley, Paul Durston, Vicki Jones and Fraser Massey, have been true critical friends and have kept me going. The long prose group at Cambridge Writers, Jane Woodnutt, Sian Salkeld, John Unwin and Jay Wharton of Crimecrackers book group, Cambridge, all helped by reading drafts. Amy Phillips stars as my technology guru. And Glyn made me tea – thousands and thousands of cups of tea.

About the author

Jane Phillips is a psychologist. This gives her an unhealthy interest in the criminal mind. To counterbalance, she has a husband, two children and four grandchildren. They do their best to keep her on the straight and narrow.

2nd May 2010

The ear-splitting boom, the stench of cordite and petrol, the searing heat of the fireball, vivid orange, reaching up and out as the car disintegrates into a mass of flying metal and glass. Pieces, bright with fire, flung high in the air, illuminate her body as it is jerked upwards, arching and falling in front of him, clothes shredded and a void where her face should have been.

Next comes numbness, followed by the despair of knowing that there is no hope; that everything he values is lost. Last of all, he watches as that last piece of shrapnel falls, tumbling towards him and hitting the side of his head.

Each time, that was when he awoke.

Chapter 1

Two years later

Monday 28th May 2012

Ben drove the hearse into their back yard and sat perfectly still. His gaze raked the walls and corners to make sure it was safe. He listened to the silence. Only then did he emerge from the protection of the car and walk into the sunlight.

He looked towards the window of their tiny kitchen and saw his Uncle Maurice shuffling about. He called, 'Mo, I'm back. Come and give me a hand.' He waited while Maurice placed his black hat firmly on his head, walked solemnly into the yard then raised his hat while bowing to the hearse. 'Come in, my friend. Welcome to our humble abode.' For sixteen years this had been Maurice's greeting to every corpse as it crossed the boundary of their back room to begin the final stage of its ultimate journey.

The humble abode was clean to the point of sterility, walls and surfaces white or steely. Two living people provided the only colour – pink for faces, green for overalls, blue for gloves and boots. The dead man rested in shades of white and grey. Maurice glanced through the paperwork. 'Cause of death ain't here. You say he died of thirst. Must be a bugger that, and murdered to boot. Don't think we've ever prepped a murder victim. Surprised they released his body so quickly. Anyways, makes our job easier.' He paused just long enough to take a breath. 'Ben, you listening?'

The words reverberated around the walls in tones that Ben had always thought of as 'the echoes of the dead'. But Ben was not listening; his thoughts were elsewhere.

'Sorry Mo, I was miles away. Give me ten minutes, will you?' He listened as Maurice's steps took him away to the kitchen. He heard the kettle being switched on for one of Maurice's innumerable cups of tea, so he knew that he would have time for peaceful contemplation of the body. First, he checked the band on the wrist and the one, for further confirmation, around the ankle.

This was indeed the body of Stanley Murdock, aged fifty-five. You poor sod, he thought. What a way to go.

The world retreated from Ben's consciousness as he became intent on his initial examination. Beneath the emaciated structure he could see a tall man, neat haircut, full head of hair, expensive teeth. For his age, he would have been an attractive man.

Ben's chat with the pathologist had brought enough information to raise questions in his mind about Stanley Murdock's death. His body had been found in a disused farmhouse in the fens where he'd been tied up and allowed to die of thirst. At the family's request, their solicitor had been the one to identify the body. Ben looked again at the corpse and shuddered. Violent death. It could tear you apart. He'd never buried a murder victim but he knew the effect this would be having on the grieving relatives.

What of the weeks and months ahead when the police investigation would intrude on their grief? And then, the trial. He knew that his part in this unfolding story would be brief and he took it for granted that he must make it as painless as possible for everybody.

He continued his perusal. The post-mortem scars on Stanley's head were well hidden. The incision on his chest was neatly sewn. He had a sucked-in look – but the hollowed cheeks were probably the result of his recent incarceration. They'd need to work on his face to flesh it out. A photo from the family would decide that.

Ben carefully examined each arm in turn. The rope burns on the chest, the upper arms and wrists would be covered by clothes and cuffs drawn down. His nails were broken and would need some work.

Then he stared intently at the hands. He turned them over several times and looked from one to the other. He placed them side by side, palms up, to compare them. He was so surprised that he spoke out loud, 'Well, I'll be...' He knew he wouldn't be able to ask the grieving relatives but, with luck, they might let something slip. He took his magnifying glass from the shelf behind him and played it over the hands. Then he cleaned the glass with an antiseptic wipe and replaced it on the shelf.

He examined the rest of the torso, then the legs and feet.

Next, he picked up his camera from the same shelf and took a series of shots of the hands. He glanced at the clock on the wall. He could hear Maurice washing his cup. As he held the sheet ready to cover Stanley Murdock's face, he spoke directly to him, 'We'll look after you. You'll have the dignity in death that you lost in life and we'll care for your family as best we can. Go in peace.' He placed the sheet gently over the face of Stanley Murdock and his thoughts turned to a more personal problem – Katy, his beautiful Katy.

* * *

'Fancy a brew?'

As Maurice bustled round, making tea, Ben removed his gloves and carefully scrubbed his hands. He smiled. Mo, for all his annoying habits, was the person who had been with him through his dark times. He knew him better than anyone, and, best of all, he was always cheerful.

'My mate down the nick, gave him a bell while you was in there with our gent. Tells me it was a kidnapping. They reckon it went wrong and they left him to die. Bloody awful way to go.'

Maurice handed him a cup of weak tea. Ben poured half down the sink, swirled the tea in the pot and filled his cup. It was coming out black now, just as he liked it. 'How'd they know it was a kidnapping?'

'Seems there was some ransom notes. Miracle it hasn't broken in the press. They're as leaky as a sieve at Parkside.'

That reminded him that he must tell the police what he'd found. 'Did your mate tell you who's in charge of the investigation?'

'Yep, that wanker, Turnbull. When I retired, he was a DC. Now he's a DI, God help us. He was useless. Good at shouting.' Maurice frowned. 'Why d'you want to know?'

'I've seen a couple of things he may have missed. They might be useful – might not.'

'You won't get any sense out of him. What've you found?'

'I'll show you when Katy gets here.' He looked at his watch. 'It's nearly time. Shouldn't be late on her first day. I'll give her a bollocking if she is.'

Maurice sniffed loudly. 'Nah, you won't. You'll have that

disappointed look. Works much better. Anyways, you're as soft as the proverbial where your kids're concerned. Katy and Sarah both. Look, Ben, you done a grand job, being mum and dad to them all these years. They're two lovely girls. But both of them know exactly how to wind you round their little finger. I'll wait till hell freezes for you to give either of them a bollocking.' Maurice busied himself, tidying the worktop, then looked up when Ben hadn't replied. 'You're looking worried. Not that geezer, is it?'

'No, it's Katy. I tried to stop her. But you know what she's like. A terrier. She gets her teeth into something and won't let go.'

'Well, that's good, ain't it? People call that focus and determination. You wanted her to go to university and she wanted to leave school and join the firm. She knows her own mind, that one. Always has.' Maurice grinned. 'And when you're as old as me, you'll want to put your feet up and let her take over. Just remind me, wasn't there a certain young man who ignored his father and joined the army? Now who would that be?'

Ben pointed to the scar on his forehead, 'And look where it got me.' He sighed. 'I told her she should begin by helping you with Mrs Walker but then I made the mistake of telling her about this one. So now she's adamant.' With hands on hips, he started to mimic his daughter's voice. 'A murder victim is sooo much more interesting than an old lady and if Sarah can deal with gory crime, then so can I.' He turned to Maurice, 'Mo, what can I do? They're both too young to be dealing with violent death.'

'Gimme your cup and stop worrying.'

'Wish I could. Hyper-vigilance is a bugger. I'm aiming for just normal parental worry – and that'll be bad enough!'

They went to re-join the corpse. Maurice uncovered Stanley Murdock's face, 'Don't look too good, do he? At least they closed his eyes, that's the bit that still gets me; them eyes – blank or worse.' Maurice patted him on the shoulder. 'Listen, Ben, you've got to let em go. They're adults now. And, remember, you wasn't much older when you came up against death in a much more violent way.'

'And you, of all people, know what that did to me. See if you can persuade her.'

'Which "her" are you talking about? Me, I suppose.'

Neither of them had heard Katy approach and they both jumped at the sound of her voice. 'And persuade me of what?'

Ben was the first to recover. He drew the sheet over Stanley Murdock's face while Maurice turned to his great-niece. 'Katy! Don't do that! You could've had two heart attack victims on your hands as well as old Mrs Walker and this gent here. And a "Good morning, Dad, good morning, Uncle Mo" wouldn't go amiss.'

Katy smiled demurely, 'Good morning, Dad. Good morning, Uncle Mo.'

'That's better. Now, your dad wants to ease you in gently. Wants you to deal with a nice simple death. Apart from this gentleman, we've got Mrs Walker and that's straightforward. Been no messing with her body. But, this one, different kettle altogether. There's been a post-mortem so your dad wants you to leave it to him. You and me can get Mrs Walker tidied up, looking peaceful, no trouble. What d'you say?'

Katy grinned at her great-uncle. 'I'd love to help with Mrs Walker.'

Ben began to relax – lulled into a false sense of security by that smile – until she added, 'But there's no way I'm going to miss out on this! It could be years before we get another murder.' She retrieved a battered copy of the *Cambridge News* from her bag. 'Have you seen today's piece?'

Ben had known the story would be big news and he just hoped it wouldn't bring the news-hounds to their door.

Katy continued, 'So, was he mutilated? Says here it was a vicious killing. Quotes the police as "following several leads" but Sarah says they always say that. She would though, just to be one up on me.' She wagged a finger at her father. 'Dad, I know you're trying to protect me but I'm not a kid any more, and if Sarah can do it, then so can I.' She put her hands on her hips just as her father had done. 'I'm fed up of her stories about all the exciting things she's done. One minute all mysterious then letting on that she was the one to solve the crime. She's only a PC for God's sake. You'd think she was the bloody Chief Constable the way she goes on.' Katy's voice took on the honeyed tones that had always worked in the past, 'Dad, please, I don't want to be Sarah's little shadow all my life and I promise you, if it gets too much for me, I'll retreat to Mrs Walker.

Deal?'

She held up her hand for a high five and Ben reluctantly met it with his own. He exchanged a shrug with Maurice and held out a set of overalls to Katy. He pointed her towards the boots and gloves. 'Firstly, no, he is not mutilated. There's no way you'd get round me if he was. You can tell he's suffered but there are no wounds to speak of. Promise me though, that you'll go out if it's at all upsetting for you. He had a hard death. We'll do the preliminaries together but I'm doing the embalming without you. No arguments. I'll talk you through it and you ask anything that's not clear. OK?

'Before I uncover him, we'll go through a few things. Just remember that this body was once a living, breathing person who deserves our utmost respect. His family also deserve every consideration. They may want to come and pay their respects and see him for the last time so we'll try to make him look as natural as possible. When we've finished he'll look as though he's sleeping.'

'Ugh! Dad, that's so spooky. Sleeping in a coffin. Like, as if he was a vampire!'

Ben did his best to look stern and ignore Maurice's grinning face. 'Stop right there, Katy. Forget vampires. If you're going to be a professional undertaker, you must act the part. You need to think of each of these bodies as a person that someone loved and our job is to make this as easy as we can for everyone. We'll get him ready to be visited. The family can then decide whether they want to see him. I'm going to uncover him. You need to know that his mouth is open and his eyes are closed. We'll have to close his mouth to make him look natural but often we have to do the eyes too.'

Ben slowly turned down the sheet so that Stanley Murdock's head and torso were exposed. 'They closed his eyes when they did the post-mortem. You can tell it's Jim Spire's work. See how neatly he's sewn up after the pm. They do one whenever a death is unexpected, but not everyone is as neat or careful as Jim.'

He looked over at Katy. 'The difference here is that our man was restrained before death so there are added marks for us to cover or disguise. That's the important bit for us – to make him look as he did before the kidnapping – for his family's sake.'

He turned to Katy and Maurice. Katy had moved in to get a better view. She was intent on examining Stanley's corpse. Ben pointed, 'Now look at his hands.'

Maurice replied, 'Ooh, nasty wrists. Broken nails but we can sort them. Nothing we can't fix.'

'Look how they've cleaned his nails. They'd have been looking for evidence. Looks like they had trouble because there's not much left of them. He must have tried to struggle free, poor bugger.'

Ben stopped and looked at his daughter. She seemed a little paler than when she'd arrived. 'The bodies are usually easier to deal with than this one, Katy. You still OK?'

'I'm fine, Dad. He suffered and it's hard not to get sucked into that.'

'It's a balance. Empathy and professionalism. You'll learn.' He pointed to the hands of the cadaver. 'If we look further, there's this. At first, I thought it was just a freckle but it's a small spot of ink. It's not biro and, if you look closely, you can see it's purple.' He handed Katy the magnifying glass and watched as she inspected the ink spot and then passed the glass to Maurice. Ben continued, 'See the way the ink's spread. I think it was from a fountain pen. How many people use a fountain pen these days? And purple ink? I don't know if the police have twigged how unusual this is. And then, there's this.'

He gently placed the hands together, palms upward, so the little fingers touched. 'Look at the length of his little fingers. His left one is much longer than his right. Not sure if the police need this but no harm in telling them. It could be inherited but it could be he was a child prodigy on the violin or guitar and that made his finger grow.'

He could see Maurice and Katy exchanging a look. Then Maurice guffawed. He turned to Ben. 'Listen, Sherlock, we're all glad that you're making changes in your life. It's good you've gone back to studying and using that good brain of yours.' He paused, puffed out his chest and pretended to smoke a pipe. 'But, in truth, Holmes, since you embarked on that criminology degree, you've been a mine of useless information. Fingers – phooey. Perchance, your methods of induction might take a back seat and allow us to put this poor fellow into the fridge and apply ourselves to the paperwork?'

11

'OK, Watson, but before we do that – any questions, Katy?'

'Yep, I've got lots, especially about murder. But first, in my new and very professional role, I need to know what comes next with Mr Murdock. And I know we're absolutely the best but why did we get him? Did his family choose us or was it just random?'

'Katy, you know about as much as I do about murder.'

Maurice interrupted, 'That's not quite true, Ben.'

Ben's look was enough to silence his uncle. He turned back to his daughter. 'Our next job is to see the family and find out what they want. It could be tricky. They're probably in shock so they'll need a lot of support. If I remember rightly, we buried his wife six months ago. Will you check that, Mo?'

Maurice looked perplexed, 'Buried his wife? Don't remember a Murdock. Hang on, I'll look.'

Ben had covered the body and was sliding it into the fridge when Maurice returned with the file. 'No wonder I couldn't remember. Called herself Margaret Muredach, but next of kin, one Stanley Murdock – our gent here. She was Catholic. Now this is interesting. Stanley insisted she had a non-denominational cremation. The rest of the family didn't complain so that's what we organised.'

Katy looked straight at her father. 'Dad! That's awful. How could he do that? If she was Catholic, surely she'd want a requiem mass and all that Catholic stuff, even if he thought it was a load of mumbo-jumbo.'

'Whoa now, Katy.'

'But it's true. That lot should've thought of her not themselves.'

'Thank you, Katy. We don't know the circumstances; she may have abandoned her religion. It was their decision to make, not ours.'

Katy was not mollified. 'Well, I think it's gross. Couldn't we have done something for her?'

Ben's voice was firm, 'Katy, we can advise but, no matter whether we agree or not, if it's legal, it's their decision not ours.'

Maurice scrabbled through the notes that had arrived with Stanley Murdock's body. 'He's down as Presbyterian Church of Ireland. That's Northern Irish protestant, in't it? Do we read anything into that?'

'No time for reading. We've got work to do. I hear Mrs Walker calling to you two and I've got some phone-calls to make.'

He ushered them from the room and took out his phone. He could hear Maurice's voice retreating towards their small office. 'I love this one, Katy. It's normal and it's boring and it's how I want to go when me time comes. Mrs Walker, ninety-two, playing bowls. Plays her shot, turns to her friend and says, "Lord, Mavis, if I didn't get so tired I could be club champion," sits down and stops breathing. Just like that. That's the way to go. The family want a right good knees-up cos that's what she'd've loved.'

While Maurice and Katy discussed Mrs Walker's funeral, Ben made two calls. The first, to Detective Inspector Turnbull, confirmed that Maurice's description of the man had been accurate. He was put through to a junior officer on the murder enquiry and told her about the little finger and the ink. The woman noted his message and details and said that someone would follow it up 'in due course'. In the background, he could hear a male voice bellowing and he ventured to say, 'That must be Turnbull.'

'Yes, and I'd better go or he'll be on to me next.' And the phone went dead.

He made his second call. He now had a picture in his mind of the three Murdock siblings at the time of the cremation of Margaret, Stanley's second wife. It was a cloudy picture as they had not featured significantly in the proceedings. He recalled that their father had taken the lead in a simple and short ceremony, but the three offspring had been conspicuous by their lack of involvement.

The call was answered by Lucien, the eldest Murdock. The result, Ben could only describe as a summons. He was required to attend the house the following day at ten a.m. When he'd asked if he could bring an associate to take notes, the reply had been intriguing. 'Bring them all. They'll all need to be involved anyway.'

As he put the phone down, Katy rushed in. She groaned and clapped her palm to her forehead. 'Oh, shit. Sorry, sorry, sorry. Dad, I am soooo sorry. Someone phoned yesterday at home and left a message. He said it was dead important. I didn't understand half of it so I wrote it all down.' She giggled. 'Then I made him say it again cos he had this real sexy voice.' She struggled with her gown and reached into her jeans' pocket. She extracted a crumpled note, handed it to her father and quickly left the room.

Ben read the note, then clenched it into a ball and hurled it across the room. But he could remember the words precisely. 'Chris phoned. Said look after Stanley. Said remember him to Rosemary. I told him that's stupid, we don't know a Rosemary. Said he'd be in touch. Love you oodles – he didn't say that, I did :-)'

He groaned and screwed up his eyes. 'Remember me to Rosemary'. It was the code he'd abandoned sixteen years ago. Bloody people, barging into his life again after all this time. He wanted rid of them all. One thing was certain, there was no way he was going to contact this Chris. He picked up the crumpled note and placed it in the bag for the incinerator.

Chapter 2

Tuesday 29th May 2012

It came in sequence: the infernal noise pounding his ears, the scorching heat blasting his face, the reek of burnt flesh in his nostrils, the vision of his dead wife lying at his feet, then the pain as the metal struck his head.

Ben sat up, shaking and sweating. Worse than the last time. Why now? It had been more than two years. He rubbed his scar gently to take the pain away. He knew that his screams would have been silent and would not have woken Katy. In the hospital they'd told him that he never uttered a sound. He just woke silently, reliving a semblance of the truth. And this semblance of truth was all that he had, because, in his conscious state, he remembered nothing of the bomb that had changed his life. They'd told him the details but even now, he had no recollection of events before, during or after the bomb that had stolen his wife and made him a hero. His thoughts turned again to the question he'd been asking himself for sixteen years. Why had she been there? She'd never been to the barracks before. But that day, she'd come. Why? If only he knew. If only.

This must be a one-off and if he ignored it, it would go away again. Bloody Chris. He'd have to shrug off Bloody Chris – tell him precisely where to go. Then he should be able to bury the dream for ever. He looked at his watch. Five o'clock – he'd start the day early and get ahead of things. That was how to deal with it. Move on, don't look back.

* * *

So, here they stood at 10 a.m., Ben, Maurice and Katy looking up at the enormous, carved oak double doors, centrally placed between two imposing wings of a mansion in Grantchester. Although only four miles south of Cambridge, traffic had been the usual problem and the dazzling sun hadn't helped. Katy whistled as she pointed to a Porsche parked snugly next to an Aston Martin, both overshadowed by a muddy Range Rover. Maurice checked around the front door for hidden keys and nodded approvingly when he couldn't find any. Once a cop, thought Ben.

As they were about to ring the bell, a police officer marched round from the back. Ben recognised her immediately. 'Hello, it's Pam, isn't it? Friend of Sarah's? My daughter?'

'Oh, hello, Mr Burton. Of course I remember you. Hi Katy. I guess you must be doing the funeral?' She nodded towards the house and lowered her voice. 'Don't envy you. Weird family. I'm supposed to be their Family Liaison Officer. They've just kicked me out. Well, suggested I leave and "get on with real policing". I've put a call through to DI Turnbull to find out what I should do. I can't just abandon them. I'm supposed to be keeping an eye on them – you know – it *is* a murder. I think I'd better go and try him again.' She waved to them all. 'See you, Katy.'

Ben pulled the antique brass door chain. Big Ben chimes clanged so loudly that they all stepped back in unison. 'Blimey, Dad, even in mourning they have to tell the world they have visitors.'

He looked at his beautiful daughter and appreciated again the care with which she had presented herself. She'd removed the rings from her piercings and replaced them with innocuous studs. She'd smoothed her spiky hair into the semblance of a style. On this, her first visit to a client, she almost looked the young professional she was trying to become.

The door opened and they faced a hawk-nosed woman. Ben recognised her as Virginia, daughter of Margaret Muredach, cremated six months previously, and Stanley Murdock, now refrigerated and awaiting embalming, and thence his last resting place. He reckoned that she must be in her twenties although she looked much older. He particularly noticed her clothes. He hadn't seen a woman wearing a twin-set and pearls since his mother had died. 'Follow me,' she said. 'Wipe your feet and close the door behind you. And, for next time, the tradesman's entrance is round the side.'

Katy winked at her dad. Ben gave a slight shake of his head. He could see that Virginia was on the verge of collapse. Her eyes were dry, but her neck tendons stood proud and her jaw was so firmly set that he thought her teeth might break under the strain.

Their feet echoed on the marble floor as Virginia led them through the square hall. Ben could see Katy looking round in awe. This level of wealth was certainly way beyond that of their usual clients. Virginia waved a hand towards a large and handsomely furnished room. 'Wait in the morning room while I call my brothers.'

They listened as her peremptory calls echoed through the house, some loud, others from a distance. This was a sprawling house, and Ben suspected that the brothers had ensconced themselves, in solitude or duplicity, as far as possible from their overwrought sister.

The three visitors studied a room where every surface was adorned with matching funeral bouquets in white and purple. Either side of the French doors stood an arrangement of white lilies and roses reaching from floor to ceiling. The scent of lilies was overpowering. Katy pulled her father towards her and whispered, 'Jeez, Dad, this place is more like a morgue than ours. Should be mourning room with a "u".'

Ben's voice was low but firm. 'Hush, Katy. People react in different ways to death. Don't forget their father has just been abandoned to die a painful death. Put yourself in their place. Would you be your own sweet self if that had happened to me?'

Katy looked contrite. They were interrupted as the bereaved family assembled and Lucien, obviously the eldest, introduced himself. He stepped forward, shook Ben firmly by the hand then nodded to Maurice and Katy. He introduced his siblings, Virginia and Alistair.

Ben made a first assessment of their states of mind. Lucien looked to have his emotions fully under control. His face was impassive, his hands quite still. Possibly a buttoned-up sort of person, or he might just be uncaring. It was possible that father and son had not been close, although their physical resemblance was startling. Alistair was hard to judge as he would not raise his head, but his body language and morbidly thin physique suggested someone cowed by life or possibly by the circumstances around his father's death. Virginia was sitting ramrod straight and was keeping control of herself – just.

Ben gave each a card with twenty-four-hour contact details. Lucien took his and, without looking, placed it in his jacket pocket. Virginia's hand shook violently as she took hers. Alistair kept his head down, his face hidden by a mop of floppy hair. He mumbled a brief and unintelligible reply to Ben's words of condolence. His card dropped to the floor without him noticing. Katy retrieved it and gave it back to him.

Lucien began to explain the family's predicament. His voice was clear and steady. 'You know that our father died a particularly gruesome death, abandoned in a farmhouse in the fens. The police have advised us to inform you of certain details. You will need these in order to ensure confidentiality. They are not to be divulged to anyone.' He looked imperiously at the three Burtons and added, 'Is that quite clear?'

Ben was usually sympathetic to clients but he was already taking a dislike to Lucien. Perhaps it was his supercilious expression, or the assumption of power and control. He couldn't quite put his finger on the basis for his feeling of disquiet.

Lucien continued. 'Our father was the victim of a very nasty kidnap which went horribly wrong. We had received three ransom notes in his handwriting and were acting with the police in order to secure his release. But that was not to be.'

A stifled mew from Virginia caused him to pause. Ben handed her a clean white handkerchief. She smiled wanly and proceeded to knead the hankie between her fingers.

Lucien gave her a contemptuous look and continued, 'A fourth note was delivered on the day he died. The kidnappers knew we had contacted the police. The final note was typed and stated that we would never see him alive again. That same day, the police received an anonymous note to say where the body was to be found. I have told you all this because we have been advised by the police not to publicise the means of his death, as this could impede their investigations. From our past association with you in dealing with my step-mother's death, we believe we can trust you to respect both our wishes and the directions of the police.'

He looked expectantly at Ben whose response was immediate. 'Yes, of course. We will, as always, respect confidentiality, both from your perspective and from that of the police.'

The loudest sound in the room was Virginia's stifled sob. Lucien continued without looking at her. 'Our main problem is that our father has laid certain unusual requirements in his will. The important aspect for you relates to the disposal of his body. I think it best that you visit his solicitor yourself to ensure that you carry out his wishes precisely.'

Ben interjected gently, 'We don't normally liaise personally with our clients' solicitors. We leave that to the family. We see our remit generally as ensuring the well-being of family members as best we can.' He paused and looked at Virginia, 'And organising the funeral service and the burial or cremation of their loved-one's remains. We can also arrange for caterers to provide some sustenance after the funeral. This is especially useful if mourners have come some distance.'

Lucien's response made clear his priorities. 'As a family, we have decided that we want to have as little as possible to do with our father's funeral. If we could, we would leave it entirely to you, but, unfortunately, we will have to have some involvement. There are stipulations in the will about his burial and these will have to be adhered to. His solicitor will give you the details. And, if cost is an issue, let me put your minds at rest.' He waved his hand around the opulent room. 'As you can see, my father was an extremely wealthy man. He has stipulated that the sum of forty thousand pounds is to be spent on his funeral. If that amount is not spent, it affects the conditions for our inheritance. Your time will be rewarded generously and appropriately.'

Ben glanced at Katy and spoke before she could react. 'Please, let me assure you that fees were not uppermost in our minds. We will, of course, carry out your father's wishes to the best of our ability. If you give us with the name of his solicitor, I will go to see him immediately.'

'Or her,' Katy added quietly.

He nodded and smiled at his daughter, 'Or her.' Then he turned back to Lucien and continued, 'We'll also need a recent photograph of your father and a set of his clothes. The day after tomorrow you'll be able to come to view his body if you wish.'

It was at this point that Virginia's dam broke. 'No, no. God, no, please no. I can't do that. I can't see him. Please don't make me!'

Virginia heaved a shuddering sigh, then sobbed quietly. She rocked back and forth obsessively while her brothers looked on in horror. Ben was pleased to see that Katy had instinctively moved to sit beside Virginia and had put an arm around her shoulders. Maurice silently took his notebook from his top pocket and continued Katy's note-taking duties.

Lucien was the first of the siblings to recover.

'Ginny, I'm sure these people do not want to hear your views. I have not yet shared with you all of the contents of Father's will. There are parts of it that we will all find distasteful. He was quite clear. If you want to inherit, you are going to have to view his corpse. We all have to take flowers. Now, I think you'd better go to your room until you have composed yourself.'

As Katy stood to lead the stooped and sobbing Virginia from the room, Lucien spoke directly to her, 'Miss Burton, my sister does not need any assistance. Please wait here while I find a photograph.'

Lucien went to a corner of the room where a stack of framed photographs lay face down. He raised each ornate frame in turn. Ben could see that each held a picture of Stanley with a famous person. Lucien dismissed the first few until he had one full-faced and smiling, as Stanley posed shaking hands with someone that Ben recognised as a former Cabinet Minister but couldn't quite put a name to.

Lucien studied it for a moment. 'Talking to power. His favourite occupation. If you can make him look like this, he'll smile up at you from the place where he's gone.'

Not knowing how to react to this, Ben turned to the still silent member of the Murdock trio. 'Alistair, is there anything you want to add?'

'I just want my share of the money.' Then he looked up at Ben through thick, dark lashes. His delicate features and startling blue eyes held a hint of bravado. 'Then I'm moving to Brighton to be myself. I'm not going to be a neutered nobody any more.'

Lucien again took charge, 'Alistair, go and get a decent suit of Father's.' He turned to Ben, 'Underclothes and shoes?'

'Yes please. A full set of clothes.'

When Alistair had left the room, Lucien ostentatiously looked at his watch. 'And then you will, I hope, leave us in peace. We all want this business to be concluded as quickly as possible. We will do whatever is necessary to comply with the terms of our father's will but, apart from that, we will leave you to earn your substantial fee.' He handed Ben a business card. 'Details of the solicitor. Now, wait here while Alistair gets you those clothes.' And with that he marched from the room, and they heard his footsteps mounting the stairs.

Maurice turned to Ben and Katy. He lowered his voice to a whisper, 'Odd, ain't it, that they don't want to be involved at all.'

Ben replied after a moment's thought. 'Maybe not so very odd when you think back to their mother's cremation. They weren't much involved then either.' They fell into silence as Alistair came into the room carrying a calfskin suitcase.

'You don't need to bother bringing the suitcase back. It's just one more thing to get rid of. Can't wait till this whole ghastly charade is over.' He glanced across at the three of them. 'Pity we didn't meet in better circumstances.' He looked at Ben. 'You're cool. Stood up to Lucien.' He turned and waved into the air. Then, he too left them alone with only the heavy scent of the lilies for company.

'I assume we see ourselves out,' said Katy. 'Now is it front door or tradesman's?'

They walked to their car in silence. Once settled inside, Maurice said, 'Well, what do you make of that?' He held up his hand as Katy was about to interrupt. 'Hold on. Them being odd ain't the half of it. If I was back in the Force, I'd be asking who blew the gaff so the kidnappers got to know that the police was involved. And why did the kidnappers inform the police? Why not just abandon the body? But, in this job, I'm asking, how the hell can someone spend forty thousand quid on a funeral? Gold coffin handles, silk shroud; we could buy in a hundred followers, I suppose.'

Ben replied, 'They were the same when the mother died. Held themselves apart. Stanley made all the decisions then. When I meet the solicitor, I'll see what I can find out about them and perhaps he...' He smiled at Katy. 'Or she will have an answer to the money question, but I don't think kidnappers will be within the solicitor's remit.'

Katy grabbed her father's arm. 'Hey, isn't this great! I really hope the job is always this exciting. Like Pam said, they're seriously weird and that house is worth mega, megabucks. Do you think the three of them murdered him to get their hands on all that loot? Like that thing on the train – you know – where they're all in it together?'

'Katy. Their father was rich. He was kidnapped. Something went wrong and he was left to die. It's the job of the police to find out who did it. Now, come back to the real world. We've got a job to do.'

Katy was silent all the way home. Ben had learnt, from long experience, that it was best to leave her to come out of her sulk in her own time. He would be delighted when she stopped being a teenager, and he wondered how long he would have to wait. But, more urgently, he had to deal with Bloody Chris.

Chapter 3

Wednesday 30ᵗʰ May 2012

They'd told him he was brave. He had a medal to prove it. But that meant nothing. The dream again. Two nights running. Worse than before. Years ago, at The Friary, they'd said that he should go back over the few days before each dream to see if he could find the trigger. If he could find the trigger, he might find the cause. And, if he could find the cause, he would have a hope of finding the cure.

He looked at his watch. Four a.m. Sleep would be impossible. What had been different in the last few days? He'd done all the usual, boring things. He'd been to see the Murdocks. That had been different. He hadn't felt his usual congruence with the family. And that was strange, because he had more in common with them than they knew. He sat up in bed and plumped his pillows. He picked up a notepad and began to write a list:
1. We've both had a close relative die suddenly and in desperate circumstances.
2. We both have Northern Ireland connections.
3. Bloody Chris and the bloody Services.

He put down his pencil. He could think of nothing else that was different. What about before her death? He'd always pushed that away. Tried not to remember. The last thing he saw… She was running towards him, red hair flying in all directions as it always did. Then nothing. Why had she come to the barracks that day? He'd been asking himself that same question for sixteen years.

* * *

At seven o'clock he called The Friary. His emergency appointment meant that his usual counsellor was not available but there was another he could see. Then he phoned Maurice and told him where he was going and that, on no account, was he to worry Katy. He refused Maurice's offer of a lift and told him to look after Katy and keep her busy.

As soon as he arrived at the clinic, a petite, dark-haired

woman approached and held out her hand. 'Mr Burton? Alison Clare. Your usual counsellor is with clients all day. I'm a psychologist and I believe I can help. Is that OK?' He nodded abstractedly.

He was led to a door at the end of the corridor. He read the name on the door. 'Dr Alison Clare, Forensic Psychologist'. He wondered what a forensic psychologist was doing here. Surely they only dealt with criminals. Then he dismissed it from his mind.

'Do you want to sit or lie down?'

'I've always had that semi-recliner and faced away. I find it easier.'

'It's your session. I'm just here to ease you forward towards your goals.' When he had settled onto the reclining chair, she continued, 'I've read your notes and I see that you have annual check-ups for your head injury but, apart from that, you hadn't been back for some time. Now you're here for an emergency session, so something must have happened. Can you tell me what that is?'

He closed his eyes. He felt his brow creasing, pulling on his scar. He used his breathing techniques to relax his muscles. Only when his face was perfectly relaxed did he start to speak. 'I think I need to tell you some history. For several years, I've only really needed to come after I'd had the dream. Then the dream stopped. Now it's back. I thought I'd cracked it and moved on but now I know I haven't. So it feels worse, much worse. Does that make sense?'

'Perfect sense. So, tell me what you can about the dream.'

He sat in silence, breathing deeply and listening to the tick of an electric clock. He noticed that precisely sixty ticks had passed before Dr Clare spoke again.

This time he replied. 'I can only tell you that it ends with Diane landing dead at my feet. People talk flippantly about their worst nightmare. They have no idea what they're talking about.'

'Let's try to get at it another way. Can we go back to the time of the bomb and just after? I know this is painful but I think it might help. You had a head injury. Can you tell me about that?'

This was easier; this was physical. 'Some shrapnel is lodged in the side of my head.' Ben pointed to his scar. 'I have to have it looked at every year to see if it's moved. So far, it's just sitting there. As long as it doesn't move, the surgeon thinks it's safer to leave it – rather than to try to remove it.'

'Does it give you pain?'

'No, well, occasionally – yes.'

Ben could hear the scratching of notes being made. Then she spoke, 'Can we talk about before and after your head injury. Do you think it's made a difference to your life?'

He didn't need to think. He'd rehearsed this explanation too many times to have to pause. 'God, yes. Downside, I'm not nearly as clever as I used to be. Upside, I'm a better person and I think differently.'

'Better?'

'Kinder, more time for people. I understand their problems. Looking back on the young man I was, I don't think I'd have liked myself.'

'Why is that?'

'Before the injury, I was an officer with a bright future – going places.' He gave a short laugh. 'You know the sort: pushy, in a hurry, arrogant. The Brass thought I'd rise to the heights. I did too; I was well on my way to a chest full of medals and braids.' He paused. 'But I'm not unhappy. I've settled into a niche that fits. I'm good at my job and I get satisfaction from looking after people when they are at their most vulnerable. Different life but a good one.'

'I'm glad to hear it. You say, less clever. How does that manifest itself?'

Ben wondered if she'd changed to a less noisy pen because he could hear no notes being made but felt sure there would be. He replied, 'Slower. Can't do the higher computational stuff I was into.' He thought for a moment. 'And I don't read people in the same way.'

'Not sure I understand that.'

'Me neither. I've only just thought of it. Give me a moment.'

They sat in silence. There was just the sound of the ticking clock. He looked at the walls. He wondered what that colour was. Taupe? He'd have to look it up later. Then he spoke. 'I don't know if this is less or more clever. In the job I was in before the bomb, it was a weakness to trust people. You had to be on your guard all the time. Now, I can take people at face value – it's been a liberation. Part of being a better person, I suppose.'

'And does this "taking people at face value" cause you any problems?'

'Surprisingly few. I find that if you trust people, they tend to be trustworthy. We've had no bad payers. Some need a little time to settle but, eventually, we get a fair deal.'

'And you said you think differently. What do you mean by that?'

'This one's really odd. I seem to have acquired some sort of photographic memory. I can look at things or hear them and remember them precisely. I thought a head injury would make my memory worse but in some ways it seems to have made it better. Does that make any sort of sense to you?'

'Oh, yes. It certainly does. This is really exciting.' She came round and stood in front of him. 'Damage to the left anterior temporal lobe.' She studied him for a moment then went back to her position behind him. She continued, 'I'm so sorry. This is your session, but this is a research area of mine. Yours could be a case of Acquired Savant Syndrome, and it's rare.'

'And...'

Dr Clare took a deep in-breath. 'I'm sure you've been told that every head injury is different.'

He nodded.

She continued. 'In recovery, there's always some re-routing of nerve pathways and now we believe regrowth of nerve cells is possible. There are several competing theories. My research focusses on whether you've re-routed down a new and interesting pathway and these are newly created skills, or if you're using the original pathway but the injury knocked out the pathways that repressed this ability. Does that make sense?'

'Yeah. And I won't knock it cos it's really useful for the job.'

'I know this is an enormous ask, but I'd like to make a case study of you. When we've sorted out your problems, of course?'

'Glad to help.'

'Now, what about the rest of your life? How is that going?'

'To be honest, I don't have much of a social life. I'm happy in my own company and I have my family.'

He could hear the slight rustle of papers. 'Two daughters and an uncle. Your daughters? Must be nearly grown up now. How are you with that?'

He laughed. 'Hyper-vigilant. I know what you're getting at. And it's true. I am. With both my girls. Perhaps not so much with Sarah but Katy's just like her mum and I know I overly worry about her. I'm casebook PTSD there, always thinking that the worst could happen. I'm trying to work through it but it's hard.'

'First step is recognising it, so that's good. Friends?'

'A few good friends – the sort you can turn to.'

'Is everyone you meet trustworthy?'

'Course not. But I can sort of tell.' He paused again briefly and wriggled into a more comfortable position. 'I see families in shock or grief, and they don't always say what they mean.' He gave a short laugh. 'And sometimes they say precisely what they mean but have never uttered it before. That can be a revelation for the rest of the family!'

'And do you see it as part of your job to fix that?'

'No, but sometimes I can help. I've become a good listener.'

'Part of the job?'

'Yeah. I feel responsible for making their lives that bit easier. I see them when they're at their lowest.'

'Can I take it then, that you're reasonably happy with your life?'

'Yep. Got a job I love and a wonderful family. Two lovely daughters and an uncle who keeps an eye on me.'

'So life is good apart from...'

'The dream. Look, you said we could stop at any time. I'm feeling much better. I've sort of got over the shock of the flash-backs.' He sat up on the recliner and turned towards Dr Clare. He noticed that she had a sad smile and wondered what her problem was. Not his business. 'I know I've got to crack it but I don't think I'm quite ready to face it yet. I like talking to you. Can I make another appointment?'

'Sure. There are a couple of new therapies I'd like to talk over with you. They weren't around when you last had treatment.

How long do you think you'll need before coming back?'

He considered this for a moment. 'Three weeks? I've got a big job on at the moment, so after that would suit me best.'

'OK. Let's go and make that appointment.'

Chapter 4

At eleven o'clock Ben marched across Parker's Piece towards the offices of Marriott, Henson and Finlay. He was barely aware of the cries of the undergraduates enjoying their games of cricket and rounders after exams, and before they really had to get their heads down for the important task of enjoying May Balls and the like. He was totally occupied with the extraordinary meeting with the Murdocks. Was their unhappiness the result of the trauma they were suffering, or... what? He'd already decided that Lucien was a cold fish, Virginia was living on her nerves and Alistair had been constrained but was probably about to come out in glorious technicolour. Of the three, it seemed that only Virginia was showing any sign of grief.

As soon as he entered the building he could see that these solicitors were not cheap. He was led to a spacious seating area to await the arrival of J. Finlay LLB. LLD. (Cantab). The paintings hanging on all four walls looked expensive and he fancied that these were the real deal. The chairs were plush and comfortable. Several large bouquets graced porcelain vases and the mirror-bright wooden surfaces gave off a scent of beeswax and lavender which led him to suspect that spray polish would never be used here. His coffee was excellent and the little twiddly biscuit melted in his mouth. Unfortunately, it was still melting when a tall, svelte woman approached him.

'Josephine Finlay. Welcome Mr Burton. Sorry. I can't shake hands. I have an allergy and, at the moment, it's causing me some difficulty. I hope I haven't kept you long.'

Ben spluttered in reply, 'No, no, Mrs...'

'It's Miss Finlay, but please call me Josephine. Sorry to have caught you in mid-swallow. Would you care to bring your coffee with you? I'm afraid it may take a while to get the late Mr Murdock's affairs in order. He was a complicated man. I think we could be working together for some time.'

She smiled a mischievous smile. 'Shall I lead on?'

He followed the bouncing auburn hair and couldn't help but appreciate the taut bottom that preceded him into a large and well-appointed office. They sat, not at the immaculately tidy desk, but on easy chairs beside a low table. Several papers were placed neatly in order in front of them.

'I am the sole executor of Stanley Murdock's will, although I must say that it was drawn up contrary to my advice and signed and witnessed just six weeks before he died. I'm sure he hadn't anticipated such an imminent demise, let alone one abandoned in that dreadful place.'

He was struck by her use of the word 'abandoned'. He'd heard it several times in the last few days and it seemed a fitting adjective to describe the Murdock family, both the victim and his children.

Josephine continued, 'Mr Murdock had set up several complex trust arrangements which will take some time to unravel. I have the impression from Lucien that the family wants this burial to take place as quickly as possible. I'll clarify that this afternoon. Mr Murdock – the deceased Mr Murdock – has specified that he wants to be buried not cremated. That is the least problematic of his list of requirements.' She looked across at Ben and said, 'I've never dealt with a murder before. Have you?' To Ben's shake of the head, she gave him a dazzling smile. 'Blind leading the blind then, but I must say, I was surprised that the body was released for burial so quickly. I'm relieved that we can get matters under way without delay. I'm certain that we all want to see Mr Murdock safely despatched as soon as possible.'

Josephine leaned towards him and looked conspiratorial, 'I'm speaking to you as one professional to another. You won't want him cluttering up your fridge and I won't want his strange arrangements to keep his case in my in-box for longer than is necessary. The sooner we can pop him in the ground, the better for all of us.'

As Josephine had leant forward, he'd caught a glimpse of cleavage surrounded by white lace. Since Diane's death, and much to his daughters' chagrin, he'd not shown the slightest interest in forming another relationship. Hence, the tingling feeling that accompanied that flash of feminine curves took him completely by surprise.

Josephine apologised, 'I'm sorry, you look surprised. Was that a little too informal? Of course, I take the job seriously, but it just gets too tedious being on my best behaviour all the time.'

She smiled broadly, showing perfect white teeth. He gave a nervous laugh. He had the feeling that he was moving into deep water and he wasn't sure of the speed or direction of the current. 'No, no, please don't apologise – it was me. I'm not used to dealing with solicitors, just grieving relatives and dead bodies. They usually speak in riddles.' He took a quick breath. 'I often have to decipher the codes that people use around death. One of my clients said his father had "gone to shake hands with the grim reaper"'.

He realised he was prattling so stopped abruptly. Josephine laughed and leant forward again, briefly touching his sleeve.

'It seems, Ben – may I call you Ben?' She didn't wait for a reply. 'That you have a more difficult job than I'd imagined.'

She laughed quietly, and Ben felt himself being pulled towards that sound. It came to him that he had not laughed in that intimate way with a woman for many years and he very much wanted Josephine to laugh again.

She brought him swiftly back to the present. 'Stanley Murdock has written a list of requirements for his funeral. Many would call them bizarre and, in this case, I'd count myself among the many.' She picked out a sheet of paper. 'He has provided a list of names and requires that they be summoned – his word not mine – to attend his funeral. It's a long list.'

She handed the paper to Ben. The list was indeed long and, as he thumbed through it, he saw that it contained several names he recognised. Obviously, those of the rich and famous who had adorned the pictures in Stanley's morning room, were to be summoned to his funeral. He wondered how many would accept the 'invitation'. Then one name jumped out at him – Professor Dobson. He'd not seen or heard of that man in thirty years, even though they lived within a mile of each other. He wondered if Dobson was still devious and objectionable. Ben looked up from the list. 'Is this copy for me?'

Josephine nodded. 'There is to be a service conducted by a Presbyterian minister followed by interment in a plot Mr Murdock has reserved. He has chosen the hymns and the prayers. Here are the details of the service and the church he has chosen.' Josephine handed him a second sheet of paper.

'Then it becomes a little less usual. I'll be able to help you with some of these requirements – if that's agreeable with you. Let's start with the easy ones. He has stipulated that Lucien, Virginia and Alistair are to view his body and to put a flower into the casket with him. He doesn't specify the flower and that seems to be the only decision he has left to them. He wants his birth certificate, his two marriage certificates and the death certificates of his two wives to be buried with him. There will probably be copies in the house but, if not, I can track those down for you. Now it becomes more arduous. Also, in his coffin, he wants the coroners' reports of both his wives' deaths. I can contact the coroner's office so, if you need help, I can assist with those.'

He felt he ought to protest. 'Miss Finlay, Josephine, I'm not sure you should be doing all this. It is very kind of you, but I think I should be earning this forty thousand.'

Josephine laughed again, making him feel that he should protest more often. 'Don't worry. I have an ulterior motive. I'm hoping that if I take some of these chores from you, then you'll reciprocate and do some parts of my job that you'll find easier than I will. Is that OK?'

For reasons that were none too clear to him, he replied, 'Sounds OK to me.'

'Good. I'd hoped you'd agree. Accompanying the will were several letters. Mr Murdock specified that they were only to be opened, or delivered, after his death. A couple of these, I'd like help with. Also, there is one which relates specifically to you. It contains the combination of his personal safe and instructions that everything therein is to remain sealed and be buried with him. I have checked and can find no legal reason why this requirement should not be adhered to. I think it prudent that there are independent witnesses present when the safe is opened. Perhaps you and another from your establishment?'

He nodded. The evidence so far suggested that Stanley Murdock had been a controlling father and as Josephine had said, 'a complicated man'. His interest was aroused and, in addition, this very attractive woman was smiling at him.

'What is it you want help with?'

'It's to do with some of the letters. Most can be sent by messenger and tracked. But there are a couple that have special requirements. Stanley has a cousin in prison. He inherits Stanley's violin and I need him to sign some papers. I've written to inform him of the bequest, but I'm not a criminal lawyer and I'm a bit squeamish about visiting a men's prison. I'd like you to visit him on my behalf. Could you do that?'

That suited him perfectly. His pending assignment was on the motivations of criminals. The chance to visit a prisoner and gain some first-hand information was a godsend. He beamed at Josephine and only half listened to her next comment.

'There is another letter that I'd like help with. This one is to be handed personally to someone who works in one of the colleges. I don't find Cambridge colleges nearly as intimidating as men's prisons but I'd feel happier if I had someone to hold my hand. Could you do that?'

She smiled again and Ben felt that the water he was treading had suddenly got deeper. She was an attractive woman and she was asking for help with things he was certain she could accomplish very well on her own. Was she flirting with him? He was never sure. To his surprise, he found himself saying, 'I'd be delighted.'

'Brilliant. I so hoped you'd help me. And I suppose, if we're being mercenary, that will help you earn some of the forty thousand. Now, details of the funeral, shall we have some more coffee and talk about that?'

Without waiting for a reply, she phoned through for coffee and began looking through the nearest pile of papers. 'Ah, here it is.' She picked out a hand-written list. 'I've noted all that I think needs doing, but it's really for my benefit. I've divided it into what you're doing and what I'm doing. Can you look over the list and make sure I haven't left anything out?'

He surveyed the perfect script. As far as he could see, there were no omissions. 'That all looks fine. There are a few things that we wouldn't normally do – organising the caterers and venue.' He smiled across at Josephine, 'I'm paraphrasing here – making it a boozy do with posh food.' He flicked the paper with his finger.

'That could spend a good portion of his forty grand. I've no idea what solicitors normally do but my bit looks fine. Can I have a copy of this?'

'Sure. I'm afraid it will be in black and white – that's all my copier will do at the moment.'

'No problem,' he replied. But there was a problem, a niggle in the back of his mind that he couldn't put his finger on. Was it that she'd said she couldn't shake hands but had been happy to touch his sleeve? Or was it just that he was finding her disturbingly attractive? It had been so long. Too long. He made a decision.

'We're having a Jubilee Party on the third, a sort of street party. Would you like to come?'

She looked surprised, then pleased, then disappointed. 'Oh, I'm sorry. I have something else arranged for that day.'

Of course you have, he thought.

'But I'm sure I can pop in for a short while. Give me the address and time and I'll do my very best to be there.'

Chapter 5

Sunday 3rd June 2012

Ben was not enjoying the street party. It was cold and wet – flaming June – but not in a good way. He'd spent half his time watching to see if she'd come, and the other half berating himself for acting like a teenager. He'd detached himself from the crowd and decided he'd watch the first of the flotilla on television, then take himself off to start his assignment. It was due in a week and he still hadn't started. He was usually punctual but, since Stanley's corpse had arrived in his establishment, he'd been unsettled. He was deep in these thoughts when a voice at his side said, 'Sorry. I couldn't get here earlier. I'm afraid I can only stay ten minutes, but I thought I'd just pop by to say hello.'

She looked fabulous. She was wearing summer clothes which showed off her figure, but with what he thought might be called a pashmina thrown casually around her shoulders. She looked at his glass, then at the table where the multitude of drinks was arranged. 'I'm driving, but I could manage one small glass of wine. Is that OK? As an interloper?'

They moved over to the table together and Ben noticed several heads turn as they passed. And why not, he thought. She looks stunning.

As he poured her drink, he opened the conversation in the traditional English way. 'Miserable weather, isn't it?'

'Oh, so depressing for the Queen. I'm definitely a royalist – what about you?'

'Not really. But I do feel sorry for her. She'll have to stand around for hours in this weather. I wouldn't change places with her for the world.'

Josephine looked thoughtful. 'Sometimes I feel I'd like to be someone else.' She smiled up at him. 'But I'm not sure who I'd want to be. No one famous – that's for sure.' She held up her glass. 'This wine's delicious. I must admit I thought, street party – rubbishy wine. What is it?'

He picked up a bottle and looked at the label. 'Villa Maria, from New Zealand. It is good, isn't it.'

She briefly touched his arm. 'I'll have to get some and invite you round to share it.'

Ben was surprised. 'I'd like that. Thanks.'

'D'you think it will rain for the flotilla? Such a pity if it does. I've agreed to go to a party given by someone from the office. I'm sorry I committed myself now.' She looked at her watch. 'Just a brief bit of business before I go. I'll phone you after I've talked to the Murdocks. We need to agree a time for the ceremonial opening of the safe.' She drained her glass and handed it back to him. 'Thanks for the drink. And I won't forget – Villa Maria. And I will invite you round. Bye.'

He watched her departing figure. He didn't quite know how to react, how to interpret the signals. He didn't have time to decide, as he was grabbed from behind by his two daughters. They both spoke at once so he couldn't make out what they were saying. Then Katy said, in a voice louder than her sister's, 'Wow, Dad – *who is she?*'

Sarah joined in before he could answer. 'Is she a new neighbour? If it's attracting her sort, I'll move back here!'

Before he could answer, Maurice came bounding up. 'Ben, you dark horse. Kept her quiet. And she's disappeared before you could introduce me. Shame on you. Couldn't stand the competition, eh?'

Ben held up his hands and they all waited for him to speak. 'She's Stanley's solicitor, so you'll be meeting her soon.'

It was as though he'd burst their balloon. It was Katy who expressed their obvious disappointment. 'Duh! We thought you'd chatted her up. Looked like there was chemistry. Anything like that?'

He hoped he looked non-committal, but realised he probably looked po-faced. 'We'll be working together, so I think we should keep it on a professional basis.'

Sarah responded first. 'Dad, that's complete bollocks – and don't tell me off for swearing. I'm an adult now and a police officer, and you should see what goes on there. There's loads of professional relationships happening in someone's bed somewhere

– or, disgusting this – in a broom cupboard at the station. So, you don't have to worry that we'll be all disapproving and stuff. You're still young enough to enjoy yourself.' She dug him in the ribs and added, 'But hey, not in a broom cupboard — unless that's her thing!'

Katy added, 'Yeah, Dad. If you want me to, I'll go and stay with Sarah. Leave the coast clear.'

'No.'

'Oh, come on, Dad. Next year, you'll be the big five-o.' She wagged her finger at him. 'You'll be too old to really enjoy yourself. Do it now!'

Maurice joined in. 'Hang on a cotton-picking minute, young lady. I've got near on twenty years on your dad and I'm still young enough to enjoy meself.'

This switched the focus to Maurice, and Katy gave him a quick hug. 'Oooh, Uncle Mo's got a girlfriend and he's not telling us.'

'Well no, but I would have if I could find someone who could jive like a dream. My perfect woman.'

'Well, Dad,' said Katy. 'That solicitor looks pretty perfect to me. And you look really good together. What Uncle Mo would call "a handsome couple". Don't look round now, but Mary was watching you all the time.'

He gave a perplexed gesture as Katy continued, 'I said don't look round. Dad, honestly! Haven't you noticed that she makes eyes at you every time she asks you to "do a little job for her". She fancies the pants off you. I thought you knew. Men!' As Ben started to turn, Katy hissed, 'I said, don't turn round.'

He thought back to all the times Mary had got him to fix a tap washer, a light bulb she couldn't reach or some other DIY problem. He'd thought he was just being neighbourly. He was sure he was right and the girls were reading too much into it.

Sarah joined in. 'Dad, you must go round with your eyes shut. You're a catch. Widower, mid-forties-ish.' She laughed and poked him in the ribs. 'Well, you look younger than you are. Tall, fit, good bod, children more or less off your hands, thriving business and you're not bad looking in a silver fox sort of way. You could hook up easily if you took an interest. Plenty of merry widows like Mary around. Heh, fancy joining a dating site? We could set it up for you.'

'No!'

Katy joined in. 'Ha! He's scared he's getting past it.' She put her arm through her father's. 'Look, Dad. You've been hiding away far too long. Uncle Mo agrees.'

At this point, Maurice looked surprised but kept quiet as Katy ploughed on. 'We *all* think it's time you put yourself about a bit.'

Ben looked at his watch and up at the sky. 'I'm going in. It's spitting, and the flotilla is about to start. I'll watch the beginning, then I'll have an afternoon nap – like old people do.'

But his family had already moved off to speak to some new neighbours.

As he turned his key in the lock, the phone rang. He picked up and a voice intoned slowly, 'I know who killed Diane.' Then the line went dead.

Chapter 6

Monday 4th June

It had taken him a long time to get to sleep. His body had tossed and turned just as his brain had done. Try as he might, he could not place the voice on the phone. It had been disguised but he had the feeling he knew it. Eventually, he fell into a fitful doze.

He woke to that same acrid smell – the smell of explosion and death. The same dream but worse. There was still that stench, still the roar of the blast and the heat of the fireball, still the metal flying towards him and the body of his wife falling at his feet. But this time a figure had stood on the edge of his vision – a murky figure. Who was it?

Suddenly, he was scared. For years, he'd been pushing his traumas into a little box in the back of his mind. Now his subconscious was pushing them back out and the time was coming when he would have to face them.

For years they'd been telling him it would help if he could analyse his dream – lay it to rest – but he'd never been able to. He'd just hoped that, like his other symptoms, it would gradually fade. He looked at the time. Five o'clock. He could be at work easily by six, missing the traffic. He could make a start on Stanley without interruption. Embalming him was going to be a long and difficult job – it always was after a post-mortem – but, the pungency of the formaldehyde would replace the smells of death, both past and present, and his brain would be engaged in intricate work. He relished the challenge.

* * *

'Cup of tea waiting for you, Ben.' He emerged from the back room to greet Maurice and Katy at the start of their day. Although it was a Bank holiday, they had agreed to work the morning. His three uninterrupted hours had provided a good start to Stanley Murdock's rehabilitation from the grey tones of death to a healthy pink hue. He looked at his tea and was immediately suspicious. It was dark

39

brown.

Katy winked at him. 'I made your tea, Dad. I know how you like it. And I've made Uncle Mo's, it looks like cat's pee but he seems happy. Oh, and we found this in the letter box. It's from that Chris.' She handed Ben a plain white card scrawled with a name and phone number. He glanced at it, then stuffed it in his pocket.

Maurice grunted at Katy. 'Now then, young lady. Just cos you've left school don't mean you can be cheeky to an old man. I'm sure tea that strong ain't good for your stomach. Ben, want more milk?'

He smiled. 'No thanks. This is fine. We'd better get on. Lots to do.' He went through to the office and returned with a sheaf of papers. 'There's the usual stuff to get sorted.' He handed some of the paperwork to Maurice. 'Mo, can you deal with that? And then there's the additional for Stanley. There's a long list of mourners he wanted to be present. Most have email addresses, so, Katy, I'd like you to try to contact them. We haven't got a date or time for the funeral yet, but if you could just alert them that it's upcoming. Some of them are very busy people, so we want to give them as much notice as possible. Do them all separately and show me the emails before you send them.' Katy nodded as he continued, 'He was thorough, our Stanley. I'll give him that. He's provided contact details, but Josephine doesn't know how old the list is so some may be out of date.'

He leaned over to show Katy, and ran his finger down the list, but she interrupted, 'Hear that, Uncle Mo? It's "Josephine". Heh, Dad, do we think this is forevs?'

'Katy! Enough! Work!' He prodded the list. 'There are some well-known and influential people here so they may be difficult to contact. See what you can do, but don't be downhearted if you get the brush-off.' He handed the list to Katy. 'I'll go and finish making Mr Murdock presentable. The family will all be viewing – even Virginia – and heaven knows how she'll react.'

Chapter 7

The study was opulent. An enormous mahogany desk filled one end of the room. A leather chesterfield and two large button-backed chairs occupied the other. A pale Chinese carpet covered the floor between. On the walls were several more pictures of Stanley glad-handing people that Ben felt he should recognise. Above the fireplace, an oil painting of Stanley dominated the room. Ben thought again how like his father Lucien looked. He glanced across at Virginia and Alistair. They both had delicate features – so different from their half-brother.

   The Murdock siblings sat, silently assembled, there to witness the opening of their father's safe. Josephine beckoned Ben to join her. She pointed to the wall behind Stanley's desk. 'See anything?'

   He moved closer. There was a paler rectangle where a picture had hung. He looked around and saw, propped against the wall, a large framed photograph of Stanley, beaming down at Margaret Thatcher.

   'No. Should I?'

   'Well, if I hadn't had instructions from my erstwhile client, I wouldn't either. It's ingenious.' She pressed a small button next to the wall light and a panel swung open. The safe now loomed, in dark grey menace, over the room.

   Josephine oozed efficiency in her tailored grey suit. 'Good. You've brought a lockable suitcase. I'll explain the process to the family and then we'll crack on.' She took her place beside the safe. All eyes turned towards her. 'Your father left several letters and codicils to accompany his will. In one of these, he required that the contents of his safe be interred with him, without scrutiny by anyone. I have taken advice, and there is no suggestion that your late father was involved in any criminal activity. Therefore, I see no legal reason for countering that request.' She looked at each of the Murdocks and asked, 'Does any of you have an objection to Mr Burton taking the entire contents of the safe and placing them in your father's coffin?'

At the mention of the coffin, Virginia began to shake violently. Katy was the first to move to comfort her. She took Virginia's hand and held it between hers, squeezing it gently. Katy breathed deeply, 'Take deep breaths, like this. Concentrate on your breathing. It will help.'

As Virginia regained control, she gave Katy a faltering smile. Alistair continued to slump in his chair. He mumbled to his sister, 'Ginny, get a grip. It's nearly over. Not long now and we'll be free.' He flicked back his hair and, with his head on one side, looked up through long lashes. 'Mr Burton, we will do whatever it takes to be free of that man. Please do whatever you can to help us.'

Ben was bemused. What was this reference to freedom? He chose his words carefully. 'Mr Murdock, I can see that, both in life and in death, your father may not have acted as you would have wished. I will try to make this time as easy as possible for you.'

Lucien stood up and again assumed leadership of his siblings. He spoke sharply. 'For God's sake, let's get back to the job in hand. We never even knew that our father had a safe. We don't know what he kept in it nor do we want to. Miss Finlay, you've told us that you have what you need to organise and conclude his financial affairs. That is all we need to know, so we are content for you to carry out his wishes. I'm sure that Mr Burton will, in order to receive his full fee, conduct himself honourably.'

Ben's face remained impassive at this implied insult. Maurice, who was standing behind the Murdocks, glared at Lucien with a look of suppressed rage. Katy stifled a giggle by turning it into a yawn. Josephine had turned to open the safe so her expression was hidden. One by one, she carefully placed the contents of the safe on to Stanley's desk.

'One locked metal cash box – no key. One, two, three, four small, sealed envelopes, one large, sealed envelope, one brown paper package also sealed. That's all. Perhaps, Mr Burton, you would check that the safe is empty and then place all these items in your suitcase and lock it.'

As he stood beside her and started to fill the suitcase, she added quietly so only he could hear, 'Fee or no fee, I'm certain that you will act honourably.'

He locked the suitcase and then surveyed the Murdocks. Lucien was looking at his watch. Katy was comforting the weeping Virginia. Alistair looked over at Ben and winked.

On the way out he glimpsed a uniformed policeman sitting in the morning room, reading the paper. The man made no move to greet him nor even to acknowledge his presence. There was no sign of Pam.

Chapter 8

Late the following afternoon, Ben, Katy and Maurice stood in a line outside their funeral chapel awaiting the arrival of Lucien, Virginia and Alistair Murdock. Ben had phoned to ask if they wanted their solicitor to be present and had felt elated when Lucien had said yes.

He looked over at Katy and smiled. He wished that Diane could see how her girls had turned out. It had been a hard road for all of them, but either the steep path was levelling or they were getting used to the gradient. There was just one obstacle to conquer. He felt that if he just reached out...

Maurice nudged him. 'Looks like a wedding reception, all of us in a line, waiting to shake hands with the guests. How come we're doing this? We usually wait inside.'

'Not sure, but I thought we should show respect for the mourners. Not that they are mourners – except Virginia. The other two don't seem bothered. Hang on, this looks like them now.'

A gleaming green Range Rover swung round the corner and braked sharply in front of them. Lucien leapt down, followed by Virginia and Alistair. Lucien strode round to the boot and produced a wilting bunch of purple honesty flowers. Virginia held a single drooping wallflower and Alistair held a healthy purple pansy still in its pot.

Alistair smiled brightly. 'We brought what we thought might be appropriate. We checked with Miss Finlay that they were within the terms.'

As if on cue, Josephine's Mini swung in neatly beside the Range Rover. As she uncurled herself from its interior, Ben felt himself blushing. Maurice nudged Katy and gave a stage wink. He whispered to her, 'See that lassie? Best keep an eye on your dad.'

'Shall we proceed,' said Ben in a level voice, leading the way into their chapel of rest. The Murdocks and Josephine followed in procession. Maurice and Katy joined in at the back, with heads bowed.

In the chapel of rest, a large oak casket lay closed and

surrounded by elaborate floral tributes. Katy positioned herself next to Virginia and pressed her arm lightly. Virginia smiled and placed her hand on Katy's proffered arm. The wallflower dropped a few petals. Maurice scooped them up.

Alistair held his plant in front of him. He kept his gaze on it as though it were a talisman – which it may well have been.

Lucien stood at the head end of the casket, back straight with arms hanging loosely by his sides, the honesty flowers sweeping the ground. Josephine stood back against the wall and eyed the scene with an unreadable expression.

'Let's get this ghastly business over with. Ginny, hold on, old girl.' Lucien sounded almost kindly.

Ben explained, 'In a moment, I will open the casket. Your father's body has been embalmed and presented in a way that is as lifelike as possible. He will seem to be merely asleep. For some relatives, this can be unsettling. According to his instructions, you are each to place a flower in the casket. There is space in the casket for you to do so without having to touch your father's body. Do you have any questions before we proceed?'

Virginia spoke in a low voice, 'Will he smell?'

'No. The only scent will be that of the flowers in the room.'

'And will his eyes be open?'

'No. He will look to be asleep and at peace.'

Alistair looked mischievous. 'I have a question. I've heard that dead bodies sometimes fart. Will he blow raspberries at us in death like he did in life?'

Ben answered levelly, 'No, there will be no escape of gas.'

Lucien was becoming impatient. 'For God's sake Allie, stop being ridiculous and let's get this farce over and done with.'

Ben leaned over and opened the casket. Virginia took a deep breath and, without looking, flung her flower into the casket, wheeled round and left the room. Katy silently turned and followed her. Lucien moved forward, looked long and hard at his father's corpse and smiled. Then he carefully placed his bunch of honesty flowers so the tips were resting over Stanley's right hand breast pocket.

He turned to Ben, 'And I don't want them moved.'

Then he too left the room.

Alistair stepped up and peered at his father's corpse. 'Handsome bugger, wasn't he? But he didn't look like that when he was alive. Not with us anyway. He always had his mouth turned down at one corner in a sneering sort of smile. You've made him look benevolent. He was never that.' Then he leaned over and tipped the pot of pansies and soil over his father's chest. 'There old man, they'll put the lid down on you and that'll be that. Who's in the closet now?'

Then he spat in his father's face and walked out. Maurice followed him leaving Ben and Josephine alone with the coffin. Ben carefully closed the lid. Josephine uttered a short giggle, then turned away from the closed door and put her hand over her mouth. When she took her hand away, she had a thoughtful look.

'Well, whoever killed Stanley Murdock certainly did them a favour. Did you see that look on Virginia's face? No? Well, I could see her as she left. I think she was terrified of him.' She laid a hand lightly on Ben's arm. 'I'll be as glad to get out of here as they were. How about you see them off the premises and then we go for a drink somewhere. I'm parched.'

He was taken aback but regained his composure rapidly. 'Wonderful idea. I'll be as quick as I can.' And he hurried out to say goodbye to the Murdocks before Josephine could change her mind.

* * *

In the short walk to the Cambridge Blue, Josephine surprised Ben by saying that she needed to talk to him as a fellow professional, in confidence, and would this be OK? Having agreed that it would, she proceeded to expound on the idiosyncrasies of the Murdock finances. Ben learned that the family had money – lots of it; with much of it stowed away abroad. It seemed that Stanley's finances were complex and that it would take some time and ingenuity to unravel them. He learnt that a vast sum had come from each of Stanley's two wives and that he had made some very shrewd investments. But Josephine said that the accountant was having difficulty in tracing the origin of some of his capital accrued during his time in Northern Ireland. She was certain, though, that all would become clear in time.

By the time they reached the pub, Ben knew a great deal more about the Murdock family than it was proper for their solicitor to have divulged. As he held the door open for her, a waft of sweet, yeasty air greeted them. The pub was warm and comfortably full, with enough background noise that silences mightn't be a problem. A few of the older regulars were stashed away in corners, their hands nursing their drinks in a proprietorial way. One or two nodded to Ben, then returned to the serious business of silently contemplating their beer. Some younger drinkers were gathered round the bar. Ben and Josephine manoeuvred themselves, with difficulty, to an empty table.

'What would you like to drink?'

'I'd love a beer – a pint? Something local and light.'

At the bar, six rowdy students were obviously enjoying several end of term drinks and it took Ben some time to burrow through. As he worked his way into the throng, a particularly ebullient young man stepped backwards and bumped into him. Ben smiled and held out both hands to steady him. The student apologised profusely, slapped Ben on the back and offered to buy him a drink. Ben refused, adding that he hoped they all had done well in their exams. In turn, the six of them raised their glasses in unison and insisted on shaking his hand. As they went back to their revelries, he smiled at distant memories of an untroubled student life. He was still smiling as he took their drinks back to their table

'A pint of Dionysus and a pint of Justinian – both light and with a hint of citrus, or so the barman tells me.'

Josephine smiled up at him. 'Dionysus and Justinian – only in Cambridge would you have beer named after Greek Gods and Roman Emperors. I'll go for Dionysus, the god of the grape.' She took a sip. 'Beautiful. Just as I like it.' She pointed towards the students who were now trying to drink from the wrong side of their glasses. 'They obviously like it here. How about you? Have you always lived in Cambridge?'

'Most of my life. I did a stint in the army but apart from that, yes. You?'

'Nearby, anyway. Lived with my mother in Cherry Hinton till she died. Three years ago, now. She worked at one of the colleges so we used to get the bus in together. Now I've moved into one of those new flats over the fire-station. No commuting.'

'Which college?'

He noticed a slight hesitation before she replied. 'She worked at lots of colleges. She never stayed at one for long. She was always moving on.'

'And you like living in the city?'

'Love it. The flat is all clean lines and everything that the house in Cherry Hinton wasn't. It's modern and completely clear of clutter and I love sitting on the balcony after work, even if I have to sit in my coat and gloves. The balcony looks out over Parker's Piece.'

Josephine took a sip of her beer. 'In winter when the trees are bare, I can just see over the wall into the grounds of St Etheldreda's. It's beautiful in there. And there's even the bonus that the flat's handy for work and for going out in town. What about you? Do you live in the city?'

'Yes, in one of those Victorian houses off Hills Road. It's been in the family since it was built, I think – three generations anyway. And now I rattle around there with Katy. She'll be leaving home soon, no doubt, and then I'll rattle round even more.'

The moment had passed to tell her that he had studied at Etheldreda's, but anyway, that had been another life.

'And your wife?'

That took him off balance. Of course she would ask about the wife he hadn't mentioned. 'She died sixteen years ago. I haven't got over it but I've sort of got used to it.'

'I'm so sorry. I hope I haven't opened old wounds.' Then with an abrupt change of subject, 'You mentioned the army? Maybe I'm wrong, but you don't seem like the army type.'

Josephine paused and leaned towards him, taking another sip of her drink. He swallowed a gulp of his beer.

'I signed up on a whim because of a family argument. My father wanted me to come into the firm, but I couldn't work with him. So I joined the army, was invalided out, and then went into the family firm anyway. The old man was ill by then and died soon after, so I took over. Been there ever since. The firm's doing well. Don't get much repeat business though!'

He winced inwardly as soon as the words came out and then

relaxed as Josephine replied. 'Yes, I gather fathers can be a problem. I didn't know mine. He died when I was very young. So my mum brought me up on her own. It was hard for her. Enough said.' And again she took him off-guard, 'So, your father? Why couldn't you work with him?'

Ben had the feeling that he was in the witness box. 'It was because he didn't understand honesty. He always did what was expedient. You know, always took the easy option which was not necessarily the right one. Sorry, that sounds pompous, but I just couldn't deal with it.'

She looked thoughtfully at him. 'Not pompous. Just honest. I admire that. In my job I meet so many shady people. It's really refreshing to have someone declare themselves to be honest. I wish there were more like you.' She sat back again, doubling the space between them and added, 'Families eh? But I like Katy. Tell me about her.'

'Well, she's seventeen. She'd insist she's nearly eighteen. She's beautiful, she's clever, she works hard, and she's very like her mother.'

God, thought Ben. Must I go on about my dead wife? He looked at Josephine but she was still smiling so he ploughed on. 'Katy decided not to go to uni and, I must admit, I was disappointed. She's young for her age, she has a few good friends but she needs to get out more. Much as I'd miss her, I think it would have done her good to get away from home. Anyway, she wanted to join the firm. She's got all the right qualities to make a good fist of it. But then, maybe I'm just a tiny bit biased.' He smiled. 'Also biased about Sarah, my other daughter – she's nineteen. She's clever and confident and will go far. She's just joined the police.'

'They sound delightful. I'd like to meet Sarah too. Is she working on the murder?'

He downed the rest of his pint, realising he was drinking too fast. 'I'm sure Sarah would love to meet you. She keeps pushing me to go out more.' He paused and pointed to Josephine's glass, which was still half full. To fill in the silence, he asked, 'Are you ready for another? Looks clearer at the bar, now that lot have subsided into chairs.'

She smiled up at him, her lips parting just enough for him to glimpse her white teeth. His heart missed a beat.

'That would be lovely,' she said. 'A half this time, I think. But before you go, you haven't answered my question. Is Sarah involved in the investigation into Stanley's murder? It must be a big thing at Parkside.'

'Fraid so. The inspector in charge is an ignorant bully and I'd rather she kept her distance. But she's full of it. Why do you ask?'

'Just professional curiosity. Stanley was my client and I'd like to know who killed him.'

He nodded. 'A half, are you sure?'

'Yes, I've got to keep a clear head. I have those favours to ask.'

As he waited to be served, he counted back to the first time he'd been out with Diane – his last first date – more than thirty years. They'd been undergrads at Ethel's, young and carefree. He weaved his way back to their table with two halves. Josephine had finished her first drink and immediately raised her new glass and said, 'Cheers, Here's to Stanley. It's because of him that we're sitting here now.' She took a sip of her beer. 'Now, tell me about your Uncle Mo. When I was chatting to him, I think he said he used to be in the police. Have I got that right?'

'Yes, he left the Force when Diane died and almost ran the business. He was my life-line. Now, I make sure he meets up regularly with his old mates.' He laughed. 'He doesn't take much persuading. There's a regular "pie and pints" session – more pints than pies, I think. And they gossip. He loves it.'

'Really? So you think old men gossip?'

'If Mo's anything to go by! He says Parkside is leaky and, as far as I can tell, he's a big part of the sieve!'

Josephine's eyes sparkled. 'I love gossip – not the stuff that hurts people – but just knowing what's going on. I'll have to have a good chat with your Uncle Mo. Now, can we talk about those favours?'

Ben's mind was turning over what she'd said, and he nodded absently as Josephine outlined the favours she wanted from him – visiting a Professor and a prison.

'You see,' she said, 'I just can't go to visit Michael

Murdock. I suffer from cleithrophobia.' At his look of complete incomprehension, she laughed. 'Yep, no one's ever heard of it. It's like claustrophobia but more refined. It's fear of being locked in. That's why I never went for the criminal side. I just couldn't bear the thought of going into a prison. And going to see that prof – I think that's my mother's influence – they just terrify me.' At his perplexed look, she added, 'She was a bedder and scared stiff of all academics.' She looked appealingly at him. 'You'd be doing me an enormous favour if you could help me with this.' Again, she smiled as she looked up from under her lashes. He felt confused. What did she want from him? He could find no answer.

Chapter 9

The next morning, after his run, Ben arrived at work to see Katy and Maurice sorting piles of paper. Katy stopped immediately. 'Brilliant! You're here. Save me from this. It's so boring. Come on Dad, give us the low-down. How did it go? Are you seeing her again?' Katy bounced up and down as she waited for his response. Maurice looked equally impatient but refrained from bouncing. He leaned towards the silent Ben. 'A drink, you said. I phoned you at ten and you still wasn't in. That was one helluva long drink. By the look of that sheepish smirk, it went well. Put us both out of our misery. Tell us!'

Ben laughed. 'We talked for a long time about Stanley's violin. It's worth a fortune. A Garnerius, I think she called it. Something beginning with G anyway. Like a Stradivarius. And I was right.' He turned to Maurice and poked him in the chest. 'So, Doctor Watson, the Holmesian stuff isn't nonsense after all. Stanley was an accomplished violinist. That could account for the long little finger.' He smiled before continuing, 'Have I told you the theory about the little fingers of young violinists?'

'Yes!' They yelled in unison.

'And the opposing theory that it's hereditary.'

'Yes!' they yelled again.

'Now,' Katy added, 'Tell us about last night!'

'OK, so Josephine knows a lot about Stanley. It seems he studied music at Ethel's, got a Starred First and was expected to go on to great things. Solo stuff. But, after graduating, he dropped out of the music scene altogether – disappeared – and emerged some years later as a businessman with money. I asked Josephine if she knew where he'd been in those missing years. She said she didn't, but she was cagey. I think she knows much more than she's letting on, but it's a matter of client confidentiality.'

Katy butted in, 'I bet he was in jail. Now you've made him look lifelike, there's a mean look to him. And his kids hate him. And there's that cousin in jail so it might be in the genes.'

'Katy! Your imagination will get you into trouble one day. For God's sake don't say things like that outside these four walls. Promise?' Katy nodded solemnly. He continued, 'The cousin should be pleased. Stanley's left him the violin. Josephine's put it in some secure vault for when he gets out of prison. She wrote to tell him about it but didn't know then that it was worth millions. Apparently, they do this dendrochronology test somewhere in Sussex and you can get an immediate date so she's ninety-nine per cent certain it's genuine, but she says she'll get a second opinion. She wants me to visit Michael Murdock in prison and tell him about his good fortune. And then maybe I can ask him about criminal motivations. I need to get this bloody assignment done.'

Katy and Maurice looked not in the least impressed and it was Maurice who voiced their thoughts, 'Bugger the violin and your assignment. What about Josephine? Are you going to see her again?'

'Oh, yes. I think so. Do you think dinner or the cinema? Which would you choose?'

'Dinner,' said Maurice.

'Cinema,' said Katy. 'Then you can hold her hand in the dark.'

'Cinema, it is.'

Katy flung her arms around her father's neck. 'I'm so happy. Ha-ha, I'll just go and phone Sarah. This time, I'll be the first with the news!'

As she hurried from the room, Maurice said in a half-whisper, 'Didn't want to say in front of Katy – know how she makes mountains – but I managed to get copies of them ransom notes. They're odd. Only about a sentence in each and no mention of a ransom.' Just as Ben was about to take a look at the notes, the shop door pinged.

As he walked through to the shop, he was surprised to see Sarah, looking flustered. 'I didn't expect to see you so soon. You OK? Has something happened?'

'Well, yes. It's Turnbull. He's relieved Pam of her Family Liaison duties and he's sent me to ask you a few questions.'

Ben could hear the slight wobble in her voice. All thought of ransom notes left him and he was immediately in dad mode. 'Not to worry, love. I'll answer all your questions. Come through to the back.'

As he made tea, Sarah took out her notebook. 'To be honest, Dad, I'm not sure what to ask you. I was in such a state that I didn't take in what Turnbully said. I don't like being shouted at – especially in front of everyone.' She shrugged her shoulders. 'But I suppose I'll have to get used to it.' She took a deep breath and the tremor left her voice. 'I was so keen to join the force but now I'm not sure it's the job for me.'

He asked gently, 'When Turnbull was shouting, was it to do with fingers and ink?'

Sarah sniffed. 'I think so. He was making such a row about it, and all the others were watching, so I couldn't ask him to tell me again. All I remember is that he said some nutter had called in, and he gave me your name and address. I know you're not a nutter, so I queried that and he told me to get the f… Well, you know what I mean. So, I came and now I don't know what to do.'

'Don't worry. I know what you'll need. Photos of Mr Murdock's hands. I'll print some off. You should get some from your police photographer too. They might not be as clear as mine but you should ask. I didn't clean off the spot of ink – just in case it was needed. Then, if you want, I'll take you through to show you his hands for yourself.'

As he searched his computer, he fumed about Sarah and her boss. He fumed about Chris and his entry into his ordered existence, and he fumed about dating and how he'd forgotten how to do it. He printed the best pictures of Stanley's hands and took them back to find Katy and Sarah deep in conversation. As soon as he entered the room, their babble dissolved into silence. Katy was the first to recover.

'Dad, I was telling Sarah how they'd tried to scrape under his nails to get evidence. Well, she knew about that so we decided we'd treat ourselves to the new nail bar in town. And don't worry, I'll have something discreet.' Her voice took on a tone that Ben recognised. 'Dad… how d'you fancy treating me to some new nails? Like, to add to my new professional image?' She giggled. 'Promise, not black.'

'No, Katy. The best I'll do is offer you an advance on this

month's salary.'

Sarah added, 'Hellooo, Katy. Welcome to the real world!'

'Well, a girl has to try. And before you ask, I'm well into that list but some are out of date, so I've got some internet searching to do.'

Ben smiled at her, spread the photos out in front of Sarah and pointed to the little fingers and the small spot of purple ink. He explained that he thought the ink was important because it was a rarity and that the long little finger might be of passing interest. While he talked, Sarah took copious notes. He finished with, 'Have you ever seen the body of a murder victim?' She shook her head. 'Well, this one is looking presentable – apart from a patch of soil on his shirt. So how about a peep? Then, when you see the first one in the job, it won't be such a big deal.'

'Thanks, Dad. I've always said you were dench. Ready when you are.'

Ben had no idea what 'dench' was but he thanked her for the compliment – and wished he was dench enough for her to confide in him.

* * *

He waved Sarah goodbye, telling her to come back if there was anything more he could do. He returned to the office to find Katy and Maurice staring at the computer. 'Look at this, Dad. It's gross. I sort of got side-tracked searching and found what happens when you die of thirst. Did you know it's a form of torture? Know what I think? I think they were trying to get information from him and he wouldn't tell so they gave up and left him to die. What d'you think?'

'Katy, I think you are wonderful and I love you, but I also think you have a vivid imagination and a job to do. He had money. He was kidnapped. It went wrong. Now he's dead. And he's left a list of people to be informed.' He added, 'Josephine tells me the funeral is going to be a big deal. Now we've got the date, she's put details in the local paper and a few of the nationals have latched on. There's been a lot of interest. How's it going with contacting that list of mourners? There are some famous names – could be difficult to get through to them.'

'Well, Dad, that's where you're sooo wrong. There were ninety-four on the list and I've emailed and phoned almost all. There are three playing hard-to-get, and there's a couple who've moved on that I'm trying to find. Seems Stanley had some clout with all of them. As soon as I mentioned it was to do with his funeral, they all spoke to me and said they'd be there. Real eager, like. I'm thinking this funeral will be full of ghouls.'

Katy's ghost impersonation made Maurice laugh. 'You're doing a grand job, lassie. You could be a private detective, but don't think all our jobs are like this. It's mostly boring, boring. Oh, and did I say dull?'

Katy gave Maurice a friendly punch and continued, 'The Cambridge dons and the businessmen were dead easy. There's a few in Northern Ireland that took a bit of tracking down, but they're coming. This one's a bit different.' She pointed to a name near the end of the list. 'Michael Murdock, the cousin who's serving the prison sentence. They put me on to the governor, no less, and I'm waiting to hear if he'll be allowed out.'

Ben leaned forward. 'Josephine told me he's near the end of his sentence so they'll probably let him come.'

Katy looked pleased with herself. 'I asked the governor what he was in for, just in case he was the violent type. It was money laundering but, seems there could be a problem about letting him out for the funeral. Not sure why.'

'What about the three hard-to-gets?'

'They're all being elusive. The contact details from Stanley seem to be right, but I get zipped answers from all of them. Like I was one of those cold callers – which I suppose I am. The people who answered the phone took all the details but wouldn't give out any info. When I tried to pin down when I'd hear from them, no joy. I'll try again now I know that Stanley's funeral is going to be a big draw.'

'Great. You're doing a grand job. We've organised the extra staff. Mo, can you chase up the hotel and food people? That's the bit that worries me most. It's out of our control and it all has to be perfect. I'm pretty sure the press will be there, and I don't want us to be the story.'

* * *

As he re-entered the back room, Ben's thoughts jumped between Chris, who would undoubtedly bring 'the Services' back on to his radar, and Josephine, who confused him.

With thoughts elsewhere, he unlocked the suitcase containing Stanley's secrets and started to unpack the mystery parcels. His mind was so far from the job that it was only when he heard the metallic thunk as the cash box hit the floor, that he realised his elbow had sent it flying. He swivelled to see the clattering of the single item revealed as the box burst open. A small gun was skittering across the tiled floor. It came to rest beside the far wall. He slowly bent to pick up the box. It was a long time since he'd seen any firearms, or had any in his possession. It seemed to Ben that this one stared at him through its single eye. Ben stared back.

Time slowed. Still watching the gun, he carefully took a clean handkerchief from his pocket and gently lifted the gun, pointing it away from himself. He checked and found that it was loaded. He removed the cylinder and put the gun and ammunition separately into the box. He ensured that the barrel pointed down into its recesses, necessary because the now dented box made it impossible for it all to fit snugly inside.

'Fee or no fee,' he said, 'I've buggered this one up.' He called for Maurice. Katy followed like a shadow.

* * *

Maurice was adamant. 'We're doing them a good service so they don't need to know.'

Ben remained unconvinced. 'I keep thinking of Josephine saying that we could comply with his wishes as there's no evidence of criminality. Maybe he was involved. Otherwise, why would he have a gun? And if he was, we should be taking this to the police.'

'Whoa there, Ben. Some people have guns and they're legit. If Stanley had a firearms certificate, then there's no criminality in owning a gun. Before we go high-tailing it to the police and perhaps wasting Turnbull's precious time, we need to know whether this gun was licensed to Stanley. If it was, then owning it is not a crime.'

'Uncle Mo's right. Turnbull already thinks you're a nutter.' Katy gave his arm a squeeze and added, 'Do you want to talk it over with Josephine to see what she thinks?'

He definitely did not want to discuss this with Josephine. She'd said that she expected him to act honourably. He didn't plan on admitting that he was doing precisely the opposite. He made a decision. 'I feel bad about this. It's going against the client's wishes but I think we should keep this between ourselves unless we find evidence of criminality. That means we have to look for the firearms certificate, and, if it exists, it will probably be in one of those envelopes next door. Mo, D'you know what these certificates look like?'

Maurice nodded. 'I've seen them. Come on. Sooner we get started, sooner we'll know.'

They agreed to open the four small envelopes, one by one, and stop when they found the firearms certificate. The large envelope would be next and the package, last. Ben carefully opened the first small envelope. It contained six documents co-signed by Stanley and Lucien. Each was an IOU showing that, over the past two years, Lucien had borrowed substantial sums from his father.

'Blimey, Dad, this adds up to eight hundred thou. He must be chucking it away to get through that in two years.'

Maurice laughed. 'Lassie, if it's that much money, it's usually gambling. I've seen millionaires brought low by it. Gets to be an obsession. They're addicted to the next win.'

Ben intervened, 'He was probably buying a house. And even if it was gambling, that's not criminal, so let's move on.'

He opened the second envelope and withdrew a single photograph of Virginia walking arm in arm with an older man in soldier's uniform. He was looking straight at the camera while Virginia smiled up at him. On the back was written in rounded script, 'With Simon – now he'll have to marry me.'

Katy took the photo and stared at it. 'She looks so happy there. Must be five, ten years ago? D'you think she was pregnant?'

Ben looked glum. 'Seems the likeliest explanation. No sign

now of Simon or a child. I wonder what happened to them and to the happy Virginia we see here. All gone the same way, I suspect. Next please.'

Maurice opened the third envelope and the photographs that fell out were of a completely different nature. Ben quickly gathered them and covered them with his hands. Looking over at Katy, he shrugged in seeming apology.

'Don't worry Dad, I've seen worse. It's gay porn but very mild. Let's have a look.'

He looked to Maurice for guidance, but Maurice avoided his gaze.

'Dad, I think I recognise some of them. I think I went to college with them.'

With a final show of reluctance, Ben handed over the photos.

'Yep, that's Jodie. He was in my year. And that's his brother, Peter, Paul, something like that. He was a year older and a real bad lad. The others were in his year. I recognise them but can't put a name to them. No idea who owns the back of that head in such an interesting position. But hey, just look at their faces. None of them seem unhappy!'

Maurice looked closely at the photos. 'They look young though. Katy, any idea how old they were when these were taken?'

'We were all at Sixth Form College so we'd all be sixteen, seventeen, about that. Wait – Jodie had a tatt done round his left nipple as soon as he was sixteen. Showed it off to all of us. It was gross. I couldn't do that for the world. Look, there it is so he must be at least sixteen. The others would all be older. Seventeen. Bloody Hell, I never knew they were up to this stuff.' She turned to her father, 'And you think I was wild. A few piercings and a Goth phase. You got off lightly!'

Ben was surprised to find that his first thought, in the midst of all this chaotic evidence, was relief that his daughter did not have any tattoos.

Maurice nodded. 'They were over the age of consent so not criminal. Dirty pictures to lay to rest with Stanley. The more I hear and see of that man, the more he disgusts me.'

Ben looked thoughtful. 'Three small envelopes, three

Murdocks. Lucien owed his father money. Virginia – who knows what that picture means – but it means something to her. And the third… I think the back of that head belongs to Alistair. I think Stanley had a hold over each of them and these envelopes held the evidence.'

Katy's lips curled in distaste. 'Dirty pictures. I can see why he might like to have dick pics, but you're saying he blackmailed his own children? That is so gross!'

Ben responded. 'I didn't say blackmail, but perhaps it's the same thing. Maybe Stanley used these to control them. You should ask Sarah about coercive control. It's a big new thing on my course.'

Katy's lips curled further. 'How disgusting! Now I understand why they all wanted him dead. Let's have lunch. I'm starving.'

* * *

As they sat eating sandwiches, Ben was deep in thought. He watched Katy munching away and envied the resilience of youth. He'd just wanted a quiet life but through his blunder they'd strayed into forbidden territory. They'd uncovered secrets which a dead man had wanted to accompany him to his grave. Now the three of them were party to those secrets. He'd felt gratified by Josephine's description of him as an honest and honourable man. He'd always shown respect for his clients, – the more so because they were dead. Over the lunch he could not eat, he asked, 'What I'm saying is, should we continue?'

'Yes,' came the reply in unison.

'Dad, you're too hard on yourself. You found a gun. You found that our client was a nasty man. At the moment we can't be certain he was into anything illegal. We got into this by accident but we need to finish what we started. If we find evidence that the police could use, we'll hand it over and take the consequences. Deal?'

Ben pushed his half-eaten sandwich away. He wasn't going to share with his daughter that they now had evidence the Murdock offspring all had a motive for killing their father. He looked across at Maurice and could see him coming to a similar conclusion. He caught Maurice's eye and surreptitiously shook his head. He mouthed 'Later.' Maurice nodded.

He collected the rest of the items retrieved from Stanley Murdock's safe. He picked up the fourth small envelope, this one padded. Drawn on the front was a square with 'Tom' written inside. 'Any idea what that means?' The other two shook their heads. Ben opened the envelope and shook out its contents – one small key. He looked inside to see if anything had been left. 'That's it. Nothing to say what the key is for.'

Maurice turned it over in his hand. 'Not a door key – too small.' He pointed to the box that the gun had resided in. 'And too big for that box. Wonder what it's for?'

Katy was examining the envelope. 'I wonder who Tom is?' She took the key from her great-uncle, turned it over in her hand and plopped it back into the envelope.

'Next, please.'

Ben opened the large envelope and spread its contents in front of them. 'Another copy of that list of mourners. No, a shorter list, but this time annotated.' He thumbed through it. 'I know this one, Dr Hallfield. He's a criminal lawyer, gave one of our lectures last term. There's a list of times and places with a question. "Ask him about Clare." Could be Clare College, a woman called Clare, County Clare? Could mean anything.' He leafed through the other pages and came across another name he knew. Dobson. The less he knew about that man the better. He shoved the papers back in their envelope, then dropped the key envelope in with them. 'Lots of paperwork but no firearm certificate.'

Maurice ripped open the brown paper surrounding the last package. 'Got it,' he shouted. 'Firearm certificate for Armscor muzzle loading pistol – in date. The gun's legit. Should have been kept at the gun club, not in his safe. Not the most heinous thing. At least it was under lock and key. But, look at this. Stacks of funny money. Says Helvetica. I thought that was a typing font.'

Ben looked closely at one of the bundles of notes. 'These are Swiss francs, loads of them. Could be millions. Why would Stanley want to bury so much money?'

A scrap of paper fluttered to the floor. Katy bent to pick it up and giggled. 'Get this! It says, "5th issue Swiss francs. Worthless. I'll get the bastard, sure as eggs is eggs."' Her face fell. 'Oh, this isn't funny. It goes on, "Margaret won't be so pretty after this." I wonder who the bastard was? And I so hope Margaret is OK. D'you think that was Stanley's wife? Why would he threaten his own wife?'

The three of them jumped as Katy's phone rang. As she left the room to take the call, Ben and Maurice gathered up Stanley's secrets. Maurice looked thoughtful. 'You know we must report this? It's evidence.'

'Don't say anything to Katy. We'll tell her later. But, yes. I'll make the call now.' He didn't want to confess to DI Turnbull so decided that the lesser of the two evils had to be Chris. He took the crumpled card from his pocket. On one side was printed in biro the name 'Chris' and a mobile number. He turned it over a few times. 'I'll phone and see what we have to do.'

Ben went to their chapel of rest and closed the door behind him. He tapped in the number on the card. Chris answered after the first ring. 'Ben, I wondered when you'd ring. I know you're not keen on us, but we do need to meet.'

Ben interrupted, 'Listen. This is important. I need advice. Stanley Murdock. There were items in his safe that he stipulated are to be buried with him unopened. I thought they were all papers but I knocked one on to the floor and it was a gun. Should I take it to the police?'

Chris's reply was loud and immediate. 'Don't do that! That's the last thing you should do. Listen, we have an interest in Stanley – you know what that means – and we don't want the boys in blue under our feet. Understand? Let me think. I'll get back to you. Two minutes.' And the line went dead.

Exactly two minutes later, his phone rang. 'You say he wanted them all buried with him? Do as he says. Tuck them all in with him and nail it down, or whatever it is you do. Don't read any of them. You hear? If they are what I think they are, they'll be safer under the ground. That all?'

'Yes. Don't you want to know if this is legal?'

'No, just do as he said.'

'Look Chris. This is serious. I think he was into major

crime. Are you sure about keeping it from the police?'

'Absolutely positive. Bury them all. Bury everything. Word from on high. National Security. Understand? Got that, Ben. Every fucking thing. Bury it.' And he rang off.

Ben returned while Katy was still in an animated phone call. He took Maurice's arm and led him further away from Katy's hearing. 'I've reported what we've found and I've been told to follow Stanley's requirements and bury his secrets with him.'

Maurice looked sceptical. 'What, he don't want it kept for evidence? That's rubbish. What kind of cop is he?'

Ben took a while to answer. 'He's not a cop. He's with the security services and they have an interest in Stanley. I don't know what that interest is and I don't want to.'

Maurice lowered his voice to a whisper. 'Security services. MI summat? Christ, what was Stanley up to? You don't want to get involved with them. We need to get him in the ground double fucking quick.'

Ben was amazed. Maurice never swore. As Maurice finished speaking, Katy strolled back in. 'You'll never guess who that was. Virginia. She's asked me to tea. She was so upset after the flower farce that I gave her my number.'

'How did she seem?'

'OK. Her voice didn't wobble. I've said yes for tomorrow. Is it OK for me to go?'

Ben thought for a moment before answering. 'Of course you must go. But please, on no account let on that you know what was in her father's safe. I've spoken to a man higher up than Turnbull. I told him what we have here, and he says we must follow Stanley's wishes to the letter.'

Katy danced from foot to foot. 'Oh! This is brilliant. Sooooo exciting. I wonder what Stanley was up to? I think he was into blackmail or maybe gun-running. And that money – what was that all about? D'you think he was a gangster… Mafia maybe?'

'Katy, stop right there. You must tell no one about this. Do you understand?'

'Can't I tell Sarah? Just Sarah.'

'No one, and especially not Sarah. Do you understand? This is the most important secret you have ever been asked to keep.'

'Yes, Dad.'

'Promise me.'

'Yes, Dad.'

'Katy, look at me. I'm telling you this now and you must tell no one. The man I called confirmed that Stanley was a dangerous man and the sooner we get shot of him the better for all of us. His secrets will go with him to his grave and then we can forget him. You're going to tea with Virginia. Let her talk but don't you tell her anything. Is that clear?' He turned to Maurice. 'And Mo, you can take that look off your face. It's going to be fine.'

Chapter 10

Monday 11th June 2012

Ben had agreed that Katy should visit the Murdock household on her own. If he'd refused, she'd have wanted to know why. Being a free spirit, he wouldn't put it past her to have gone anyway. There was a family liaison officer on the spot, so he could be pretty sure that she'd be safe – even if one of the Murdock offspring *had* killed their father. He knew that his girls needed to make their own mistakes. That was the logic, but emotionally, he was finding it almost impossible to let them.

He'd relished the peace of some time spent on his own and had looked again through the paperwork destined for Stanley's grave. The list of mourners was the most enigmatic and therefore the most interesting. Each entry was accompanied by veiled insinuations of wrongdoing. He'd recognised only two names, Professor Hallfield, whom he respected, and Professor Dobson, whom he considered to be at the other end of that spectrum. In disgust at the thought of Dobson, Ben had thrust the paperwork back in the envelope and had taken all of Stanley's illicit possessions and locked them in the fireproof box in his bedroom.

* * *

'How was the tea party, Katy? Did she tell you how the three of them staged a kidnapping and topped the hated patriarch?'

'Oh, Dad. She was terrif. Once you get behind the stroppy front she puts on. I don't think she was involved in the murder but I wouldn't put it past that Lucien. D'you know, he looked right through me. Made me feel like I wasn't good enough to be in his poxy house. I think she's lonely and once she got going, could she talk? And, get this, it all backs up what we think. I'll call Uncle Mo and tell you about it.'

Ben wondered if Maurice had been hovering just out of sight because he immediately called, 'Cuppa, you two? I'll just go and make one.'

As soon as they'd gathered, Katy told them to sit. Ben could see that she was relishing being centre stage. 'It was a real eye-opener. I think she's been bottling it up for ever. This family is incredible – weird, weird, weird, but seriously loaded. The money clocked up over the years and it seems Stanley could be a bit of a charmer. Wife number one had Lucien then upped and died. The inquest said it was accidental. Virginia says the family think it was suicide, but I think she was murdered.' Katy paused and, when there was no response from her audience, continued. 'Her money was divided between Stanley and Lucien. So that meant Lucien could leave home when he was sixteen. Virginia's never forgiven him. Says he abandoned them. Dad, can you pass me another biscuit?'

Katy stopped long enough to dunk her biscuit, lose a bit in the bottom of her mug and fish it out again. When she'd retrieved the soggy mess and eaten it, she lurched on. 'Listen, though – this is the best bit – only four months after his first wife died, Stanley marries again. Another heiress. That was Margaret, the one we buried.'

Ben smiled at Katy's use of 'we'. She hadn't been around for Margaret's funeral but was already being proprietorial about the family firm.

Katy continued, 'She had Virginia and Alistair. Stanley was so mean to them. He kept it so they had no money of their own. Margaret fell down the stairs six months ago and died, and Lucien said it was an accident because he saw it happen. Huh! Accident! No way was that an accident! But what I can't get my head round is why they didn't all leave the old bastard and start a new life without him.' She took a sip of tea and waved her free arm expansively. 'Now, what I think is, Stanley killed his two wives to get their money, then Lucien killed his father. Trouble is, that doesn't fit with the torture bit. Surely, even Lucien wouldn't torture his own father?' She stopped for a moment. 'Here's a thought. It could be the man who swindled Stanley with that Swiss money. Stanley went after him and he turned the tables. Uncle Mo, you were a cop, what do you think?'

'Ah, well, lassie. Sorry to disappoint you. I was only a wooden-top but I think your dad's right. It was a kidnapping gone wrong. I'll be going to my pie session tonight so I'll find out what the police are thinking.'

'But kidnapping for money is so boring. I want it to be exciting. I was reading this book...'

'And that, Katy, might just be the problem. Reading too much into things. Even if it is a boring murder – if there is such a thing – what you are doing is a great job in supporting Virginia. Looks like she needs it. I'll have to go and see them again. Lucien won't be pleased but, if they want to inherit, they've got to help us spend this forty grand.' He waved his finger at his daughter, 'And, Katy, no more flights of fancy.'

If Katy had been surprised that her small acts of kindness towards Virginia had wrought such a change in attitude, Ben wasn't. He suspected that this had been the first kind act that Virginia had received since her mother's death. Lucien wasn't the most sympathetic of brothers and Alistair seemed wrapped up in his own problems. Ben had clients who had told him secrets they'd never have dreamt of sharing with their nearest and dearest. Listening and then forgetting was all part of the job.

The evidence in those little envelopes suggested that Stanley had made sure he controlled his offspring. He could see how their confidence could have been eroded to such an extent that escape would seem impossible. And, anyway, where could they have gone? Stanley had money and contacts, so surely, he would have tracked them down. He knew enough about Stanley to be sure that he wouldn't have let them go if he could help it. Only a few days to go and they'd all be rid of him. Stanley would be safely stowed and they could forget him..

'Dad, come and see this.' Katy was pointing at her screen. 'I've found the answer.'

'Life, the universe and everything or something more important?'

'We got the gist of the wallflower and the pansy – they were easy. I've been trying to work out what the honesty flowers meant.'

'Well, I can't imagine that Lucien was declaring that Stanley had been a totally honest and upright citizen.'

Maurice popped his head round the door. 'Does that mean your clever daughter has worked it out?'

'Yes. And how on earth you all managed before the internet,

I'll never know. Look here. It does make sense when you know that the seed pods of honesty are also known as "the coins of Judas". Adds a whole new meaning to Lucien's offering.'

'Well, well,' said Ben. 'Clever old Lucien. A bit more subtle than his siblings. I wonder they had the courage to be so up-front with their floral tributes – especially Alistair. He's certainly come out in the last week.'

Katy added, 'And did you notice Virginia's new outfit? Make-up, clothes. She looked ten years younger. She told me she's seeing a counsellor and she's going to move away. She's determined to start afresh and get a life. Good for her. About time.'

Ben was gathering paperwork. He looked at a very long list. 'Let's see what else needs doing. They're not letting the cousin out, so I've got to go and see him. I'll do that after the funeral. Have we covered transport, flowers, catering and orders of service? All in line with Stanley's instructions? Good. We've organised the extra manpower plus the catering. It's only two days to go. We'll be in the spotlight so we've got to get this one absolutely right.'

Chapter 11

Wednesday 13th June 2012

This was the part of his job that Ben most enjoyed. The opportunity for silent contemplation. The preparation was done. The T's were all crossed and the I's dotted. Now, he stood looking down the nave of the church feeling the usual sense of tranquillity that an empty church gave him. He breathed in the essence of the place, the aura of agelessness, of generations past and those yet to come. The stillness of the air enveloped him and he felt safe from the perils of his world.

This was the church that Stanley had specified. It was a church that Ben loved. Even though he'd lost any belief in a god or an afterlife, he still came to concerts here, and wondered if he would ever be able to appreciate its beauty after Stanley's funeral. He supposed that it was his choice whether he allowed Stanley's ghost to haunt him. And what of Diane's ghost? He pushed that thought away.

He surveyed the purple and white funeral flowers hung at the end of each pew. The faint perfume of freesia and sweet peas wafted around him in pleasant undertones. The order of service booklets were stacked in neat piles at the back of the church; fatter and more ornate than was usual, including, as they did, the words of the many readings and hymns that Stanley had specified.

Stanley's casket stood at the front of the church, bathed in flowers and ultra-ornate coffin furniture. Ben had buffed the handles till they shone like fool's gold. To some this would seem like a display of wealth; a sign, as with the ancients, that this man had been important, and so took adornments with him to smooth his path into the underworld. To Ben it looked vulgar. He had the feeling that Stanley's passing – if it were to be into an underworld – would need a lot of smoothing.

Hearing a noise he looked up. A figure dressed in black was edging into place at the organ. From this distance he looked like an enormous bat until Ben realised that the man was wearing an academic robe. Stanley had specified the organist, a renowned musician and a fellow of St Etheldreda's. The organ pipes wheezed into life as the organist began the repertoire that Stanley had ordered. Ben looked at his watch. The service would not be starting for half an hour but it was usual for mourners, plus any passing tourists and interested onlookers, to arrive early.

It could have been that the music was the signal, but now the empty church began to fill. Ben nodded a further greeting to the six sturdy pall-bearers. They were regulars and knew their part well; keeping a low profile, melding into the darkness at the back of the church until the time came to remove the coffin to the plot in the churchyard beyond. He took his place beside Maurice and Katy at the main doors and began to hand out orders of service. He could see that a few people were entering through a side door – one that had previously been locked. In order to ensure that they had service booklets, Ben took a handful and advanced, with decorum, to the front of the church. The 'side door people' had begun to fill the first row of unreserved seating. Three men knelt with heads bowed and grunted in response to his suggestion that they might like an order of service. They took the booklets grudgingly and muttered something unintelligible, all the while keeping their heads down.

He retreated to the back of the church and motioned to Maurice. Maurice spoke in a low voice. 'Press photographers out front. Reckon them lot's camera shy.'

Ben looked at the other participants. He couldn't call them mourners. Several wore full academic paraphernalia. Professor Dobson was there, sitting at the front as though he was part of the family. He was talking to another begowned figure. The two men shuffled further along the pew as they were joined by five others in academic attire and Ethel hoods. So Stanley was still known at Ethel's. He wondered what the connection was.

There was a distinct buzz that was not altogether usual at a funeral. Under the cover of the music, people were chatting loudly, tapping each other on the back, renewing old acquaintance. He looked at the congregation and could see not one sad face.

At the appointed time, Lucien, Virginia and Alistair Murdock made their appearance. Lucien led the other two to the front of the church. No deference and decorum here. They strode to the front in quick time, heads held high; united in their desire to get their father deposited in the ground with what might be called indecent haste. Indecent, if you hadn't seen the three envelopes that Stanley had wanted to go with him to his grave. Only Ben knew where Stanley's list of mourners was, and it was not in his coffin. He'd kept the list, the threatening note and the innocuous key. Keeping them could be dangerous but he had a niggling belief that Stanley's story hadn't finished with his death.

He looked round to see if Josephine had arrived and noticed a nondescript figure slip into the church at the last minute and melt into the background. Ben decided that this must be Chris. Then the Minister appeared centre stage, the organ belted out Onward Christian Soldiers, the congregation rose and the service began.

* * *

'Bloody hell, I'm knackered.' Katy took off her hat and laid it on a table, spreading the chiffon trails with care. Then she kicked off her shoes and fell backwards on to the settee. 'What a day. No hiccups, thank God. And was anyone sad to see him go? And did you see those heavies from Northern Ireland? They were sooo scary.'

Maurice sank down beside her and stretched his legs in front of him. 'Yeah, a bit odd seeing them mixed with the great and good. There was some real high-ups there. And them 'heavies' was right alongside the posh lot. We had the good, the bad and the ones who was exceedingly ugly.' He took off his shoes and rubbed his feet. 'Sorry about the smell but my feet are killing me. Did you see that politician – whasisname? You know, the one caught with his fingers in the till. And that TV presenter with the orange face. Not a pretty pair.'

Ben looked at them both slumped on the sofa. 'No staying power you two. I'm going for a run. The best way to get rid of adrenalin. Anyone fancy a jog to Lammas Land?'

Maurice ignored him and continued with his tale. 'Did you see them ugly buggers – clever how some of them managed to dodge all the cameras, hats over their faces. And them ones as went in the church by the side door. Reckon they must've organised that with the vicar. Hey, though, I'm sure some of them shy ones was undercover police. They had that look about them. You get to know

71

it after a while. They wouldn't have wanted to have their cover blown.'

Katy suddenly clapped her hands and laughed. 'D'you know, I thought some of the waiters were a bit off. Maybe they were cops too. It would be a really good way to earwig. No one sees waiters, do they?' Katy looked coyly at Ben. 'And Josephine looked stunning. I bet you didn't notice, but black really suits her.'

Maurice chimed in, 'See how she charmed them uglies. She made sure she talked to all the "bad boys". I think she was making sure she kept them in order so they wouldn't kick off. Now, if she joined the firm, even the dead would sit up and take notice.'

'Enough!'

'Oooh, must be going well. Anyway Dad, do we have a day off now Stanley's safely stowed?'

'You should be so lucky, my girl. We've got someone coming in tomorrow and we've got to earn the rest of our fee. Even with all the trimmings that Stanley ordered we've got some way to go. I'll start with the cousin. A pity they wouldn't let him out. I've arranged to see him on Friday at Highpoint.'

Ben's need for a run had nothing to do with the events of the day – except one. As the Northern Irish contingent had been about to leave, the largest one had sauntered over to him and left a parting shot. The man had prodded him in the chest. Ben could remember his words precisely. 'I know you, pal.' And he'd pointed his thumb in Katy's direction. 'Yer wee girly's grown apiece since I last saw her. She'll be missing her mammy. Friendly warning, keep yer nose out.' Then he'd prodded harder. 'Yer ken my meaning?'

Ben did. And he was determined to do precisely that – keep well out of it.

Chapter 12

Friday 15th June 2012

It had taken five days to get confirmation of the visit. Ben arrived early at the gates of Highpoint prison. Apart from the tall iron grilles and the stout gates, the first sight of the buildings reminded Ben of the Council estates in Belfast, row upon row of flat concrete buildings lacking any character but that of depressed sameness. And both places had that overwhelming sense of menace hovering around them. He shuddered and shook off his feeling of doom.

Prior to his visit, he'd read the rules and had ensured that he had less than forty pounds and no sharp implement, phone, camera, chewing gum or wax, cigarettes, consumables, drugs (as if he'd know where to get any) or a toy gun. All phone and photo equipment had to be left outside, so he looked round the empty car park then hid his phone in the depths of his car.

He had been told to allow half an hour to get through security, but he was the only visitor, and one representing a solicitor. So the search was, to his mind, cursory. After the metal search, there was a rub down search which was not nearly as intrusive as he'd expected. His name was highlighted on a list – a list with just one name – and his pockets were searched. The forbidden items were read out, and he confirmed that he carried no contraband. He handed over his car key. Then he was led through a metal door which was locked with a large key in full sight of another prison officer and a surveillance camera. There followed a second and third door, also unlocked and locked in turn with the same degree of oversight. Ben followed the officer across a yard to an inner perimeter fence which loomed at least twice his height. A metal gate was opened with a fourth key. The gate swung open noiselessly and, after their entrance, swung back with a clang as the lock hit the stock closing it automatically. Inside that fence, there was not a sound; no hum of human activity, no traffic noise, no bird song.

Accompanied by the prison officer, he walked past rows of

municipal looking buildings, each one square and solid with barred windows and stout doors.

Their arrival at the door of the visits hall was prefaced by a raised voice from within. 'Where the feck is he? I've been waiting here for twenty fecking minutes and, contrary to what you people think, I haven't got all day to sit around waiting for bloody solicitors' runners.'

The prison officer turned to Ben. 'Used to be a model prisoner till that uncle of his died. Been a right pain in the arse since then.' With that parting shot, he opened the door, motioned Ben to enter, turned and walked away whistling tunelessly.

Ben entered to find another prison officer nonchalantly sprawled in a chair that was too small for him, and the back view of a tall, thin young man pacing the floor. As the man turned, his face brought Ben up short. Ben stared across the room at a reflection of Diane. This young man could have been her brother or her son. As Ben entered, the young man stopped pacing, pointed an accusing finger and shouted across the divide.

'Oh, so you've bloody deigned to arrive, have you? Well, you needn't have fecking bothered. I know about the bloody violin. Bloody Stanley has shafted me for the last time. Said he'd see me right. Left me a bloody violin. Can you credit that. It's not a fecking violin. It's a fecking fiddle, so it is.'

During this diatribe, Ben had had a chance to regain his composure. He held up both hands, palms facing the angry young man. The prison officer looked on from under hooded lids. Ben decided he might be heard if he matched Michael Murdock's words. Still holding his hands up, he said with authority, 'Michael – listen! That fecking violin is worth a fecking fortune. Do you understand? Your violin is worth millions. Enough to keep you in luxury for the rest of your life.'

Michael Murdock had obviously heard at least the gist of the message. He fell into a chair and leaned forward over the table in front of him. The anger in his eyes was gradually replaced by a creased brow of bewilderment.

'Say again.'

Ben sat down opposite but made sure to keep a safe distance from this volatile young man. He spoke softly and slowly. 'The violin that your Uncle Stanley left you is a Guarneri. One was sold recently to an anonymous buyer for nine million pounds. Nine million pounds. That's not to say that yours is worth that much, but Stanley's solicitor has had it verified and placed in a secure vault at the correct temperature and humidity.'

To Ben's consternation, Michael Murdock began to weep. Ben shook out a clean handkerchief and held it aloft and, following a nod from the warder, handed it to Michael. Michael wiped his eyes and blew his nose. Then, when Ben refused the soiled handkerchief, stuffed it into his pocket. He leaned further forward and whispered, 'You're sure? He told me he'd see me right. I thought he'd died and left me stranded. Bloody wild, I was. I've done seven years for him. That was the bargain. He'd see me right.'

Ben trod water. He needed to know what he'd waded into. He leaned forward on his chair, folded his arms lightly in front of him and said, 'Tell me.'

Michael glanced at the warder, then continued in a whisper, 'D'you know, you're the first visitor I've had in seven years. Can you believe that? It's not been great in here but could've been worse. They all think I'm UVF or IRA. Silly buggers don't know the difference. Works though. Makes them wary of getting on the wrong side of me. They think there'll be repercussions.' Michael took out Ben's hankie and blew his nose loudly then continued in a voice so low that Ben had to lean in further to hear him. 'If they'd known it was Stanley with the connections, not me, my life would've been hell. You can see why I didn't put them right. They left me alone and I've spent my time studying. I'm outa here in one month and nine days. But I'm broke, I've got nowhere to live and I don't want to go back to Belfast. So, how long before I can get the money?'

Ben didn't answer. His client, whom he'd buried four days ago, comfortably settled with at least some of his incriminating evidence was, if Michael Murdock was to be believed, a liar, a terrorist and should have been a felon if this young man hadn't taken his place. He needed to be sure. 'Tell me again – just so I'm clear. What did Stanley do?'

Michael looked over at the warder then back at Ben. Ben could see the anguish etched in Michael's face. 'That bastard – what didn't he do? I've had years to think about what he was up to.' He gave a wry laugh. 'Was too feckin' green to see it at the time. I was taken in good and proper but he was one evil bastard. Anything nasty to do with money, he was into it. Smuggling, laundering, more, but I've got no proof.' Michael smiled grimly. 'D'you know. I'm glad he's dead. Rids the world of one stinking problem.'

Ben kept his voice calm, 'I'll have to talk to Stanley's solicitor. She's his executor so she'll know. How about I come back when I've got some news.'

Michael smiled. 'I'd really like that. I'd forgotten what it was like to talk to someone human. Come back soon please.'

'Yeah, soon as I can. Anything you'd like me to bring?'

'Toothpaste.'

Ben turned to the reclining officer, 'OK if I bring toothpaste next time?'

The officer nodded then lumbered out of his seat. 'Coming back then? Mind you phone first.'

On his way out, Ben realised he'd forgotten to get the papers signed. He'd have to do that when he brought the toothpaste. As he reached the car park, empty except for his car, he could see a paper flapping under his wiper. Bloody advert, he thought. What the hell are they advertising here? When he reached the car, he saw it was a note:

'Ben, do <u>not</u> talk to anyone until you have seen me. Lives are at stake. Chris.'

He screwed the paper in his fist and shouted out loud to the empty car park.

* * *

The churning in his stomach, the little beads of sweat; Katy and Maurice had insisted, otherwise he might have backed out. But they'd looked him over and agreed that he'd scrubbed up well, and now he was approaching Parkside Place where he was meeting a beautiful woman who seemed keen to get to know him better.

He'd been surprised at the funeral, just as they were finishing up. She'd waved goodbye to the last of the 'bad boys' and had come over to congratulate him on a perfect send-off for Stanley.

Then she'd said, 'We've still got business to sort out but let's forget about Stanley and all his doings for a while. Let's go out. What are you doing Friday evening?'

He'd been doing nothing, and now here he was doing something – something he'd forgotten how to do. He was taking Josephine to see one of his all-time favourite films, 'The Man Who Fell To Earth'.

He reached the front door and pressed her button on the intercom. She responded immediately, 'Come on up – fifth floor, turn left to the end – number fifty-one.'

He hadn't felt this alive since he'd left the army. He ignored the lift and took the stairs two at a time. He arrived at the fifth floor slightly breathless so gave himself a moment to regain his composure. Josephine's head popped out of a door at the far end. 'Hello,' she said. 'I wondered where you'd got to.'

'I walked up the stairs. Not used to five flights but it was worth it for the unfolding view.'

'Come in. Do you mind taking your shoes off at the door. It's the beige carpets. So difficult to keep clean.'

'No problem.' He immediately noticed the orderliness of the flat. 'Lovely place you have here.' But he was not looking at a home. The room was decorated in those shades of beige that never offend the eye. The beige on beige was not to his taste – it reminded him of those show-homes he'd traipsed round with Sarah when she'd decided to move out. But they, at least, had had ornaments scattered around to break up the monotony. Here, there was nothing to give a clue to the owner.

'I managed to get some of that wine we had at your street party. Shall we have a glass before we go out.' As he moved to close the front door she added, 'Please leave the door ajar. Then I know it's not locked.'

Of course, he thought. Cleiso-something-or-other. He followed Josephine into the pristine kitchen. It was indeed as she'd described it – all clean lines with not a utensil in sight. He couldn't imagine his kitchen being this tidy, even after Katy eventually moved out.

He held out the bunch of flowers to Josephine. 'I couldn't come empty handed.'

'Thanks – I'll arrange these later if that's OK with you.' She took the flowers and put them in a jug of water in the sink. Then she washed and carefully dried her hands before removing two sparkling long-stemmed glasses from a cupboard and opening the fridge. It was not at all like Ben's chaotic fridge, always so stuffed with food that it was difficult to see what was inside. Neat plastic boxes met his eye – all stacked in order of size. Josephine pointed him towards a stool by the centre island. 'Have a seat while I open this.' She poured two glasses of wine to exactly the same height and handed him one. He was fascinated. He had never been in surroundings such as these. It was like sitting in a film set and he almost expected someone to leap forward and shout, 'Cut!' When no one did, he said, 'Beautiful kitchen. Are you fond of cooking?'

She looked around. 'Not really. It's a waste, isn't it? I don't have much time and I have no one to cook for. And you?'

'I love it. I do most of the cooking at home. Maurice often comes round and Sarah comes back for a good feed and, of course, Katy hasn't left home yet. They sometimes bring their friends, so it can turn into quite a party.' He could see that Josephine was looking wistful and wondered if he'd been a bit too effusive.

She looked at the clock on the wall. Ben checked his watch and realised that her clock was ten minutes fast. 'Your clock's fast,' he added.

'I know. I'm a bit paranoid about being late so I always keep it fast. Are you ready to go?'

He quickly finished his wine and stood up, even though he knew they had plenty of time to walk to the cinema. As a Bowie fan he'd been looking forward to seeing this re-run of 'The Man Who Fell to Earth'. He hoped Josephine would enjoy it too.

While she collected her bag, he idly picked up a book from the shelf in her living room. As Josephine re-entered the room, he placed the book at the end of the shelf. Without comment, she repositioned it in the place it had originally held. 'Let's go,' she said. 'We don't want to be late.'

* * *

After the film, they walked into the crowded streets of Friday-night

Cambridge. The noise of revelry was all around them. Even though most students had vacated the city for the summer, the Regal was doing a brisk trade. Young people were crowding round the doors and it was proving difficult to get past without straying on to the road. One of the over-large bouncers saw the problem and parted the crowd for them. As Ben thanked him, he replied, 'S'OK. Can trust them not to get run over when they're on their way in. End of the night, wouldn't let em near a road if I had my way. Townies are better'n students though. Do as they're told. G'night.'

It was the first time in years that Ben had heard any mention of town versus gown. As one of the few Cambridge undergraduates who had been born and brought up in Cambridge, he had been acutely aware of any differentiation based on town/gown status. The mention from the bouncer took him back to the time he'd punched a fellow student, an ignorant aristocrat, for denigrating the residents of Cambridge. He remembered the dressing down he'd received from Dobson, for starting a brawl in the college bar. Fines were imposed and he knew that his would have hit his pocket far harder than that of his adversary. It would have, if the adversary had not paid both fines and asked Ben if he would care to join the University Amateur Boxing Club as the varsity match was approaching and they needed to win back the Truelove Bowl. He had and they had. The thought of it now was anathema to him. He'd gained a full blue. His thoughts turned to his Victoria Cross. Another prize he'd won.

They were half way across Parker's Piece when Josephine's voice interrupted his thoughts. 'You thinking about the film? I enjoyed it.'

'No,' he replied. 'I was thinking about undeserved prizes.'

She looked quizzically at him and he saw that they were approaching a large puddle. It nearly blocked the entire path so he automatically took hold of her elbow to help steer her round it. He felt her stiffen then relax and wondered what was going on in her head. He replied, 'That bouncer got me thinking about my youth. I gained some prizes. Not sure I deserved them. Glad you liked the film. I was a bit worried that it wouldn't be your thing.'

'Oh, but it was a love story. And about lost families. But no happy ending. I didn't like that. I like happy endings.'

This gave Ben a whole new perspective. He'd always thought of it as a film about corporate greed. He decided he'd have to buy the DVD and look at it again.

They had reached Josephine's apartment block. 'Thank you', she said. 'I really enjoyed this evening but, if you don't mind, I won't invite you in. I've got an early start in the morning.' And she gave him a quick kiss on the cheek and disappeared inside.

Chapter 13

Monday 18th June 2012

Ben looked out at the manicured, rolled quad and the Wren church behind it. The buildings were still that pale yellow that had attracted him to this college in preference to the larger and more imposing ones. He wondered how many generations of ducks had waddled across that perfect grass. They and the dons would, he was sure, still be the only ones with permission to do so.

He must have passed this spot every week for the last sixteen years and hadn't given it a thought, not in the latter years anyway. He'd expected to feel something. But not this surge of emotion that standing at the threshold of these buildings had brought – trepidation, anticipation, a burst of sorrow and just a hint of joy. *Why joy?* He hadn't expected joy. He'd lived cheek by jowl with this world for all those years and had avoided it, at first with intent but lately it had simply slipped away from his reality. Why had he allowed himself to be sucked back in? He looked across at Josephine as she bent low to sign them in – russet hair, straight back, long legs. Was that why?

They wound their way up the stone stair and waited in an ante-room. An iron-haired woman bade them sit and disappeared into the room beyond. She reappeared immediately and pointed to the light over the heavy oak door as it blinked green. 'Professor Dobson will see you now.'

Ben's stomach lurched. She hadn't told him it was Dobson they were going to see. Sod's law – could have been any bloody professor and it had to be him!

The room looked exactly as all the others in main college: wood-panelled walls, old oak desk, a large fireplace with hefty logs set in place, sagging settees to sink into, bookcases crammed to the ceiling in higgledy fashion. The smell of the books. How he remembered that mellow, musty odour. But that was his other life. He didn't dwell any more on what might have been. Hadn't thought of it for years.

He looked across at the occupant of the room. He hadn't changed much either, tall, austere, black hair now flecked with grey. He'd always had a lined face but now the lines had deepened. Big teeth – he'd forgotten the big teeth. Dobson greeted Ben as an old friend, even though their last meeting had been less than cordial.

'Benedict, what a pleasant surprise. When Miss Finlay telephoned and said you were accompanying her, I was astonished and delighted. We've followed your progress, you know.'

Ben looked across at Josephine and shrugged. She should have told him it was Dobson. Then he would have said he knew him. Dobson continued in what Ben knew to be mock sincerity, 'I was so sorry to hear about your foreshortened army career and the death of your poor wife. But I had no idea you were burying poor Stanley. I do hope I won't be in need of those services in the near future.' He laughed – a giggle that was so out of kilter with his low and cultured voice, that it took Ben right back to tutorials in this room. Those intense sparring matches competing with this man in order to win a mathematical argument. Ben studiously avoided Josephine's gaze.

Dobson was speaking in his usual unctuous voice, 'Benedict, now we're reacquainted, I must invite you to formal hall or to one of the Master's sherry parties. There's someone I think you should meet. And Miss Finlay, I'm so pleased to meet you. It's a bit early for sherry. Would you like coffee?'

Without waiting for a response, he pressed the intercom and barked an order for coffee. The coffee arrived with such speed that the tray must have been waiting outside the door.

'Benedict, come and help me serve.'

The professor held out a cup and, as Ben took it, held on to it just long enough to allow him to whisper in Ben's ear, 'You turned me down and had the temerity to join the intelligence corps. We'll have to remedy that.'

Then aloud, he said, 'Let's get on then, shall we. Stanley was a strange fellow. I'm at a loss to know what he wanted to share with me after his demise.'

In an effort to remove thoughts of the professor's 'remedy', Ben said, 'And we've been at a loss to know how you two knew each other, and why he left a letter addressed to you. You seem to have had little in common.'

If he hadn't been in a heightened state of awareness, he might have missed the intake of breath and infinitesimal tremor in the professor's voice as he began his reply, 'Didn't you know? He read music here. Apparently, he was a brilliant violinist. Of course, Benedict, you will know that music and mathematics are intimately linked. I wish I'd known him then – alas not. However, our paths crossed later.' He pointed a thin finger at Ben. 'We do try to watch over our alumni, you know. Especially those who can support our many fund-raising events or contribute in other, more intimate, ways to the reach and influence of the college. I'm sure, Benedict, that you, of all people, will understand my meaning.' He turned to Josephine, 'Now, Miss Finlay, tell me, what do I have to do?'

After a fierce look at Ben, Josephine went through the preliminaries while Professor Dobson scrawled his signature on her form. 'Mr Murdock's instruction was that I was to await your response to the contents of this letter. Of course, you have the right to ignore his instruction. However, I am bound by it, so I must ask. Do you have any objection to opening the letter now and responding?'

While Josephine was talking, the professor's eyes were fixed on the letter in her hand, and as she held it out, he grasped it with an eagerness that, to Ben's eyes, was completely out of character. Dobson ripped open the envelope and took out a single page and another missive consisting of several sheets stapled together. Dobson took the first and scanned its contents, then fell back in his chair and laughed heartily. He stood, then marched over to the bin and, with ceremony, lit the corner of the single sheet, held it for as long as he could and only then dropped it into the bin to watch it burn. He placed the other papers in his desk drawer, closed and locked it, then turned back to face them with a smile.

'No response. That's one bit of business finished.' He fixed his eyes on Ben. 'But Benedict, if I recall correctly, we have some unfinished business of our own.'

Ben carefully placed his cup and saucer on the table and stood up. He was adamant in his reply. 'No, Professor, our business was finished thirty years ago. We will not be revisiting it. Josephine, I think it's time we left. Goodbye Professor Dobson. We won't meet again.'

The professor smiled indulgently. 'My dear boy, I'd not bet on that if I were you.'

* * *

'What was all that about?' Josephine had marched them to a café in St Andrew's Street. She had waited until he had bought two black coffees. Now her voice had a hard edge to it that Ben had not heard before. 'Why didn't you tell me?' she hissed. 'You studied maths at Cambridge and you never thought to tell me. You were a student of Professor Dobson and you thought you'd waltz in and I wouldn't notice that you knew each other.' Her voice rose. 'What kind of a fool do you take me for?'

He looked round but everyone was studiously intent on the food in front of them. He replied, 'I'm really sorry. Of course I don't think you're a fool. You didn't tell me it was Dobson we were seeing. If you had, I'd have told you. He was my tutor at Ethel's. I was there before I joined the army. I know I should have told you but the moment never seemed right. I thought it would seem like boasting. And anyway, it was another life. It's history. I'm not the same person now. Nothing like.'

He could see that she was not mollified. She pointed an accusing finger at him. 'And he was being so kind in renewing your acquaintance and you blanked him. You marched me out of that room and you were rude. So, what gives?'

'Look. We never got on. Thirty years ago he wanted me to follow a profession that I didn't want to and I told him where to go. I haven't seen him since. As I say – it's history.'

But Ben knew that history it was not. He knew that yet another call would come from Chris and that history was about to repeat itself.

Chapter 14

Wednesday 20th June 2012

St Etheldreda's by moonlight was beautiful. The pale-yellow stone had taken on an ethereal air but Ben hardly noticed. He approached the Master's Lodge with a mixture of anger and anticipation; anger at the threats that had been used to get him there and anticipation that he might, at least, get one over on Dobson.

The Master's Lodge was just as he remembered; tall windows, pristine paintwork and an impressive front door. He'd been invited there just once a year, in each of his years as an undergraduate. For that particular Master, it had been the pretty boys who had received repeated invitations and he had never been a pretty boy.

Dobson approached him immediately with that oleaginous smile. 'Benedict, I'm so pleased you could come. Let me introduce you to the Master and then there is someone you really must meet.'

Professor Dobson waved his hand to summon a waiter and took a glass of sherry from the proffered tray. Ben picked up a glass of orange juice. It had become inevitable; that 'someone' would be Chris. The first phone-call had come even before Stanley's body had crossed his threshold. Then, Chris had left his number, and later, someone had followed him to the prison. Dobson had given him the message. He was certain that the chance that his path would eventually cross with Chris's had reached inevitability. He was equally certain that he would need to keep his wits about him.

Dobson introduced him to the Master and there followed a brief conversation. It quickly became clear that the Master was unsure why an undertaker was present at this gathering; a presence which was explained neither by Dobson nor by Ben.

As they detached themselves from the Master's coterie, he turned on Dobson. 'Listen, Dobson. You got me here by threats. Don't forget that those Services that you think so highly of caused my life to disintegrate.'

'Come, come, Benedict. You exaggerate. Now, the person you need to speak to is over here.' Professor Dobson motioned towards an inconspicuous young man who, at once, detached himself from a small group and joined them as they walked to a far corner. Ben looked him over; late twenties maybe, medium height, medium build, medium everything and a face that was totally forgettable, all good attributes for a spy. Ben was gratified to see that he had been right. This was indeed the person that he had seen slip into the church at Stanley's funeral. The young man thrust out his hand and took Ben's in a pump action shake.

'Mr Burton, I'm so pleased to meet you at last. So good of the Prof to arrange this so I don't have to follow you up. I'm sure that you've twigged that I'm Chris.'

As he shook hands Ben thought, play the game, play any game you like while you find your way through to understanding what they want. It's their game and they make up the rules. Just don't make it easy for them. Make them work for it and, if in doubt, act the uncomprehending idiot.

'Hello Chris. I'm afraid you have the advantage over me. We've just met and I'm already confused. Follow me up, you say? Good God, you're not a relative of a client, are you? I am so sorry. That is unforgivable. We pride ourselves on our service to the families of our clients. If we have neglected you, I can only offer my abject apologies. We're usually very efficient. Tell me your surname and we'll be on the phone to you first thing.'

Ben was beginning to enjoy himself. Dobson was looking distinctly annoyed – in that sniffing-a-bad-smell pose that Ben remembered so well. Chris was obviously searching for the best way forward. Ben fingered the card in his pocket, Chris's card, and then went into full empathic mode.

'Chris, such a difficult time for you. Some people want to talk about their loss; others need to look inwards for a while. In our profession we see people at their most vulnerable and we always respect their wishes.' In a childish gesture, he crossed his fingers, knowing that in Stanley Murdock's case, this was certainly a lie. He continued. 'Do you want to talk about your loved one or would you rather we talked about something else?'

'Oh, for God's sake, Benedict. Take that bloody undertaker's hat off and engage your brain. I assume you still have one? You know very well for whom Chris works. You do not yet know why he needs your help.'

Ben was not going to let that barb pass without comment. 'You know, Dobson. Implying that a man with a head injury might not have a brain is so unsympathetic as to be downright cruel. And then to follow it with a request for help is inept bordering on crass. I think I deserve an apology. Wouldn't you agree, Chris?'

Chris grinned. Dobson scowled. Ben waited.

Chris looked across to Dobson and gave a slight nod. There followed a grudging and insincere, 'Apologies, my dear boy. I'd quite forgotten your unfortunate injury.'

Dobson's scowl deepened and silence ensued. Chris quickly filled the void. 'Professor Dobson, you must have other people you need to talk to. I'm sure we can amuse ourselves for a while. See you later perhaps?'

Dobson was obviously reluctant to leave and eventually replied slowly, 'Certainly, dear boy.'

As Dobson marched away, Ben's brain took in the slow speech. That voice on the phone. It had been Dobson. But, how could Dobson know who had killed Diane? He had no time to consider this as Chris brought him back to the present. 'He's a pompous old git and devious, but he's useful. Enjoyed your RADA performance just now, but let's get down to business. Firstly, did you bury that shit of Murdock's like I said?' At Ben's nod, he continued, 'Good. We were waiting for the proverbial to hit the fan when he died. It hasn't – not yet, anyway. We need a favour from you. A big favour. A very, very, big favour. It's possible that a whole bloody great edifice may come crashing about our ears. Our people will get hurt, possibly killed. You could stop this, and I'm not sure how to persuade you to help.'

Ben took a couple of breaths. He now knew he had the upper hand but Dobson had rattled him. He needed to stay calm if he was going to get what he wanted out of this encounter without falling into their clutches.

'Chris, I can tell you now that I'm not interested.'

Chris laid a hand on his arm. 'Hold on Ben. Just hear me out, please.'

Ben needed to stay. There was Michael Murdock to consider. He pretended to think for a moment. 'OK, two minutes then I go.'

'I've read a lot about you. Your army record is imp...'

'Long time ago.' Ben waved his hand dismissively. 'I'm a different person now.'

'You sure about that? Heard you tackled a mugger last month, brought down a hoodie and got an old girl's bag back. Kept it quiet too – didn't get your name in the paper. Not in the same league as what you used to do, but shows me it's still there. Not everyone puts themselves in the line of fire and walks away incognito.'

Ben looked at his watch. 'You've eaten into your two minutes and told me nothing. And flattery won't help. I'm not interested in whatever it is you people have to offer.' Then he added in an undertone, 'And the last straw? I don't take kindly to being blackmailed.'

He turned away. The move was so fast that Ben hadn't seen it coming. Chris grabbed his arm in a firm grip and would not let go. 'Ben – please – a minute? No one's blackmailing you. We hoped you'd be interested in helping your country. I know you've already done more than your share but we can see that you still have what we want. What's with this blackmail thing? Who said anything about blackmail?'

Chris was still holding his arm in what must look – although it certainly did not feel – like a friendly gesture. Ben surveyed the room, knots of men in their black ties, quaffing their drinks, a few women dotted about, and he could think of no way of disengaging himself without causing a fuss. 'Dobson, that's who. Don't forget, I know your sort. You're going to tell me you knew nothing about it. Well, it won't wash, so let go of my arm. It's time I left.'

'Dobson. Christ! I'm sorry. Look, I need to deal with him. If I let go, will you promise to hear me out.'

Ben turned towards Chris. He'd got angry and had nearly blown it. He needed to get this blackmail thing sorted; to make sure no one got hurt on his account. He nodded.

Chris let go of his arm and smoothed his sleeve. 'Sorry about that. And yes, I am going to say I knew nothing of any blackmail threat. We know a lot about you and I can't think of anything that Dobson could use against you. As far as we know, you've led an exemplary life.' He waved his arm in the direction of Dobson. 'You must have a skeleton we haven't discovered. But let me tell you – and this is for real – we can make that skeleton disappear if you'll help us.'

'And if I don't, the skeleton starts to rattle?'

'It depends. Out of my hands. I'll do my best but who knows what the brass will say. Hear me out and I'll see what I can do. Will that do for now?'

Ben nodded as his thoughts shifted back to Michael Murdock. He wasn't sure why Michael's safety was so important to him. Probably because he was just another innocent in danger. A vulnerable person in the line of fire, and he had seen too many of those to feel comfortable about allowing harm to come to any one of them. He didn't trust Chris, but Chris was his only option, so he had to listen. 'Go on.'

'Thank you. We need help, and it seems you might be the only person who can give it. You're assisting Josephine Finlay with the terms of Stanley Murdock's will. Let's just say we have an interest in Stanley and Stanley's family. We need someone to befriend the three Murdocks and their cousin Michael, and to find out what they know about Stanley. That's all we want. Not too much to ask, is it?'

Ben knew, of course, that that wouldn't be all they wanted. He'd escaped once. The intriguing question was, did he want to escape again? To his surprise he found that he was ambivalent. The tingling feeling deep in his stomach told him that he was interested. And it wasn't just that he wanted to save Michael.

Chris continued, 'We're trying to avert a disaster which would undoubtedly lead to blood-letting. Very nasty stuff. We know why Stanley Murdock was killed and we need to find out what his family know. They have no friends, no one we can approach. We've had our people talking to them, disguised as police. But no dice – they won't talk. We think that you are the perfect person to draw them out, and find out what they know.'

He considered for a moment. That little kernel of excitement was back. How long since he'd taken a risk? Too long. 'OK. I can do that. But only if we can get the blackmail sorted. That's the deal-breaker.'

'Tell me,' said Chris.

Ben nodded his head towards the group that Professor Dobson was declaiming to. 'It's not my skeleton. It's not a skeleton at all. Your friend Dobson may be Bursar here, but he's scum. He invited me here with the proviso that, if I didn't fall into line, the word would be put out that Michael Murdock has no paramilitary connections and he's gay. You know what that means in jail. If you want me to work for you, I need to know that Michael Murdock will be protected for the remainder of his sentence and that he'll be allowed to inherit Stanley's violin. If you can't guarantee those two things, I'll walk.'

Chris looked over at Dobson. 'Blimey, he takes the... Look, we can do that, no trouble. We have contacts in Highpoint who can put it about that Michael has very dangerous friends. We'll put a watch on him in prison and, if need be, we can make sure this violin isn't considered under the Proceeds of Crime Act. That's guaranteed. So will you do it?'

With the balance between apprehension and excitement just tipping towards the latter, he said, 'It just means extracting some info from the Murdocks?'

'That's all.'

Ben looked dubiously at Chris. It probably wouldn't be all. If he did this for them, they'd be back but he could cross that bridge later. 'I'll do it.'

Chris let out a long breath. 'Thanks, Ben. That is a huge load off my mind, I can tell you. I'll phone the prison now to have a watch put on Michael, and you can be sure we'll rein in Dobson. Might not have to. He'll probably have his comeuppance in October.'

Ben was intrigued. 'How come?'

'New Master next term. A woman. Very impressive and she won't take any nonsense from the likes of Dobson.'

Chris was holding out his hand. 'You may not think so, but we do believe in gentlemen's agreements. I do, anyway. So, can we shake on it?'

Solemnly, they shook hands.

'I'll be in touch tomorrow to give you your brief. I've got one call to make and then I'll phone the prison. We'll get that sorted this evening. But, thanks. Stanley Murdock has some serious shit hidden. We need to find it.'

Chris moved away and took out his phone.

As he turned to leave, Ben found Dobson blocking his path. He looked round to see if he could dodge this encounter without causing a stir and found that it was impossible. He recoiled as Dobson lightly tapped his arm.

'Benedict – a very useful evening, I'm sure you'll agree. I can see from the expression on the face of my dear friend, Chris, that he has been successful. Delighted, dear boy. Thought you would want to help your country.' Dobson gave a smile, showing those big teeth. He reminded Ben of a crocodile. Dobson continued, 'Just in case you begin to doubt that you've made the right decision, I'll add to your appetite for truth. Stanley Murdock was implicated in the blast that caused your injuries. There is evidence. Thought you'd like to know.'

* * *

'Bastard.' He spoke aloud as he walked out of St Etheldreda's and turned down St Andrew's Street towards Hills Road. He didn't know which he was referring to – Dobson for what he'd said or Stanley Murdock for what he'd done.

For the first time he had a name. He'd always been able to blame an amorphous body. There had always been the question. Which side had planted the bomb; the Catholics who wanted to disrupt the Peace Process or the Protestants who wanted to do the same? Renegades from either side could have done it. But now he had a name. Now he had someone to blame for his nightmares. On that day, his life had plummeted into chaos. He didn't need reminders. His deep depression, bringing up two daughters without their mother and the toll it had taken on Mo. And the loss – what about the loss?

But now he had a name – Stanley Murdock. And Stanley Murdock was dead – murdered. Diane dead at the barracks. Now, sixteen years later, someone had taken out her murderer. His hands clenched in convulsion and he looked down to see blood seeping where his nails had cut into his palms. If he ever met the man who had killed Stanley Murdock, he would shake him by the hand. More than that, as his pace quickened towards home, he knew that he had to find Stanley Murdock's killer before anyone else did.

Chapter 15

Thursday 21st June 2012

Ben woke with a start. He sat up. Moonlight was streaming through his open curtains and, outside the window, birds were beginning to tune up for their morning chorus. The room came slowly into focus, reassuringly familiar and ordinary. He reached over to switch on the light and to gather some tissues. The photo of Diane smiled up at him.

He shook his head to try to clear those other images. The dream – but so much worse than before. Worse because, this time, the murky figure that had been standing on the sidelines watching the unfolding carnage had morphed into Stanley Murdock. And Stanley Murdock had been laughing.

For sixteen years he'd been living this half-life, and the trauma he'd tried so hard to leave behind was unfolding again. His girls had lost their mother so they'd needed their father and that had been his lifeline. His thoughts turned to Mo and Gwen and what he owed them. They'd been settling down to a quiet middle-age when they'd had to take on his work and his family until he'd been able to cope.

He'd said to Dr Clare that he needed three weeks. But he needed her now. A new chapter of his illness was opening and he desperately wanted to be able to close it again without falling back into the abyss he'd left all those years ago.

* * *

'Hi Dad. How was the do?' Katy examined Ben's face. 'God, you look rough. Got wasted last night, did you?' Without pausing, she continued, 'Went out with Pam and Sarah. They're not supposed to talk about it but I got the inside info on Stanley's murder. We decided it was a London gang after a big ransom. But they can't have been much good cos Stanley died and they got zilch. Dad? Are you listening?'

He had never told his daughters about his nightmare and he wasn't going to change that now. 'Sorry, love. I didn't sleep well last night. What did you say?'

At that moment Maurice burst in taking his coat off as he walked over to the kettle. 'Sorry I'm late. Had a great session with the muckers last night. Found out what they know about the murder. Bugger all, that's what. Need a cuppa though – plenty of liquid – good for the head.' He pointed to the top of his head as he glanced over at Ben. 'You look like death. Pardon me for using that expression in here. You ill?' Before Ben could reply he added, 'That Turnbull is such a tosser. Piss up in a brewery. They'll have to bring in another SIO. He's lost the window. Them thugs'll be miles away by now so I don't think they'll ever solve it.'

Katy joined in. 'Well, that's just what Sarah said. She put in her report about the fingers and Turnbull didn't shout at her so she reckons it must have been OK. She said to thank dad and to give him a kiss.' She blew Ben a kiss.

When he didn't respond she looked more closely at him. 'What's up, Dad? You look dreadful.'

In the dark of the night, Ben had decided not to share his discovery with his family. Now, seeing the look of concern on the faces of Katy and Maurice, he realised he needed their support. By an effort of will, he kept his voice steady. 'I found out last night that Stanley Murdock was involved in the bomb that killed your mother and injured thirty-one people.' His voice rose. 'We've just buried that bastard with due ceremony. If the police get nowhere, it's fine by me. I don't want his killer found. Ever.'

Katy wrapped her arms round her father and gave him a hug. 'Dad, I don't know what to say. Except that I'm glad he's dead too.' She looked from Ben to Maurice. Maurice shrugged his shoulders and looked plaintive. Katy continued, 'Everyone we've met seems to be glad he's dead. Did that man ever do anything good in his life?'

Maurice seemed to have found his voice. 'You sure? How'd you find out?'

'Professor Dobson. He's got contacts. People who'd know.' He gave a hollow laugh. 'And he knew Stanley and they had something going. God, I hate them both.'

Maurice looked perplexed. 'You sure you can trust Dobson?'

'No. He's an obnoxious excuse of a man but he has no reason to lie.'

Katy took charge. 'Sit down Dad, and Uncle Mo will make you a cup of tea.' She gave a strangled gulp, half cry, half giggle. 'Can't guarantee the quality though.' Then she hugged him again. 'What else can we do for you?'

As she released him, Maurice touched Ben's arm. 'Perhaps a visit to The Friary will help? I can phone them now if you like. Then drive you there. Yes?'

Ben drew in a long breath and slumped down in his chair. 'Thanks Mo. I've already phoned. But a lift there would be good.'

While Maurice bustled round doing nothing, Katy said, 'We love you, Dad. And it will be all right. I know it will.'

Mo tapped her on the arm, 'You OK?'

She whispered back. 'Yes. It's Dad I'm worried about.'

Ben sat up straight. 'Thanks, both of you. It helps to know you're there.' He turned to Katy. 'Will you be all right here on your own?'

'Course I will, silly. And if I have a problem, I'll phone Uncle Mo, who is now going to make sure he has his phone turned on.'

She gave Maurice a reproving look, and he had the grace to look embarrassed as he shuffled his mobile out of his pocket and switched it on.

* * *

The only conversation on the way to The Friary had been for Ben to tell Maurice that he was seeing the locum he'd seen last time. Apart from that brief interchange, they had driven the fifteen miles in silence. Now they sat in the reception area. Maurice squeezed his arm. 'I'll wait here – no hurry. And good luck.'

Dr Clare came to greet them. Ben introduced her to his Uncle Mo. 'Ah,' she said, 'You must be the one who keeps an eye on him. Looks like you're doing a grand job.'

'Do me best. He's a good lad.'

Ben smiled. When was the last time he'd been called a lad?

He followed Dr Clare and, after he'd settled down in his

chair, he opened the conversation. 'I've had four dreams in a couple of weeks.' He forced a laugh. 'And I'd quite like them to go away again.'

'You're ready to talk about them?'

'I have to.'

Dr Clare walked round Ben's chair so he could see her. She pointed to some papers in her hand. 'When we've got over this crisis, there's a new therapy for you to try. It has a good track record in reducing and eventually eliminating the anxiety relating to the flash-backs.'

He sat up. 'Dr Clare, I'll try anything. If you said I had to swim in the Cam each morning and catch fish in my mouth, I'd do it.'

She smiled. 'It's not as bad as that, but we'll need at least ten sessions. Is that OK?'

He nodded.

'We'll book those in. Now, the dream? Take your time. And you can stop whenever you like.'

Ben nodded again.

She continued, 'So, what do you think has made the dream reappear? Have there been any big changes in your life?'

He didn't reply.

After a brief pause, she added, 'Was it the same dream or has it changed?'

'The second was different but I couldn't tell how. The third was worse and the last one was much worse.' He paused, 'Because I'd found out who planted the bomb.'

Without missing a beat, she asked, 'And how did that make you feel?'

'Angry. Very angry. And I've no way of venting that anger because he's dead. The person who killed my wife is dead. Someone murdered him.' He clenched both hands into fists. 'Then last night he was in the dream. He was standing at the side, laughing.'

Dr Clare spoke quietly. 'Let's leave the dreams for a while.' She rustled her papers. 'It says in your notes that there was a second bomb and that you raised the alarm before it went off and ran in and saved the lives of five men, and many more by stopping them from moving towards it. But your wife was killed and you were injured. You were awarded the Victoria Cross. This may well provide the seeds of both your good recovery and your continued problems.'

'How so?'

'Well, you're obviously brave – hence not giving in. You're working through your depression and are no longer taking medication. That's a really good sign. But you continue to have these flash-backs in your dreams. Have you any theory why this might be?'

'No. I've been asked that hundreds of times. To be honest, they'd become part of my life and I'd begun to think that finding the answer might be worse than suffering the dreams. Then they went and I thought I'd left them behind. Now, I want to be rid of them for ever and I don't know where to start. What do you think?'

She was forthright in her reply. 'Mr Burton, it's not my place to put any theory to you. It could take you in completely the wrong direction. I think it's for you to come to a conclusion, not me.'

'My problem, my solution.' Even though he saw the merit in her words, there was disappointment in his voice. 'Let's think back to what you said.' He ticked the subjects off on his fingers in perfect order. 'Bomb, alarm, saved lives, wife dead, me injured, VC. Let me think about it for a minute.'

Ben and Dr Clare sat in silence for a full minute. There was not a sound. He looked round for the ticking clock. It had gone. Then he spoke. 'I feel guilty. I couldn't save her.'

'You feel guilty for something you couldn't do. Do you think that makes sense?'

'No, but she died and I couldn't save her. I got a medal for saving all those other people but it's worthless. I don't even remember doing it. I only know that I couldn't save her.'

'And you feel guilty for something that was impossible for you to have achieved? I wonder, could you let go of that guilt? Rationalise it, perhaps?'

'I'm not sure that I can. If that's what's causing my dreams then I've been carrying it for sixteen years. It won't be easy to lay it down.'

'True – but now you've expressed it, you can try. A first

step might be to ask yourself, would she want you to be suffering after all this time? Wouldn't she have wanted you to become completely well again?'

'Of course she would. But I don't know how. How can I stop feeling guilty?'

Her response was tangential. 'Let's just say that, if you allow that guilt to disappear, you'll certainly aid your recovery.'

'Thank you. I have no idea how to go about it but I've now got something new to work on.'

'Just remember. You're not Superman. You're human like the rest of us. We all do things we regret. We all have to learn to forgive ourselves. I'm sure that you forgive other people every day. The question for you is, can you learn to forgive yourself?'

A thought flashed inside his head then disappeared. 'Forgive myself? I hadn't thought of it like that. You're right, of course.' He sat up. 'It's been a short session, but I think I'm ready to go now.'

He stood up and faced Dr Clare. The thought flashed again and this time it stayed. He saw Stanley's list in his mind's eye. The words on it stood out, perfectly imprinted. 'Ask him about Clare'. So he asked, 'Dr Clare, do you know Professor Hallfield?'

He could see her blush begin to rise before she turned away. 'Why yes,' she said brightly. 'He taught me on my forensics course. How do you know him?'

'He taught me too. Criminology. Lectured us on blackmail.' He saw the blush drain from her cheeks to be replaced by a dull grey. 'Ask him about Clare.' Ben now knew that he had found 'Clare' and surmised that Stanley had held information about Dr Clare and Professor Hallfield that neither of them had wanted made public. He waited to see if she would say more. When she remained silent, he took her hand and shook it gently. 'Thank you again.' Then he added. 'If I can ever help you in any way, any way at all, do let me know. You just have to ask.' And he picked up his things and walked back to rejoin Maurice.

Maurice stood as he approached. 'Feeling better?'

'I'm going to have a course of ten visits and they've given me something to work on, so, yes, I think I do feel better. Let's go home.'

But, as they emerged on to the steps of The Friary, Ben

looked down to see Chris lounging against the side of Maurice's car. He found that he was not surprised.

* * *

'Hello, Ben. And you must be Maurice.' They shook hands. 'Pleased to meet you. I'm Chris. I was supposed to meet Ben today and I persuaded his lovely daughter to tell me where he was. Ben, OK if we go off and have our chat now?'

Ben could see that Maurice was about to protest so he held up his hand. 'That's fine. That's absolutely fine. Don't worry, Mo.' He gestured behind him towards The Friary. 'I can cope. Chris and I have some catching up to do. Tell Katy I'm OK. And can you see that she's all right and show her how to lock up. Thanks Mo. I'll see you tomorrow.'

Ben and Chris started towards Chris's car. Chris motioned back towards The Friary. 'Want to tell me about it?'

'No.'

'Understood. We know about your PTSD. Understandable in the circumstances. They send us all for therapy after we've been in the field. No choice. Should do the same in the military. Makes sense to stop it before it takes hold. Let's take a drive out to the fens. It's empty out there. No surveillance. I'm sure that's why they took Stanley there to die.'

* * *

As they drove north, the land flattened to fen. The sky enlarged to fill all the spaces. Though it was summer and late morning, a thin layer of mist hung silently over the blank fields giving a greyness to the scene. Ben could understand why the kidnappers had chosen to bring their victim out here.

As he drove, Chris spoke. 'Good place to talk – the car. I'll fill you in. We're going to visit the scene of the crime. Out towards Wisbech. Empty country. The boys in blue found him in a barn next to a farmhouse in the dead centre of nowhere. House was empty – nearly derelict. The old guy who'd lived there topped himself. Can see why. Bloody awful place. Didn't leave a will so there it was, sitting empty. Silent. Too bloody quiet. Must admit it gave me the willies and I've seen some god-awful things. Just perfect for bringing someone for a little light torture.'

Ben knew something of fen people and their ways. He'd buried some of them. The Fens, flat and unfurling, mile upon mile, were a world apart from the bustle of Cambridge. He gazed round the far horizon and he couldn't imagine what it would be like to live or die out here. Chris switched tack with such speed that he nearly missed his question. 'What d'you know about the UVF?'

Ben was silent for a moment. 'UVF – Ulster Volunteer Force – Protestant paramilitaries, spent their time killing Catholics. Suspected of drug running and other Mafia-style activities. I've got to tell you that I've been warned off by one of the Northern Ireland contingent at the funeral. Possibly UVF.'

'Have you indeed. They're rattled, then. Before I tell you more, I've got to remind you that you're still covered by the Official Secrets Act even though it's more than twenty years since you signed. Understood?'

Ben nodded. He thought he knew where this was going. He was wrong.

Chris continued, 'Stanley Murdock was one of ours. We put him in deep cover with the UVF in the eighties and, for a while, he was one of our best.'

Ben interrupted, 'One of ours? You mean MI5?'

'Yeah – no big deal – he wasn't the only one. Anyway, we had to bring him out in ninety-six and we were sure his cover wasn't blown. Seems we were wrong. Somehow, someone must have found him out. As yet, we don't know who and we don't know how. We do know they tortured and killed him.' Chris banged the steering wheel – hard. 'We've got to find the bastards and find out how much they know. We're protecting our people as best we can. Then there's the family. The cousin should be OK till his release. That fat cop they put in charge – Turnbull – idiot put in a rookie family liaison officer. We've had her replaced by one trained by us. Protects the family and is quietly searching the house and rifling through their computers. Odd family – can't get a peep out of them.' Chris looked at Ben and Ben looked at the road, wishing that

Chris would do the same. Chris swerved to avoid a pheasant and continued, 'Fucking birds! Odd, don't you think, two grown people with money, still living at home. Only the eldest broke loose. Had someone search his flat. Stanley was good at his job. All clean so far. Anything incriminating has gone with him to his grave.'

Ben was deep in thought. This added a whole new dimension to Stanley Murdock but it still didn't excuse his actions. His thoughts roved over Stanley's papers. He could see them in his mind's eye, nestled with his important papers in his fireproof box. As far as he could remember, there was nothing to suggest that Stanley had been a spook but plenty to suggest he'd been a crook. He'd have to look through them again.

Chris turned from a B road onto what looked like a farm track. He manoeuvred the car round a large pot-hole. 'Roads out here are crap. As soon as we could, we analysed the dirt on the family's cars – see if it came from out here but they were all clean. The Range Rover had been steam cleaned. Don't know why people do that. Not good for the car. You do that with hearses?'

Again Ben had to make a quick reverse from his line of thinking. 'No, we have a car wash bay at the back. We bring in a lad to wash them before and after use. Tell me, where do the police fit into all this?'

'We're running the police investigation but Turnbull won't know it. He'll get precisely nowhere. Probably wouldn't anyhow. Useless git. Anyway, the last thing we want is publicity so we'll send him running off in all directions to keep him off our backs.'

Ben sat in silence. Every day this whole mess just got messier. Only yesterday he had thought to shake the hand of Stanley Murdock's killer. Now he found that the man who he believed to be a bullying father, a criminal, a blackmailer, a terrorist and a murderer had also been a spy. 'One of ours' was how Chris had described him. If 'one of ours' could do those evil things, did he, Ben, want to be one of theirs? At last he spoke. 'So you're saying MI5 will be the ones to find the killers. What do you see as my part in all this?'

'The Murdocks are an odd bunch but they seem to trust you as much as they trust anyone. We can't get a peep out of them. Tried all sorts. Tight as a nun's arse cheeks. All you have to do is find out what the Murdocks know about Stanley's other life – his work for us. We'll look after them. You find out what they know and we'll do the rest.'

'And if they know a lot?'

'We'll persuade them it's in their best interests to forget what they know. No violence, I promise. They'll agree. We can threaten them with the Proceeds of Crime Act – even if it doesn't apply. Get a tame solicitor to persuade them. It's amazing what people will forget when they think there's a fortune about to be whisked away from under their noses.'

'And, if they're found, will the killers come to trial?'

'It's not if – it's when. We'll find them. And I think, Ben, that's a question for us not for you.'

'I assume then that the answer is No.'

'Let's just say that you'll not interfere in finding and dealing with the killers. We'll get them. You do your bit and then you can walk away.'

'Sounds to me that the last thing you want is a trial. So you'll deal with them in your own way. Yes?'

Chris sounded grudging, 'Could say that.'

Ben knew what that meant. He had a sudden urge to smack Chris across his smiling mouth. Stanley had killed his wife. Now Chris was going after Stanley's killers. Ben needed Stanley's killers to go free. If he was going to accomplish that, he had to find the answers before Chris did.

'Right, I want more than that. I want to know who you get and I want to know when you get them. Is that a problem?'

After a pause, Chris responded, 'I think we can let you know when this operation ends.'

As they passed a small and dilapidated cottage, the farm track upgraded to a single-track metalled road. They rounded yet another pothole and Chris said, 'Nearly there. A problem we haven't cracked yet is how the hell did they know about this godforsaken hole. Means their intelligence is getting past us – not good.'

* * *

As they bumped into the abandoned farmyard, Ben's first thoughts took him back to the days of his deep, dark depression. There was an enveloping greyness, a lack of any connection with the rest of the world, a feeling of time standing still and that overwhelming sense of doom hanging in the air. He shivered himself back to the present. What a place to die.

'No police tape, no one guarding the scene?' he asked.

'No point – they'll be long gone. Our people've done their stuff here so we await results. Particularly interested in DNA. Take their time, these police bods. Either that or they're stalling. Wouldn't put it past them. Turnbull thinks it's a London gang who scarpered when it went belly-up. But we know it was Belfast based. They'll be back home safely tucked in with their alibis, so it's abandoned again.' He laughed, 'Want to buy it?' He gestured for Ben to stay still. 'Stay in the car, I'll get you some boots.'

Chris retrieved two pairs of pristine Hunter boots from the back footwell. He handed one pair to Ben, then motioned towards a path at the side of the house. 'It's that way. Muddy as hell even though it's summer.'

It was indeed churned up with what must have been more traffic in the past few weeks than it had had in years. Ben said, 'Forensics have been, but apart from that, is the scene reasonably intact?'

'He was tied to a chair. They've taken that away. Big heavy thing, came from the house. Otherwise the barn was bare, except for some long basketty things hanging on the walls. They took the ones from inside the barn.'

'How did they get into the house?'

'Could've picked the lock. Wasn't secure. Why would it need to be out here? Not many passing villains and nothing worth stealing. Empty since the old guy topped himself.'

'How long?'

'Six months. But look at it. Would you want to buy this?' Chris kicked a downpipe. It fell to the ground together with the gutter it was holding up. A shower of rust and dirt rained down on the two of them. 'Not exactly a des res, eh?'

As they rounded the corner of the house, Ben could see it was more of a shed than a barn. Hanging along both sides were those basketty things which Ben recognised as home-made eel traps. Chris took a key from his pocket and unlocked the large, shiny padlock that secured the doors. 'Help me, will you. The doors stick.' They pulled open the doors and the smell hit them like a wall. A swarm of flies buzzed out. They both backed up and turned away to breathe some sweet air. 'Poor bugger pissed and shat himself – some puke too. Let's move away till some of this goes.'

Ben followed Chris away from the open doors. 'Was the padlock here or was it secured by the police?'

Chris smiled. 'Padlock's ours. Hasp was here. It's recent. We think they put it up to shut him in. Sold exclusively to B&Q. We're checking the Northern Ireland stores. Fat chance we'll find anything. Could have bought it anywhere. Needless to say we haven't found the padlock. Ready to go in?'

Ben nodded and they walked back to the shed's entrance. Chris led the way. 'See the cleared circle – they swept it before they went. Cut the ropes binding him. They're missing too. Poor sod slid off the chair. He was found on the floor, there, see, where the stains are; been dead about eighteen hours. Anonymous letter dropped into Parkside. CCTV shows someone in a hoodie. That's all we've got. A grainy hoodie – not enough for an ID – no fingerprints, no DNA on the note. That was about nine but our friends in blue took all night to find the fucking farm. Bloody morons. Then it was another whole day before they let us know.' Chris kicked another downpipe and moved more quickly this time to avoid the rust shower. 'Should've involved us when he was kidnapped – fucking idiots – someone's head will roll for that. As soon as we got involved we had the body released to you.'

'Thought it was quick. Any trouble from the coroner?'

'Na. Sorted it with him. Independent sod but he co-operated.'

Ben peered at the cleared space then leaned over the place where Stanley's body had lain. He played his phone torch over the ground in ever increasing circles. 'Did the fingertip search throw up anything?'

'Nope. Nor the search of the house and land around. No tyre marks, no sightings, no footprints, no nothing. It bloody rained between seven and nine on the morning after he died. It might have helped if the fucking fuzz had got here earlier but it was pissing down by the time they rolled up.'

Ben leaned further in towards a small dark stain on the ground towards the centre of the cleared space. 'Any blood found here?'

'Just a few smears on the chair where he tried to get free. You've seen the body – he was tied up but no sign of violence. Not to say there wasn't any but it's not the usual MO. Odd that, but heh, I'm telling the expert here. What d'you think?'

'It's been twenty years, what would I know? Organisations change in twenty years. People change in twenty years. Maybe they've become more sophisticated. Psychological not physical – maybe. You keep saying "they" but what have you found to suggest more than one?'

'Nada – it's shit – we wait for DNA in the hope that something'll turn up. Pathetic.'

'How come you're so sure it's UVF?'

'Two things… no, three, four, five. Number one – our surveillance showed they've been gearing up to something big here on the mainland. Number two – we've been tracking increased traffic with North London and that's where Stanley has contacts. Number three – someone close to the Shankill Butchers has just been released and was followed to Cambridge last month. Our clods lost him for four hours. You see, even we employ numpties.' Chris smacked the side of the shed with the flat of his hand. It was the third sign of his frustration. He continued, 'Number four – we found his car near a pub regularly used by the UVF for buying drugs for import to Belfast. Number five – kidnap-murders were a speciality and we've got evidence it's still going on. And they came to the funeral. This fits that pattern near enough for us to be confident it's them. We'd upped the watch on them because they're sending people to Syria to learn and liaise with Daesh. One, two, three, four and five we're on to. The last one's a real bugger.'

'One of the NI contingent at the funeral threatened me. He knew me, knew Diane, knew Katy. Should I take it seriously?'

'Big fella? No front teeth?'

Ben nodded.

'I'll put tabs on him.'

That was enough to tell Ben that he should indeed take it seriously. He could take care of himself. But how could he keep Katy safe? He pushed that to the back of his mind and moved on to his next question. 'The pub. Any joy there?'

'Na. Tight-lipped – like you'd expect in a place like that. Couldn't get a peep out of them. Trailed some of them for a while but nothing. You finished here? Let's go.'

Ben wondered what Chris was holding back. He didn't have the leverage to extract further information so he tried another tack. 'Last question. What about his kids? Could they have done it?'

'Na. They've been checked out. Clean. We didn't rely on the cops. Did our own investigation. And we've got our man in their house. Nothing found. Nothing to find. Let's go – it depresses me out here. Too much bloody sky.'

* * *

They journeyed back in silence. Chris seemed to have said all he needed to and Ben was deep in thought. He didn't buy the UVF angle. Something didn't fit, so uppermost in his mind was why MI5 were so convinced when they only had circumstantial evidence. Either they were hiding something or they had focused too early. He dismissed the question – not his problem. He had to find a way to get the Murdocks to open up. That was his problem.

When they drew up outside Ben's house, Chris spoke. 'You know you could come to us full time. You were bloody good. You can be good again.' He grinned. 'And anyway, you don't want to spend the rest your life prettying up dead bodies. Think about it and let me know.' Chris looked at his watch. 'I'm off to get rat-arsed. Wanna come?' Ben would have enjoyed a beer but could think of many more agreeable people to share it with. He declined, and anyway, he had some thinking to do.

Chapter 16

Friday 22nd June 2012

Ben had a nasty taste in his mouth; the taste of dishonesty – both his and that of the people he was mixing with. He'd been for his run but that hadn't helped. He'd agreed to do a job for Chris and he would see it through. He needed to do that for his own satisfaction, but then – finish.

He had a new direction. He was going to relieve himself of his burden of guilt about Diane's death. After that he didn't know, but what he did know was that recovery wouldn't be easy. He had two funerals under control and a free morning. He phoned ahead to arrange a visit without the usual Visiting Order, then set off for HMP Highpoint. He had some news – not all good – but Michael would have to be told.

As he arrived in the car park, the sun was shining but the grey prison buildings still looked depressed. He divested himself of his contraband taking only his ID, car keys, the papers for signing and the toothpaste for Michael. He didn't know what was allowed so had bought the only make he could find in a sealed box. Boxes were cheap but sealed boxes came expensive.

The drill was the same, with the exception of the toothpaste, which he handed to the first guard. The man investigated the packet thoroughly and handed it back. 'Seeing as how you're from his solicitor, you can give it to him, personal like.'

The same officer conducted him through the maze of corridors. When they reached the room, it looked much as it had the last time, except now Michael was sitting quietly on the far side of the table chatting amicably with the semi-recumbent officer. They both stood as Ben entered.

'Is it OK if I give him the toothpaste? The other officer said to bring it in.'

'Yeah – wish half the people in here was as careful about hygiene as this one.' He nodded towards Michael. And, as he took his next breath, Ben realised that the pervading background odour was of unwashed bodies. He handed over the toothpaste.

Michael opened the box and the conversation. 'Look, I'm sorry for the way I behaved last time. Now I know Stanley's done right by me I'm the model prisoner again. Shake on it?'

Ben looked at the officer who gave a slight nod. They shook hands and Michael seemed reluctant to let go. As he gently broke contact, Michael explained, 'See, you don't get to touch people in here. Reminds me of the outside.' He wiped away a tear with the back of his hand and sniffed. He pulled out a crumpled handkerchief. 'I washed it – not well, as you can see. We don't really have the facilities in here.' He brightened. 'And, d'you know, they wouldn't even let me have an iron!' He held it towards Ben.

'I think you'd better keep it. I've got plenty more.'

'Thanks.' Michael stuffed it back in his pocket. 'Any news for me?'

'First, there's some papers to sign.' Ben looked across at the officer and held up the papers and a pen. There was an almost imperceptible nod. As Michael signed, Ben lowered his voice so the prison officer couldn't hear. 'There's good and bad. The violin's yours and it's genuine. That's the good news. The bad news is that it'll probably be about a year before you can get the money.'

Michael looked crestfallen so Ben held up a hand. 'I asked Stanley's solicitor and you should be able to get an advance if you need it, so you won't be destitute. And when you do sell, about half the money will go in fees and taxes but that will still leave you a few million the richer.'

Michael whistled silently. He looked thoughtful then smiled. 'I suppose, with prospects like that, I can borrow. So that's all good news.'

Ben leaned in further and lowered his voice more. 'So now you're in a good mood, can I ask you something?'

'Yeah, go ahead.'

'How come you got yourself into this mess?'

Michael sighed. 'Well, that's a very big question and one I've asked meself many a time.' He carefully repacked then unpacked the toothpaste tube. Then he began to systematically shred the cardboard pack. 'The thing is, I was as green as the grass in the fields back home. Eighteen, just come to England to work for me da's brother. But the da's brother stitched me up.' He settled himself more comfortably in his chair. 'See, when I was a wee boy, I knew Stanley back home. He was the great man in our family. He'd come to stay with us in Belfast. Paid the ma handsomely for his board. Threw money round in the pub. When me da was killed, it was Stanley who paid for the funeral. Big do it was.'

Ben interrupted. 'Was your father UVF too?'

'Jesus, no. He was a pacifist. Silly sod got himself caught in crossfire. It was Stanley who brought his body home.'

'I'm sorry. And then what happened?'

'Soon after, Stanley upped sticks back to England. Just sudden, like. He sent back regular money, enough that we didn't starve. And later, when the ma died, he came for the funeral and persuaded me that I'd be better off working for him in England than going to college in Belfast. He was family – my only family – so I came. He set me up in digs, paid me a pittance and got me to sign papers for him. He was money laundering. I didn't ken what was going on and I carried the can. He said I'd get a light sentence as it was a first offence and I was young. Bloody didn't. Told me he'd see me right when I got out and that was the last I saw of him.'

'What! He never came to visit?'

'No, told me it would be better if he didn't. More convincing, like. But he'd see me right when I came out.'

'Did you ever meet his children?'

Michael looked perplexed. 'Children? What children? Stanley didn't have any children. That's why he took me under his wing. I was the nearest he had to a family. He wasn't even married.'

Ben whispered, 'Did you know any of his UVF friends?'

'Na. Me da said to keep away and I loved the da so I did. By then it was easier to keep out. I really respected the da for keeping his distance throughout the Troubles. That took real guts.' He paused and sighed. 'But they killed him anyways. Glad it's over, but I never want to go back there.'

Ben made up his mind. 'How long till you get out?'

'Four weeks and four days.'

'Right, you can come and stay with us till you get sorted. If it takes a year, no problem. I'll put you to work.' He was thinking of hoisting bodies and caskets, something Maurice was getting too old for.

Michael beamed. 'That'd be grand. I've done an accountancy degree and an MBA since I've been here so I can be useful.' He was silent for a second. 'You're not a solicitor, they told me that. So, what is it you do?'

'I'm an undertaker.'

Michael threw himself backwards in his chair and laughed so much that he had to take the hankie out and wipe his eyes. 'An undertaker! That's just grand. I thought maybe you were a counsellor or a doctor or something like that. An undertaker – that's priceless.' And he laughed again. 'I'd be honoured to work for an undertaker. Thank you.'

The officer looked at his watch. 'You finished your business?'

'Yes thanks,' said Ben, and to Michael, 'See you next week.' And they shook hands once more.

Chapter 17

The next morning at eleven, Ben began his task of interviewing the Murdocks. While Virginia was at the other end of the house organising coffee, he thought again of the differences between this family and his own. He smiled at the memory of Katy falling on him, in obvious relief, on his return from The Friary. She'd sat him down, given him her best attempt at a dinner and generally mollycoddled him until he'd had to say, 'Enough'. Then she'd told him about her visit to Virginia, a trip that had completely slipped his mind.

As he waited for Virginia to bring the coffee, he ruminated about the turn his life was taking – full circle to his army days? No. He wouldn't allow that.

'Penny for them,' brought him back to the present.

'Sorry, just reliving a misspent youth. Thank you. It's good of you to see me at such short notice.'

'No problem. It's to our mutual advantage. We all want to get that stupid will sorted and get on with our lives. And I must admit I'm at a bit of a loose end, you know, finding my feet now Father's dead. Is that normal?'

'Oh yes. It's almost always like that. When everything's been organised there's a lull before life resumes.'

'And I haven't got any real friends. Father disapproved of anyone I brought home so I lost touch with them all.' She smiled at him. 'To be honest, I'm glad of the company. Help yourself to milk and sugar.' She handed him a cup of deep black coffee. 'Is it too strong? I can get some water.'

He took a sip. 'Just as I like it.'

'Do have a biscuit. Father hated what he called fancy biscuits, so I've gone a bit overboard since he died. We've got a cupboard full of anything with chocolate.' She smiled. 'We'll balloon if we eat them all.'

In the short silence that followed, he wondered whether it would be too early to move to the subject he most wanted to talk about. He decided to stick to his plan and play it as he would as an undertaker. With gentle probing, he would let the client lead the conversation.

Virginia immediately gave him an opening. 'I don't want to hark back to the funeral. It happened, nothing went wrong, it's over.' She shuddered. 'All those revolting people. I'm glad I'll never have to see them again. D'you know, one of them had the cheek to come round. Creepy man, -wanted to know about a key. And he kept asking about someone called Thomas. Wouldn't give up. I told him we had no idea who Thomas was and he'd have to get a locksmith cos we didn't have his key. In the end, I had to shut the door in his face.'

'D'you know who he was?'

'No – big teeth – that's all I remember.'

Dobson. What did Dobson know about the key with its envelope marked 'Tom' that was now safely nestling in Ben's fireproof box?

'And I definitely don't want to talk about the weeks before the funeral. So, what shall we talk about?'

This was what he was waiting for. 'I'm glad you said that. I'd like to ask you a favour.'

Virginia looked up and smiled. 'Ask away. I'll be delighted to help.'

He launched into his cover story. 'Thanks. I think you can help me with something quite apart from my job. I'm doing a part-time degree in criminology.' He gave a sheepish grin. 'I'm not finding it easy getting back to studying so I need all the help I can get. By coincidence, my next assignment is on Northern Ireland and the Troubles. I've got to find an angle to work from and I don't think the child's perspective has been explored. Katy tells me you lived there as a child, in a town called Moira?'

Virginia nodded. He continued, 'I was hoping you might help me with an outline of what it was like; give me some background. Of course, I won't name you but it will help me if I can get some personal information. You know, the child's perspective, first-hand.'

She smiled. 'Studying again – brave step.' She looked thoughtful. 'It's a long time ago but I'll do what I can. We left there when I was ten. Lucien and Allie might be able to give you a different view. Loads of things they did, I wasn't allowed to do.' She smiled. 'No women's lib in those days – not for me anyway. Father's influence. I'm sure they'd help. Especially Allie. He fancies you, you know.'

Ben shifted in his chair. He'd suspected it. He'd have to tread carefully. 'That would be great. I could maybe use the gender differences as one of my themes. Would it be all right to start now? And do you mind if I take notes?'

'Sure – no problem. I've got half an hour, then an important hairdressing appointment. Your daughter suggested a change of style and colour might raise my spirits. So, I'm taking the plunge. She's super. I bet you're proud of her.'

He smiled. 'Yes, I am. She's not had it easy. Her mother died when she was small and then I was ill for several years. She's resilient. She's had to be.'

Virginia looked perplexed. 'I didn't know. We talked for ages yesterday and she never said. She let me maunder on about my family. She was polite but I know she doesn't approve of my dress sense. Her words were that I dressed old for my age. We should go shopping.'

Ben was now the one looking perplexed. This was a different woman from the one he'd met before the funeral. In just two weeks the unhappy and disapproving woman had been transformed. He could guess the reason. He wondered if she would tell him.

She was still talking. 'I'll be glad to talk about my time in Ireland. I was happy then. And I'm beginning to think that I can be again.' She looked into the distance. 'It means "Fate", you know. "Destiny."' At his look of bewilderment, she added, 'Moira. The word means fate.' She kicked off her shoes and curled her legs beneath her on the settee. She lay back onto the backrest, closed her eyes and started to talk. As she spoke, Ben realised that he was superfluous. She was taking herself back to a time and place where she'd felt safe and happy. 'I loved Ireland. It was magical. We lived in a small town, a safe place. It was after the Anglo-Irish agreement so things were better, but we still had to be careful.' She opened her eyes. 'The only bombing in Moira was after we'd left, so the

113

Troubles didn't really affect us. Is that all right for you? The fact that we had no problems?'

He nodded and she continued. 'I suppose I can best remember from the time I went to school. It's a bit hazy before then, you know, bits and pieces that might or might not be real. I was happy because it was just me, Lucien, Allie and Mother. Father was hardly ever there. He came sometimes and stayed a day or two.' A look of distaste crossed her face. 'This, I remember. When he was home, he always went to Norman's.'

'Norman's?'

'Norman's Bar. He had to play the big man – you know – buy drinks for everyone. They all thought he was such a fine fellow. But we liked it cos, if he was there, it meant he was out of our hair.' She paused. 'Anyway, then he'd go away again and we wouldn't see him for months.'

She seemed far away so Ben gently interrupted her reminiscences. 'Do you know where he went?'

She opened her eyes and looked straight at him. There was a fierceness there that he'd not seen before. 'We didn't know and we didn't care. While he was away, we never spoke of him. Didn't even think of him. We just shut him out of our lives.' She leaned forward. 'You haven't seen this family in its best light but from what you've seen, I think you can believe this – we cried when our father arrived and we laughed when he went.'

Ben said the only thing he could say. 'I'm sorry.' And he was. Truly sorry for this unfortunate family.

Virginia leaned back again, her face relaxing once more. 'We had plenty of money, more than the other families around. A lot of it came from my mother, of course. It wasn't a poor area, but no one was what you could call rich. We went to the local school and had to mix with everyone. It was mostly Protestants like us but there were a few Catholics around and we used to call them names – like you do as kids.' She smiled. 'They called us 'proddy dogs' and we called them 'cat alights'. But that's as far as it went. Funny – I haven't thought of those names in years – or those kids. I wonder where they are now?' She paused.

This wasn't right. Surely their mother had been Catholic, but Virginia had said 'Protestants like us'. They had cremated her mother only six months before and the paperwork had definitely stated, Roman Catholic. It didn't fit. 'But I thought your mother was Catholic?'

'Oh, she was. She converted when we moved here; it was her biggest rebellion. Had Allie and me baptised too. But not Lucien. In Moira, we had to be Presbyterian. One of Father's rules. She broke that rule when we moved here. He was furious, but she wouldn't back down so there was nothing he could do.' She grimaced. 'But he got his own back when he had her cremated. We didn't complain. She was beyond his reach then, but we still had to live with him.' She looked directly at him. 'Mother was a good person. She went to mass every week, she loved us and looked after us. So, if there is a heaven, she'll be there.' She smiled a sad smile as she looked down at Ben's cup. 'More coffee?'

He held out his cup and, as she poured, he asked, 'So, when you were in Northern Ireland, how was it when he was away? Sounds like you were close.'

'Oh yes, we were. I was devastated when she died. Katy was so sympathetic yesterday and now I know why. I'll definitely phone her.' She paused while she took a notebook from her pocket and scribbled a note. While she wrote, he wondered if he should promote this budding friendship or try to obstruct it. Either way, he thought, it would make no difference. Katy would do what Katy would do. Interesting that this woman in front of him, eight years older than his daughter, had not felt able to do what she wanted. Did she kill her father? Ben doubted it, but he knew that ordinary people could be driven to extraordinary deeds.

She put her notebook away. 'You know, our father always insisted we call her Mother. Not Ma or Mam or Mammy like the other kids. I hadn't thought of it but looking back, he was a snob even then.' She laughed. Her eyes sparkled. 'D'you know, we've burned all those stupid photos of him with important people. We had a ceremonial bonfire. It felt good.' She paused. 'I'm not sure I can tell you much more. It's so long since I've even thought about life before Cambridge. But I'll give it some thought and get back to you. Will that be OK?'

'That would be brilliant. Can I ask one more thing? You came to Cambridge when?'

'1996. Some time in the autumn, I think. Lucien might know the date.'

He responded, 'And do you know why you left Ireland?'

'Father came home one day and said we needed to pack all our things. We were moving to England. His word was law so that was that. We didn't ask – but I remember it was quick. And that was when our misery started, but you don't want to know about that.'

Ben did want to know. He wanted to know about their relationship with their father – warped certainly – but crooked enough to lead to murder? He would have followed up but had no chance to do so. Virginia uncurled herself from the settee, stood up and stretched. 'I feel great. You're a good listener. You should do this for a living.' And then she laughed. 'But I suppose you do. I'll tell Lucien and Allie that they *must* talk to you about Ireland. Lucien was that bit older so he'll remember things I don't. Shall I phone when I've got some more to tell you?' Without waiting for an answer she looked at her watch and moved towards the double doors. 'Must dash. Let me show you out.'

As they moved towards the front doors, a large man in police uniform came out of one of the other rooms. He ignored Ben and Virginia as he proceeded to the back of the house. Virginia waved dismissively towards him and spoke in a voice loud enough for him to hear, 'I preferred the woman they sent. At least she was polite. He's going to be with us for at least a month. What a drag.'

Chapter 18

Lucien greeted Ben at the door with, 'Good. You're on time. I've got ten minutes. Then I'm going out. Like a fucking prison in here.'

Lucien led him into the room that had been Stanley's study. Every article that might have been a reminder of Stanley had been removed. Patches on the walls showed where pictures of the rich and famous had hung. Ben could see that a kitchen chair had been brought in and placed on the other side of the desk for him to sit on. The grey safe, though firmly hidden, seemed to face him in mute indictment of his failure to safely deliver its contents to their last resting place. He had told no one, not even Maurice, that some of them were in the fireproof box in his bedroom: the list of people that Stanley had had a hold over, the envelope with the small key, the note from Stanley about the worthless money. He'd felt he had to keep those, but had no idea why.

Lucien sat behind the desk and gestured to the other chair. 'Listen. I'll be straight with you. I'm only talking to you because of the terms of the will. I need my share pronto and Ginny tells me this'll speed things up. If it will help, I'll say you've done hours of counselling the bereaved family. Understood?' He nodded as Lucien continued, 'You want to know about Northern Ireland.'

Ben replied calmly. 'Mr Murdock, we all want the same thing. For my part, I want to get this job finished and off my books. I'm sure you all want to get on with your lives. So, let's get down to business. What can you tell me about your childhood in Northern Ireland?'

'Not much. Bloody boring. Like any small town. Nothing ever happened. High spots were the cattle markets and a fair that came once a year. OK, I was looked after, surrounded by two women – three, if you count Alistair. But even that was suffocating. And it was always bloody raining.' He stopped and twirled his pen, a Montblanc. Ben could also see clearly that Lucien had one little finger longer than the other. 'When Father came home and said we were moving to England, I was delighted. So we came to

Cambridge. That's it – end of.' He leaned back in his chair, hands clasped behind his head.

Ben nodded. 'Can I just take you briefly back to that small town? You said you were surrounded by women. So, where was your father?'

'Oh, away working in Belfast. He was never home.'

'Do you know what he did in Belfast?'

'No idea. He never said and we weren't allowed to ask questions. He was wheeler-dealering no doubt. Making his money work for him. He was good at that.' Lucien laughed mirthlessly. 'Yes, he was good with money. Always kept a tight rein on it.'

'Did you ever go to Belfast with him or meet any of his friends?'

'No. We lived in that hole in the ground. Never went anywhere. He took Allie to Belfast once, but he kept away from me. I stood up to him and he didn't like that. I'm like him, a risk-taker. But he took one risk too far and it killed him. Not sorry. We never got on.'

'Any idea where he took Allie?'

'No, but it was the only time I ever saw their mother stand up to him. No backbone, that woman. Didn't even object to his philandering, even though he rubbed her nose in it. Everyone knew, but she just kept pretending. Come to think of it, that time with Allie was the only time I saw him raise a hand to her. Didn't hit her. I got between them. He didn't dare hit me. I was as big as him. I left home when we came to Cambridge. The three of them stayed under his thumb. Rid of him now though.'

'I'm really interested in...'

'Hang on. Why the interest in my father? I thought it was Northern Irish childhood you wanted to talk about.'

Ben took a slow breath and leaned back to mirror Lucien's stance. 'Father-son relationships in a war zone could be part of my assignment. But you're right, I'm straying from my brief. From what I can gather, your childhood had two different dynamics, when he was away and when he was home. What was it like when he was home?'

Lucien looked at his watch then tapped its face. 'Look, I said ten minutes. You've had five and I've had enough. This is it in a nutshell. I never talked to the bastard if I could help it. I hated Ireland with him or without him. I don't remember much and I've told you all you need to know.'

Lucien stood up. Ben followed and faced him. 'Thanks for your time. This has nothing to do with Ireland but I'm curious. Who contacted the police when he was kidnapped?'

Lucien looked surprised, then his brows drew together. 'I did. It was either that or pay the ransom.'

Chapter 19

Thursday morning found Ben walking slowly up the drive towards the front doors of the Murdock house. He had not been looking forward to this meeting with Alistair and had put it off for as long as possible. The thirty-minute walk from home had given him time to analyse his fears. Yes, he knew that Alistair could be vulnerable having just buried his father, though it had become clear that there had been no love lost and no grief felt. But he had to admit that his fundamental fear was that he didn't know how to handle the situation.

He'd heard back from Virginia that she had more to tell him and he'd agreed to meet her, though he doubted it would add to what he already knew. That call from Virginia had spurred him on to organising this meeting with Alistair. He needed to learn more about Lucien's revelation that their father had 'taken Allie to Belfast once'.

The door was opened by Virginia who greeted him like an old friend, immediately asking what he thought of her new hair style. His response was obviously not as enthusiastic as she'd expected as she pouted and said, 'Can't you do better than "It looks nice?"'

He was taken aback by this latest change in Virginia. 'Er. Very nice?'

She smiled. 'I suppose that will have to do. Allie's waiting for you. He's bought some new clothes. He's been preening all morning and he wants you to admire them.'

Ben's heart sank.

'He's in the kitchen. Go on through,' and she pointed towards a door leading from the hall to the back of the house. On his way through the hall, he glanced sideways into a small study. Chris's man was sitting there reading the newspaper. Ben said a hearty 'Good morning'. He glanced up, grunted and returned to his paper. No wonder the Murdocks wouldn't talk to him.

Ben walked quietly up to the kitchen door and peered round

it to see Alistair seated on a tall stool by the breakfast bar. He appeared oblivious to the small television on the worktop that was loudly playing a film. Ben looked round the room. The kitchen covered the entire width of the house with two sets of French doors leading out to an immaculate garden which stretched into the distance. This kitchen was better described as a kitchen, dining room, living room in one. He suspected that Josephine would approve the clean lines and wondered if she'd ever been in here. The thought of Josephine reminded him that he must phone her.

Alistair did not immediately notice Ben, so he knocked loudly. The contrast between the two men couldn't have been clearer. It was obvious that Alistair had spent a long time choosing his clothes and styling his hair. He was dressed entirely in skinny black which contrasted starkly with his pale skin and bright pink hair, held upright seemingly by anti-gravity. What was not obvious was that Ben had also spent an inordinate amount of time choosing his attire for this meeting. He was dressed in loose, ill-fitting jeans and a brown flannelette checked shirt that he had found at the back of his wardrobe. He'd omitted to shave for a couple of days and was finding the stubble irritating, especially the rasping sound it made when he scratched it. He had little idea what attracted gay men, but the effect of his choice was, he hoped, going to make him look thoroughly unattractive.

Alistair turned and looked him up and down. His first words told Ben that he had chosen wrongly. 'Ben, how wonderful. Love the cowboy look. So retro! And the designer stubble so suits you. Sets off that rinky dinky little scar. I'd do stubble but I don't think the butch look would be me. I'm more of a twink, don't you think?'

Ben's heart dived further. He decided to ignore the compliment and also to refrain from commenting on Alistair's changed appearance. He didn't know what a twink was but he could guess. He would try to keep the conversation brief and impersonal. It was going to require a high-wire act to get what might be crucial information from Alistair whilst not encouraging him in any way. 'Thank you for agreeing to help with my research. Can we turn the sound down?'

Alistair pointed to the television. 'Ever seen Priscilla? Now he's dead I can watch it every day.' He found the remote and switched the television to mute.

'Thanks. And thanks again for agreeing to see me. I've had a great response from your sister. She's been really helpful.'

Alistair waved his hand. 'Ginny's cool.' He pointed to his drink. 'I'm having a mojito. Want to join me?'

'No thanks, I've got to work this afternoon.' He decided that the straightforward approach would be best. 'Look, Alistair, giving me some of your time will get you nearer to your inheritance and I think you can help me with my assignment. But I've got to tell you, I'm one hundred per cent hetero. I'm not interested. So can we get that out of the way?' He didn't wait for a reply but pushed forward with his first questions. 'Do you remember much about Ireland? Your sister tells me you were quite young when you left.'

Alistair looked dejected for just a second. Then he let out a giggle. 'They all say that, so I won't give up hope.'

Alistair walked over to the enormous fridge and took out the makings of another cocktail. He started chopping and the scent of fresh mint filled the air. Ben couldn't help but notice how delicate Alistair was in all his actions. He looked away as Alistair raised his gaze and asked, 'What was the question? Oh yeah – Ireland. Not the best place for a sensitive lad. Still bad now, and the North is worse than the South. Who'd have believed that? Bloody awful place. Hated it. They had to be dragged into decriminalisation and they've been queer bashing ever since.' There was bitterness in his voice. 'I suppose when they stopped being terrorists, those thugs had to find *something* to do.'

He raised his knife and pointed it towards Ben. Watching the knife waving, Ben was glad the island bar was between them. 'Men like him. My fucking father. He was a thug too.'

Ben interrupted. 'Your father? I thought you were his favourite. Virginia told me he chose you to take to Belfast. Have I got that right?'

Alistair aimed a scornful look at him. 'God, I thought you were cleverer than that. Having a "pansy boy" was not what he wanted. He wanted to toughen me up.' Alistair giggled. 'Didn't work though, did it?'

Ben sidled in the question he really wanted to ask. 'So, where did he take you?'

'We went delivering leaflets in Belfast. Kept lecturing me about being tough, and how shameful it was to be "a pansy". That sort of thing. Then we met up with this friend of his – Jack Something. Anyway, he was supposed to be a real hard man. But this is the funny thing.' Alistair stopped and a wide smile appeared, and then he laughed a great whooping laugh. 'Yeah, that was great. He was so mad. Oh God, yes. I'd forgotten. We were in this pub, yeah, and this friend started feeling me up. This mate who was supposed to be so hard. This Jacko fella was a kiddy fiddler. He liked little boys – specially little boys like me. I was dragged out like Hell was on fire. My father didn't say a word and I laughed all the way home. But only inside. It didn't pay to make him mad.'

He wanted to ask if Stanley Murdock had been violent but there were some more pressing questions he needed to ask.

'This man Jacko, can you tell me anything about him?'

'Na, we left pdq.' Alistair thought for a moment. 'He must have been important though cos everyone stayed well clear. Made a path for him through to our table. You know – like in the movies – when the crowd opens up cos they're scared of the bad guy. We left Ireland soon after so I never saw him again. That's all I know about Jacko.'

'Do you know what was in the leaflets?'

'No. They were all folded up with little writing. Too small for me to read. I was only seven. All I had to do was go up to the door and post them. He stood on the pavement and waited for me. We walked bloody miles.'

Alistair took a lime from the fridge and started to squeeze it. He pointed to his empty glass. 'Sure you won't have one? Go on. It's cooling – just right for this weather. I promise I won't jump you or even flirt with you. Well, not much anyway. I won't even tell you how hot you are. And then you can ask me some more questions about our dysfunctional family.'

Ben felt disorientated, just as he'd felt when talking to Virginia. This wasn't the young man he'd first met just a couple of weeks ago. How could the removal of a tyrannical father – for that's how he now thought of Stanley – have brought such a change in the two people who'd lived with him? He could only think of rubber balls that had been squashed and then released and had started bouncing round the room. He realised that he wanted to find out more than just the remit from Chris. He wanted to know how a parent could exert such influence on his children that they were cowed, as these two had been. He'd seen some evidence in the contents of Stanley's safe but he wanted a first-hand account from the victims and crucially, he wanted to know if any of them had garnered enough courage to rid themselves of their oppressor. He allowed himself to be persuaded. 'Okay, thanks. I'll try a mojito. What's in it?'

'Bacardi, lime, sugar, fizz and mint – oh, and green, lots of green. I add a shot of melon liqueur. Love the colour. Looks good eh?'

Ben tentatively took a glass of the verdant liquid and sniffed it. Alistair laughed. 'Smells like a fruit bowl and kicks like a mule. Since the old man's gone I've been a bit naughty. It's started to go to my waistline so I've got to cut back but hey, a toast.' He raised his glass high, 'Here's to the dead arsehole. May he rot in Hell!' And he downed his drink in one. He waved his empty glass. 'You're supposed to say "to the arsehole" and down yours. But I don't s'pose that's your scene!' He laughed at his joke as he went to make himself another. He looked over at Ben. 'Now, drink that down and have another. Then you can ask me anything, anything you like.'

Ben hesitated a moment then downed his drink in one. It tasted good and it wasn't kicking yet. He found he was beginning to like this young man – perhaps not a good idea as he was a potential suspect. He handed his glass back to Alistair. 'Right, then, tell me about your father. What did he do in Northern Ireland?'

Alistair took a slurp of green liquid. 'You know, I have no fucking idea. Don't know what he did in Cambridge either. Made our lives a misery – that's what he did.' He added a hiccup to his reply.

Ben asked, 'How come he had such a hold on you both?'

Alistair continued chopping the mint and remained silent. Ben began to think he had gone too far when Alistair looked up with a pained expression. 'I've asked myself that since the day he died. You know, it seems like this enormous weight has been lifted from us. I s'pose we just got used to it. He kept tabs on us all the time, and what he said was law. We sort of lost all power or even the will to argue. Can you believe this? One of my mates managed to disable the tracker on my phone so I escaped his evil eye for a while. When he found he couldn't follow me, he stopped my money for a month. I was twenty-three for God's sake but who could I go to. Who would believe me?'

'He tracked you?'

'All of us 'cept Lucien. He managed to get away but he had his own money from his mother. Father gave us enough to live on but not enough to move out.'

'Didn't you have paid jobs? Earn your own money?'

'Wouldn't allow it. Said we were his children so we shouldn't need to work. It was like he owned us. It just became normal.' He laughed and raised his full glass. 'But hey, now we're in a new normal. We can do what we like. Drink mojitos all day and watch Priscilla.' He passed a glass to Ben and chinked the two together. 'Here's to the new normal. Fun, fun, fun.'

Alistair downed yet another glass. It was obvious that he had started drinking some time before Ben had arrived and was now in the euphoric stage of inebriation. This was a time to get some truthful answers. Before he had time to ask, Alistair pulled open the door of the fridge and called across, 'Let's eat? I'm starving.'

As Ben watched Alistair rifling in the fridge he decided it would be safer if he volunteered to do the cooking.

Alistair brandished some bacon. 'Bacon sandwich OK?'

'Great. Let me cook it. Fried or grilled?'

'Oooh, fried. I'll diet tomorrow.'

Ben began on the bacon sandwiches. 'What I don't understand is why he brought you all back to England? It seems that it was done in a hurry. Did he ever tell you why?'

'God, it's obvious you never knew my father. He never told us anything. We asked Mother and all she would say was that England was safer. S'pose she was right. There was a bomb in Moira soon after we left.'

Ben was interested to see that, as they'd got deeper into conversation, Alistair's campness, much in evidence when he'd arrived, was diminishing. 'Didn't you even have a clue what he did while you were in Ireland? You must have had some idea.'

'Yeah, we thought he was mixed up in some criminal stuff but we didn't care. As long as he was in Belfast or wherever, and not with us, we didn't give a shit what he was doing. We were as surprised as anyone at that lot at his funeral. Never met any of them before and never want to again. Not my type, if you get my drift.' He giggled. 'Except Father thought Jacko wasn't my type either. Now you would be a wow on the scene.'

Ben's response, though muffled by a slurp of mojito, was clear.

Alistair grinned and took a bite of his sandwich. 'Hey, great sandwich. Want to come and cook for us? Ginny's not much good at it.'

Ben began to feel that his brain didn't quite belong to him. He had to concentrate to think. Was it the mojito kicking in? He sighed inwardly; life had been so simple before Stanley's corpse had landed in his fridge.

'She needs a man. And one that can cook. The only one she was ever really keen on let her down.'

Ben half knew the answer but asked disingenuously, 'What happened to him?'

'Simon? Disappeared without saying goodbye. Broke her heart. It's more than five – could be eight years – and she's still not over it. Poor Ginny. She needs looking after.'

'Didn't anyone try to find him?'

Alistair gave him a sideways look. 'Father said he did. Told Ginny that Simon didn't want to see her any more. I never believed him but – whatever.' He shrugged and went back to his limes. 'Let's call her and watch Priscilla.' He went to the door and called, 'Ginny! Ben wants you to come and watch Priscilla with us. He thinks he'll be safe with you around. And he makes a mean bacon sandwich. Want one?'

* * *

Ben sat between Virginia and Alistair watching 'Priscilla, Queen of the Desert' and singing along. He was glad he hadn't driven here. The walk back would sober him up but meanwhile, he would relax and enjoy this silly film. He realised he hadn't been this happy for a long time and hoped like hell that these two were innocent of their father's murder. He would have to find that out – and fast.

Chapter 20

Friday 29th June 2012

He wondered if this was going to be habit-forming. They'd had a pleasant drink in a pleasant pub. They'd talked about his work, the local election results – old news – the miserable weather at the beginning of the month and how much better it was now, the Queen and the Jubilee, the upcoming Olympics and other non-controversial topics. This was their third date and Ben was beginning to wonder if he would ever crack that shell that surrounded Josephine Finlay. Whenever he asked her anything about herself, she adroitly changed the subject. Today, he'd skirted around anything personal.

He returned from the bar with two more beers and decided it was time to ask the question he'd been avoiding all evening. He took a deep breath. 'Katy wants you to come to dinner with us – you, me, Katy and Sarah. I must warn you, she's not the best cook in the world. But she is enthusiastic.' He let his breath out as he awaited her rejection. He knew this was taking them into more intimate waters. Dinner with the family. He'd thought it too early but Katy had insisted that he ask. He knew Katy would be disappointed at the refusal.

'And Mo? Will he be there?'

'If you like, we can invite him too.'

'I would. He's one of nature's gentlemen. I don't meet many of those. Yes, I'd love to come.'

He was so surprised that it took a moment for him to respond. 'That's great. Katy will be pleased. She suggested Saturday, tomorrow. I know it's short notice but is that any good for you?'

Josephine checked her phone. 'Yes, that works. I'm seeing the Murdocks at five. Lucien wanted a Saturday meeting so I agreed. Need some more info from him about Northern Ireland. Would seven-thirty be OK?'

'Sure. I'll tell the family.' He wondered what Josephine

would be asking at the Murdock house. Whatever else she would be doing, he suspected that she would not be laughing uproariously while eating bacon sandwiches, drinking mojitos and watching Priscilla, Queen of the Desert.

She asked, 'How's it going with earning your fee? Been to see the Murdocks yet?'

'Ever seen Priscilla, Queen of the Desert?' His reply had obviously thrown her.

'No. What's that got to do with anything?'

'I watched it with Virginia and Alistair. We sang along and we drank mojitos. I'm beginning to think we've all wasted a huge chunk of our lives. Them, because their father wouldn't let them live and me, because I wouldn't let me live. They seem to be getting the hang of it. Anyway,' he shrugged and shook himself. 'Let's not get maudlin.'

'No, but I know what you mean. People think life's easy for me, looks, brains, good job, money. Well, it's not.' Then she added, 'That's enough about me. I'm glad the Murdocks are moving on with their lives. I like those two. Lucien, I'm not sure about. He's being careful with me and I don't know why. Maybe I'll get to the bottom of it tomorrow.'

* * *

They shooed him out of the kitchen. They wanted to have 'girl talk'. He listened at intervals throughout the afternoon and several times he'd had to walk away. On the whole they were working well together. It seemed that Katy was in charge. Ben assumed that was because she was still in residence. And Sarah was taking her role as second fiddle with reasonably good grace. She was again regaling Katy with tales of the Force. He listened particularly closely and moved nearer the door when she mentioned Inspector Turnbull and the murder enquiry.

'They're mostly OK, but I'm staying away from Turnbull. All Uniform call him Turnbully and you can see why. Pam says he's getting worse cos we're getting nowhere. Shouts at everyone. We had a hot lead from a Met informer and followed that for days, but it went cold. When they found him, he had the best alibi – like being inside – duh!' She laughed. 'Can't get more solid than that. Couldn't pin anything on his known associates either. And, this is hot news, seems the Met is taking an interest in the case. S'pose because it's got media attention. Mind you – that footballer up on a rape charge – that took the heat off us. The nationals all whooshed off up north to doorstep him. D'you think these carrots are small enough?'

He couldn't hear Katy's reply but it seemed the carrots were fine because Sarah continued, 'D'you want the beans cut in half? Oh, and listen to this.' He could imagine Sarah's triumphant expression and felt more than a little sorry for Katy.

'This is even hotter news, and we're really not supposed to know this, so you mustn't tell a soul. Understand?'

There was a pause – surely done for effect. And then Sarah continued in a lower voice so he had to strain to hear. 'The word is that they're going to bring in an SIO from outside Cambridge. Smack in the face for Turnbully. Wouldn't like to be anywhere near him when that happens.'

At this point, it seemed, Katy had heard enough. 'Well, we know stuff about the victim that you don't.'

Ben pushed open the door and said lightly, 'How's it going? Need any help?'

He looked reprovingly at Katy and almost imperceptibly shook his head. She blushed and turned away. 'Thanks Dad, I think we're on track. We're doing healthy cos she's thin and we think she'll like that. I thought roasts were simple but they're not. Sarah's got this amazing app. It tells us when to put everything on so it's all ready together. Show Dad.'

Sarah held out her phone. 'See, Dad, you could use this.'

Ah, even the old man could manage it.

'You just type in the meal plan or look up a recipe on the web, put in the time you want to eat and it works it all out for you. We so want to impress her. Katy says she's just typical of a solicitor cos she asks loads of questions. But she's stunning looking – so not your typical Duty Solicitor. God, they're boring. There's one that tries to hit on me every time he's in the station.'

Katy interrupted. 'If you've quite finished with your exploits, we need to get on with the fruit salad.'

Sarah looked sideways at her father. 'Heh, Dad, you going to marry Josephine? If she's as clever as Kate says, you'll have to be quick. Someone else might nab her.'

'Good God, child, do I ask you about your boyfriends? No, cos I know you wouldn't tell me; not the truth anyway. How is young Mark, by the way? Am I going to meet him? Are you going to marry him?'

As he said this, he saw the sidelong look that passed between Sarah and Katy and again, he wondered when Sarah was going to tell him. Did she really think he would disapprove?

Obviously, this was not the right time for disclosure as Sarah grinned and gave her father a thumbs-up. 'Nice one, Dad. Evasive action taken.'

Meanwhile Katy was on task. 'Dad, have you got the wine sorted?'

'Yes, and Mo's arriving at seven so we can all be prepared. Anyone would think the Queen was coming.'

Sarah replied, 'Duh! You don't think we'd do all this for the Queen? This is far more important.'

He sighed and again wondered where all this was going. He retreated and left them to their fruit chopping.

* * *

Josephine was precisely on time. The meal arrived on the table within minutes of the initial pleasantries, leaving little time for anything other than small talk. To Ben's relief, Mo was garrulous throughout the meal, chatting away to Josephine about Cambridge, the weather, the Jubilee celebrations and the upcoming Olympics. All the things that he and Josephine had discussed in the pub. He noticed that she was much more animated with Maurice than she had been with him. Ben decided that Josephine's suggestion that Mo be invited had been inspired. It lessened the potential for uncomfortable pauses. The only slight pause had been when Josephine had asked why Mo had never married. She had been effusively apologetic when he'd told her that his Gwennie had died three years ago. 'Same time as my Mum.' She paused. 'But they're always with you, aren't they?'

Then, lightening the atmosphere, Mo told a funny story about an ineffective burglar who'd managed to break into his brother's house by mistake, causing a row heard by the neighbours which brought the police to the door. No arrest of course. He finished his tale with tears running down his cheeks, 'Blood's thicker than... but I bet the barney's still going on!'

Josephine, in return, told a tale about an ancient client who had been in the habit of hiding her will in a different place each week until the day she forgot where she'd put it. She'd turned the house upside down and only found it after she'd made a new one. She'd left that one with Josephine.

Ben could top that with the will that had been lost until he'd discovered it inside the corset of the dead person.

The girls brought in the coffee and sat down looking tired but satisfied. Josephine was the first to congratulate them. She leaned towards them and smiled a dazzling smile. 'Thank you, both of you. That was great. I have to tell you that I don't even attempt roast dinner. I could never get it all ready at the same time. I think you're really clever.' She lifted her wine glass. 'To the cooks!'

They all raised their glasses, even the cooks. 'Glad that's over. I don't think I'll ever cook again!' was Katy's only offering.

Josephine was talking to Sarah. 'I'm fascinated by your job. I don't do much work in criminal law, so I only know about that side of it from my colleagues. They tell me it's mostly boring, but I suppose catching Stanley's killer would be pretty exciting. How's it going? The investigation, I mean.'

Sarah moved her chair closer to Josephine's and leaned in. 'I was only telling Kate earlier. Not good. Me and my mate Pam have a terrible time on it cos our boss is a monster. I've only just been brought in. I was pi... miffed at first to be left out – big crime etc. But Turnbull is such a prat that I'm almost sorry I'm on it.'

As she paused for breath Josephine intervened. 'But you must know what's going on?'

'Yeh, but it's totally boring. Before, when I was on indecent assaults on Midsummer Common; that was interesting. Now they're thinking of putting in someone under cover to flush him out. I think it's a great idea. I was going to volunteer till they moved me to the murder. Anyway, the high-ups are holding out, worried about entrapment and all that. But they're all bloody men so they don't see what it does to the women.'

Josephine smiled. 'Fighting for women. Good for you.'

Before she could say more, Sarah added, 'Domestic violence too. They say they take it seriously but I don't think they understand. D'you do anything with DV victims?'

'Not my area. My work is dull compared to yours. That's why I'm keen to know what's happening with my only murdered client. Sounds morbid, but it brightens up my day.'

Ben could see that Katy was getting more and more agitated as she watched Sarah monopolising Josephine. He watched as Katy closed in.

Katy moved her chair so she was close up on Josephine's other side. She tapped her index finger on the table. 'What if your murdered client was a monster? What if he wasn't a good guy at all? What if he was into domestic violence? Would you still do work for him?'

Ben saw Josephine stiffen, her face tense, her hands clenching the arms of her chair.

He intervened. 'Katy! That's enough.'

Josephine breathed deeply, then smiled at Katy and held a hand up to Ben. The tension was released. 'It's all right. It's a perfectly reasonable question. Solicitors do have to decide whether they can act for a client. For Stanley, I'm acting only on the disbursements of his will. As long as there is no evidence of criminality in relation to that, I can continue. But what makes you think he wasn't a good guy? Do you have any evidence?'

Ben intervened. 'No, we don't have anything. I think Katy was just being hypothetical.' He wondered what it was with Josephine and domestic violence.

Maurice had been sitting quietly for some time and now he roared with laughter. 'Katy, you're an absolute star. My star. Here's a new career for you. How's about you write all this down, get to be a crime writer and keep your dad and me in our old age?' He turned to Josephine. 'She's got such an imagination. It's wasted. Look, lassie. He was rich, he was kidnapped, he died and the gang got a big fat zero for its pains. But I got some news about your man.'

Ben silently thanked Mo for getting them out of that corner.

He knew he could rely on him to be discreet. 'Out with it then, Mo. What have you heard?'

Maurice settled himself back in his chair with all eyes on him. He paused for a moment, then spoke low and slow, 'Well, see. This is what I heard. My mates tell me they're getting nowhere fast. Just like Sarah said. Nothing incriminating at the scene and DNA's come back inconclusive. That's what they was banking on – DNA. Got bugger all else.' He looked across at Josephine. 'Ooops. Begging your pardon.'

'Mo, don't worry. I'm hooked. What *do* they know? Are they anywhere near an arrest?'

'Well, no. They ain't. Seems they got one trace and they ain't got a match. So, I'm asking. This gang, how come only one of them left any DNA? And how come it ain't anyone who's been nicked before?'

Sarah was looking thoughtful. 'Maybe they all had suits like we wear so we don't contaminate the scene. If they were professional, they'd know about DNA. Maybe that's why there isn't any.'

Now it was Josephine's turn to look thoughtful. 'But the police, if they don't have a match, they sometimes keep it on file. Mo, Sarah, is there anything else they can do with the DNA evidence?'

Maurice answered. 'Nah. There's rules. If they're charged and get off, then, they just keeps it and hope they gets em for summat else.'

Katy jumped in. 'Anyone who watches TV knows they all wear masks and things. We have to sometimes, like if there's any way we can be contaminated. Those suits are dead easy to get.'

Ben added, 'Mo, did your mates say they were men?'

'Don't think so… but it must be, mustn't it? Them gangs ain't known for their gender equality.'

Josephine added, 'And, from what I hear, Stanley had to be moved to get him to the farmhouse. It would need someone strong to do that, so probably a man.'

Sarah wagged her finger. 'Huh – no! There's strong women too. We've got some real heavy women in the Force. And you should see the ones at the fire station. They're not wussy, girly types. Sure a woman could do it, but I reckon he'd have to be drugged if it was only one suspect. Might not have to if it was a gang.' She turned to her father. 'Were there marks of a struggle on the body?'

Ben motioned to Katy to answer. She beamed at him then turned to her sister. 'He was tied up so there were rope burns. Nothing else. We don't think there was a struggle to get him there. He did struggle to get free – we know that from his nails. Uncle Mo, d'you know if there was any drug found in the body?'

'Well, lassie, he was missing for about a week before he died. If he'd been drugged to get him out there, I'd be surprised if any traces were left. Sarah, know anything?' She shook her head so he continued, 'I'll see what I can find out, though it beats me what difference it makes.'

'Well', said Katy, 'What I'd really like to do is find the murderer.' She looked straight at her sister. 'That'd be one in the eye for the cops.'

'Katy, no!' The sudden outburst from Josephine surprised them all. She stopped, then continued in a quieter voice, 'That would be so dangerous. In my job, I hear about violent criminals and you wouldn't want to be anywhere near them. Promise me you'll leave it to the police. Please.'

'Heh, don't worry. I was only kidding. I wouldn't know where to start. But in my next life I'm going to be Katy Burton, PI.'

Maurice laughed. 'Is that after the crime writing? Anyways, you haven't heard the end of my news. The word is that them high-ups is getting twitchy and they're going to bring in someone from the Met to lead it. Someone who knows what they're doing.'

Sarah concurred. 'Yep, that's what I heard. Might get a result then.'

But a result was just what Ben did not want. Whoever had killed Stanley Murdock had done him and the world a favour. And, for different reasons, he knew that a result was just what Chris didn't want. He sighed. He was going to have to phone him.

The party broke up, with Maurice offering to walk Josephine home; an offer that she quickly accepted. Ben was again left wondering why Josephine was so much more at ease with his daughters and his uncle than she was with him. And why had she reacted so strongly to what Katy had said about domestic violence? He looked at his watch. Not too late to phone Chris. Turnbully would have to stay and Chris would have to organise it.

Chapter 21

Monday 2nd July

Ben's brief phone-call to Chris had brought a request for him to return to the Murdocks to get something concrete to assure The Service that the family knew nothing of their father's involvement with MI5. Ben had tried to explain to Chris that this was impossible; that proving a negative was only possible in maths because it was in the abstract. In the tangible world, it could not be done. Chris had been dismissive. Maths, what did maths have to do with information gathering? Ben had briefly thought about his own time agent-handling and decided that Chris had a lot to learn.

As he swung the car slowly onto the Murdock forecourt, Alistair was sweeping the pebbles.

'Hi,' said Ben. 'Thought you'd have someone to do that.'

'Gardener twice a week – came yesterday.'

Ben put on a perplexed look. 'Then, why?'

'Lucien messed it up when he was leaving. Ginny wanted it sorted.' Alistair leaned on his broom and smiled. 'See anything different?'

Ben could. The pink hair had reverted to brown; the skinny black had been replaced by jeans and t-shirt and the overly gay gestures had disappeared. Alistair laughed. 'Been to see Ginny's shrink. Told me rebelling was keeping his memory alive. Told me ghosts only live if you feed them. Clever eh? So I've stopped feeding him. Coffee?'

'Yeah, great. Sounds like good advice. Lucien not here? I need to see him.'

'Nah, went off in a bad mood. Does that. Glad we don't have to live with him. He's a bugger when he's riled.'

'Do the moods last long?'

'Depends. With Father, it could be all day, the two of 'em at it like bloody gladiators. Alpha males. You know.'

As they passed through to the kitchen, Ben glanced to where the miserable policeman usually sat. He nodded towards the empty chair. 'Where's our little ray of sunshine today?'

'Dunno. Phoned this morning to say he had a meeting and he'd be in later. Means we get to read the paper first.'

Virginia greeted them in the kitchen. 'Just the person I want to see.' She held up a whole salmon. 'I got a recipe and it says salmon fillets. How do I get fillets from this?'

As Ben filleted one side of the fish, he explained what he was doing and showed them how to pin-bone the fillet with Virginia's tweezers. Then he suggested that one of them try filleting the other side. They took it in turns and, between them, produced a raggedy fillet. He was sure that it contained no bones but it didn't contain much fish either. He put the fish carcass in a saucepan explaining about fish stock.

'Coffee,' said Virginia. 'I need one!'

Over coffee, Ben put in, 'Allie says Lucien's like your father.' Then he waited for one of them to fill the vacuum.

It didn't take long. Virginia looked thoughtful. 'God, yes.' Then she went silent. Ben slowly drank his coffee and waited. Alistair poked at the fish bones in the pan. After a pause, Virginia continued, 'Yep, angry, both of them. But Father kept his under control. Lucien's not so good at that. Allie, should I talk to Fiona about him?'

'Fiona?' asked Ben.

Alistair answered. 'Our counsellor.' Then he turned to his sister, 'Yeah maybe. Can't do any harm.'

Ben could see an opening. 'Sounds like a good idea. I've been going to a counsellor for years. I was wondering if Michael would need some help when he's released?'

Alistair immediately asked, 'What's he like? We'd never heard of him before the will.'

'Your father brought him over to England to work for him.'

Virginia banged the flat of her hand down on the worktop. The sound reverberated as she rubbed her reddened palm. 'Another bloody secret. The more I hear, the more I realise we never even knew him. A bloody stranger who controlled our lives.'

But Alistair was not to be thwarted. 'Anyway, is he violent? A hardened criminal? A smack-head?'

'No. Just a lost boy really. He's your cousin. His brother's son. I like him. But I'm amazed your father never mentioned him.'

'I'm not. We always knew he had secrets. But whatever they are, I just don't want to know.'

Alistair hugged his sister. 'Me neither, but, what d'you think, Ben? Maybe we should get to know this cousin. He's family. Our only family. At least I think so! Could be hundreds of cousins for all we know. How do we find out?'

Before he could answer, Virginia butted in. 'We'll ask Michael.' She smiled at Ben. 'And you're going to help us.'

'Sure.' At least then, he'd know what they were saying.

Chapter 22

Tuesday 3rd July 2012

Ben looked at his watch. She should be home by now. He pushed the buzzer and waited. 'Hello.'

'Hi, Josephine, it's Ben. Can I come up?'

There was a slight pause, 'Of course,' and he knew he should have phoned first. He'd thought about it and had decided to surprise her. Wrong choice. He took the lift and arrived at her door just as she was opening it.

'Happy birthday!' Ben produced a dozen yellow roses from behind his back. He had a present in his pocket but he'd give that to her later. Josephine looked startled.

'How did you know?'

'I have spies everywhere.'

Josephine's look made him wonder if he'd said the wrong thing but then she smiled and stood back to let him in.

He removed his shoes and placed them neatly by the door, then surveyed the room. The flat was as immaculate as ever. Not a cushion out of place, each placed perfectly straight in a line on the back of the settee. He couldn't imagine his house ever being this tidy. There were always books, CDs, newspapers and magazines strewn around and plates that he'd not yet managed to fit into the dishwasher. Katy's coats, shoes, bags left where she'd dropped them. He made a mental pledge that they would be tidier.

He looked round the room and turned to Josephine. 'Your flat is perfect. I thought maybe you tidied for me, but today you didn't know I was coming.' Josephine's expression told him he'd said too much so he added, 'I just don't know how you manage to keep it like this. Look, I'm sorry. I should have phoned first.'

'No, no, don't worry. You just caught me unawares. And it's lovely to see you when I wasn't expecting to. Let's have a drink.' She led him through to the immaculate kitchen, opened the pristine fridge and took out a bottle of Sancerre. He was fascinated by her but hardly understood her. The thought of an exotic butterfly flitted across his mind.

'So, how did you know?'

'About your birthday? Simple. When I called to pick you up at your office, I heard one of the receptionists ask if you were going to do anything special on Tuesday. I went back and asked what was special about Tuesday. I know they shouldn't have told me but I said that I wanted to celebrate with you. Don't be cross with them.'

'Of course not. And thank you for taking all this trouble. It was thoughtful.'

'No trouble. I've clocked up a few birthdays and I still like to celebrate.' He held up his glass. 'Here's to you and I hope you have a wonderful year. Any plans you want to share?'

For a moment her eyes were distant then she smiled. 'Oh, I forgot to say. Thank you for that delicious dinner with your family. Do give my thanks to your girls. Aren't they just gorgeous?' She motioned for him to sit down. He perched on the side of the settee, not wishing to disturb the perfect cushions. 'And Mo was so kind, insisted on bringing me all the way home. He kept me amused all the way. Regaled me with stories about his life in the police. And told me about helping to bring up your two.'

'Yes. I was ill for quite a while after Diane died. Post-traumatic stress disorder. I was a mess and Mo and Gwen were wonderful. It took a few years to get back to some sort of normality.' He smiled. 'But here I am – relatively normal.'

She sat down, leaned towards him, her face full of compassion. 'You don't have to answer this, but I've had a couple of clients with PTSD.' She hesitated. 'Was Diane's death sudden?'

'She was killed by a bomb in Northern Ireland while I was stationed there. It's sixteen years and I'm still coming to terms with it.' He didn't add that Dobson had told him that Stanley, her client, had planted that bomb. He held his glass of wine aloft. 'But life goes on and I'm a better person than I was then. So it's not all bad. Come on. Let's not get depressed. It's your birthday. And you haven't told me your plans.'

For a moment she held his look then glanced away. 'Oh, some good news. As soon as you send in your invoice, we should be able to do a final settlement of your bill. Then you can really celebrate. Things are moving quickly. Faster than I thought possible. The Murdocks will be pleased, especially Lucien. He's been pushing hard.'

The thought of the Murdocks reminded him that he had to talk to Lucien again – and then possibly Alistair. With his mind still on the Murdock family and their problems, he took the gift from his pocket.

'I got you a present. Just something small. Close your eyes and hold out your hands.' As she hesitated, he smiled, 'Go on. It won't bite.'

As he placed the small package in her hands his mind began to race. Something was stirring in the back of his consciousness and he began to grasp its implications. No, it couldn't be. What exactly had Lucien said? And Alistair? It could all be falling into place in a way that he'd never imagined. He'd thought Chris was off beam. He knew the police were off beam. Now he had more digging to do to see if he'd also been off beam. He wanted to get on to it straight away. 'Look, I just came to give you this and to wish you a happy birthday.' He looked at his watch. 'I'm going to have to go soon, and I'm sure you've got things to do.' He raised his glass again. 'Happy Birthday, Josephine. Shall we celebrate properly on Saturday?'

'Yes – of course. That would be nice.'

'Where would you like to go?'

'Oh, I don't know. You choose.'

'I'll see if we can get into Midsummer House. I've wanted to go ever since he was on TV but I've never had the excuse before.'

'Oh no! It's far too expensive. I couldn't possibly...'

'Yes, you could. And you've just told me I'm about to get the bulk of forty grand, so we can both celebrate.' He looked at his watch. 'I'm sorry but I do have to go.'

'That's okay.'

He hadn't told her that he'd already booked the table, or that he was putting two and two together and might just be coming up with four. And, he hadn't told her that his ordered world had just suffered another tremor.

She showed him to the door. 'Thank you for being so kind. You're a very nice man and I appreciate you. See you Saturday.'

And she kissed him lightly on the lips.

As he descended in the lift he swore quietly. He would have to ask a favour of Dobson. That was about the last thing on earth he wanted but he couldn't see any other way.

* * *

He arrived home to an empty house. 'Katy! Katy… You home?' No answer. He looked at his watch, eight-thirty. He wondered which of her friends she was with. Time for a quiet supper and something relaxing on the TV. No chatter. Just time to himself. As he prepared his meal, he looked for a note. She usually left a note propped against the kettle. Not there. Unusual, but she sometimes forgot to leave one. Then she'd phone because she knew he'd be worried. He wandered out to the phone in the hall and there was a flashing light, a message. He pressed play. That pseudo-voice again. 'You have one new message', then Maurice's voice boomed out. 'Ben, when you get this. Phone me. Nothing to worry about. Just need to talk.' He dialled immediately and Maurice answered on the first ring. 'Thank Heavens. Is Katy there?'

'No. I've just got in. She's out somewhere. D'you need to talk to her?'

'Ben, I'm coming over. Five minutes.' And the line went dead. Ben's heart thudded in his chest. He needed to use those five minutes – needed to keep busy. He paced through the house looking to see if there was anything out of place. Katy's room was its usual mess but there was no sign of anything untoward. His mind went back to the threat at the funeral. He hadn't done anything to incite the hard men from Ulster. Maybe Chris had rattled their cages. If he had and Katy was harmed…

As he went through the house, he didn't want to admit it, but he was searching for signs of a struggle. Everything was perfectly normal, just as he'd left it. He was finishing in the sitting room when the he heard the key turn in the front door. Must be Katy. He ran to the door, relief flooding his veins. Maurice held up his hands and said, 'Look, don't worry. It's probably nothing.'

Ben's voice rose. 'What do you mean "don't worry"? What's happened?'

'Well, it's probably a new boyfriend or sommat. After you left, Katy was right off. She was hiding something. I asked her where she was off to, sort of casual, like. She wouldn't look at me and mumbled that she was meeting some mates. I knew she wasn't being straight with me.'

'Did you try to stop her?'

'Stop her? How could I? I let her go. What else could I do?' He shrugged. 'But, a bit later, I tries ringing and her phone's switched off. You know these young girls, never turn off their phones.'

'What time did she go out?'

'Bout half six.'

Ben scrolled his contacts and called Katy's number. Not available. His thoughts raced as he paced the floor. He gave a forced laugh. 'I'm the one who's supposed to be hyper-vigilant.' He rubbed his forehead round his scar. It was beginning to throb. 'You're right. Probably a simple explanation. New boyfriend's the most likely. Mo, we're just going to have to sit this out and wait for her to come waltzing through the door.' He looked at his watch – nine o'clock. 'If she's not back in half an hour, we begin to worry. OK?'

Maurice nodded. Ben gestured towards the kitchen. 'I'll get us some food to take our minds off it.'

He rattled pans with ferocity. It had been her suggestion that she made sure she was always contactable. And now she wasn't. He could feel his guts twisting. Of course nothing would have happened to her.

For the next half hour Ben and Maurice took it in turns to pace the floor. Then, they took it in turns to try to call Katy. Then, they took it in turns to pace the floor again. When the sound of Ben's phone pierced the air, they both jumped and stared at it. Katy's name was on the display. He answered quickly. 'Katy?' With an affirmative, he breathed a huge sigh and continued, 'Are you OK?' He listened to her reply then said, 'Yes, yes, of course. Stay right where you are. We're coming now.' He turned to Maurice. 'She's shaken but she's all right. Come on.'

* * *

They drove in silence towards Shelford. Traffic was light and they made good progress. 'She said she'd be outside the garden centre.'

'There she is!' Maurice shouted, and he pointed to a small, dishevelled figure standing under an ornate palm tree. They swung up to the entrance and, as soon as Ben had skidded to a halt, he leapt out of the car and ran to her, hugging her to him as she snivelled into his collar. When her whimpering had stopped, he gently pushed her away and looked at her. Her face was blotchy, her clothes dirty and torn. He immediately suspected the worst and did not know what to say. He started with, 'You OK?' which she patently was not.

She nodded. 'Dad, I'm so sorry,' and she immediately burst into noisy sobs. He could see Maurice approaching. He gently shook his head as Maurice opened his mouth to speak. Maurice closed his mouth and stood looking mournful.

Ben squeezed her gently and said, 'Ready to come home?' All the while he was thinking, ready to go to the police – or Chris? If there was evidence, it would need to be preserved.

'Yes,' she whispered. 'And my bike's gone.'

'Never mind the bike. Come on.' And he half-led, half-carried her to the car. 'Mo, you drive and I'll sit in the back with Katy.'

He put his arm round her and she relaxed against his shoulder. She started talking as soon as they were on their way. 'It's all my fault. I'm so stupid.'

'Nonsense, of course it's not your fault. Can you tell me what happened? Just tell me what you can.'

Ben braced himself to hear what no father ever wants to hear. But what she told him was not at all what he expected. 'I know it was stupid, so please, please don't tell me off. I don't need you to be angry with me. I'm angry enough with myself.'

She looked up at him and he replied, 'I won't be angry with you.'

She gulped. 'It all started when I said to Josephine that I wanted to be a P.I. I've been thinking about it ever since, so I decided to try to follow someone. Virginia told me that Lucien goes round there nearly every day since the murder, so I thought I'd see if I could trail him on my bike. That bit worked fine. The traffic from Grantchester meant that I could keep up but then I made a big mistake.'

He couldn't keep quiet any longer. He spoke through gritted teeth, 'What did he do to you?'

Katy looked surprised. 'Why, nothing. It was me.'

'Just tell me what happened.'

'He got to his block of flats and went in, but he left the door on the latch. I looked in and then I crept up the stairs to his door. That door was open too, so I pushed it a little. I couldn't see Lucien so I went in.' Ben was about to speak but she held up her hand to stop him. 'I could hear him in the kitchen and I realised I was trespassing. I was just going to turn round and creep back out, but then, this gigantic man was coming up the stairs. Huge.' She spread her arms as wide as they could go in the confines of the car. 'So I ran and hid in the bedroom. In the wardrobe. The man crashed open the living room door and I could hear them talking. That went on for ages then the man got angry and I could hear him breaking things. I swear I stopped breathing, I was so scared. The crashing went on and on. I heard Lucien trying to stop him. Then it all went quiet. I thought he might have killed Lucien but then he said real loud so I could hear every word. "Get it by the end of the week or it'll be you." And then I heard the door slam.' She stopped and blew her nose noisily. This was too much for Maurice.

'Lassie, tell us! What happened next?'

'I couldn't go back out the front so I climbed out the bedroom window and sort of landed in the bushes. Then I called you.' Her voice had gone quieter as her tale unfolded. 'Dad, Uncle Mo, please, please don't tell Sarah. I'll never be so stupid again and I'll die if she knows.'

Ben knew that neither of these was likely. Katy was Katy, so, yes, she would probably be as stupid again. And no, she wouldn't die if Sarah found out. But he was so relieved that his worst imaginings were just that, that he hugged her and laughed. Tomorrow was the time for lectures. Tonight, they'd go home, Katy would have a warm bath, he and Maurice would thank their stars that she was alive and well. He would give her a warm drink and sit with her till she fell asleep, just as he used to when she was small.

And tomorrow? Tomorrow, the repercussions.

Chapter 23

Wednesday 4th July 2012

Ben looked at the red light over the door and spoke to Dobson's secretary. 'Has he got anyone with him?' He gave her his best smile and wondered how her wire-grey hair stayed so perfectly in place.

'No. But he won't take kindly to being disturbed.' She reached for a ledger. 'Shall I make an appointment for you. He can see you next week. Thursday or Friday?'

But Ben didn't have time to wait till next week. 'I'll see him now.' He knocked on the door and waited. A testy response came from within. 'What is it, woman? I said I was *not* to be disturbed.'

Ben opened the door and poked his head inside. 'Sorry to disturb you, but I have a question that can't wait. Can I come in?'

'Why, Benedict. I thought you'd been avoiding me. Yes, of course. Come in. Sit down. What can I do for you? Would you like a sherry or coffee?'

Ben didn't want to exchange small talk so he came straight to the point. 'Neither, thanks. But I do need some information. It's about Stanley Murdock. It seems he had an eye for the ladies?' Dobson inclined his head. Ben took that as affirmation and continued. 'I wondered if you could find out about his time as an undergrad here. I need to know if there were any peccadilloes that had repercussions here, in college. Can you find that out for me?'

Ben looked at Dobson and immediately knew he had miscalculated. He should have said that Chris needed the info. Dobson stood up and his face took on a look of outrage. He spoiled the effect by giving that high-pitched laugh. 'My dear boy! What a thing to ask! What happens in College stays in College. You should know that. I couldn't possibly divulge College matters, even to you. I don't know how you have the temerity to ask that of me.'

Ben felt anger rising in his throat. He knew that Dobson wanted him to grovel and he wouldn't do that. He swallowed hard. 'So you won't help me?'

'Certainly not. As an alumnus, you surely know that information here is privileged.' He paused and looked sideways at

Ben. 'However, I could make an exception, but I would need something in return.'

Ben was immediately wary. 'What would that be?'

'I don't know at present, but I'll think of something. I'm sure you'll be able to do me a favour in return at some point.'

'No Dobson, I don't think so.'

Dobson smiled showing his mouthful of big teeth. Despite his rising anger, Ben could think only of a donkey about to bray. He knew that he needed to sound conciliatory. 'OK. Perhaps we could come to some arrangement.'

Dobson let out his falsetto giggle and waved a hand towards the door. 'Well, Benedict, you were too slow. I think I've changed my mind.' He moved towards the door then turned. 'But a small piece of advice, dear boy. If I were you, I'd be careful. Very, very careful. It seems that you are intent on digging up history that should remain buried. Powerful men have powerful allies. I'm sure you get my drift.' Then he called out in a peremptory manner. 'Mrs Jones. See Mr Burton out and don't let anyone else disturb my thought processes.'

Ben stomped out of Dobson's study. He'd asked just a simple question, one that he could easily have answered. Dobson had taken great delight in fobbing him off. But, threats? What was the meaning of the veiled threats?

Suddenly he wanted to get out of this college and leave Dobson and his ilk far behind. He hurried round the corner towards the porters' lodge and bumped full-tilt into the Head Porter, who held out a steadying hand to make sure that Ben stayed on his feet.

'Easy, Sir. You could do yourself a damage rushing round like that. There's always undergrads wandering head-in-the-clouds or head-in-the-phones, so you need to look where you're going.' He stepped back and looked Ben up and down. 'Well, well, if it isn't – no, don't tell me. It'll come. Haven't seen you in many a long year.'

Ben opened his mouth but the porter held up a hand to stop him. 'No. Let me think. I pride myself in remembering all our young men and women. Here in the eighties. Maths – Senior Wrangler – don't tell me – name begins with a B. You used to run every morning. I must be getting old. The name's gone for the moment.'

'Burton, Ben Burton. And you're Fisher. Your father was Head Porter then, and you were as young and innocent as I was.'

'Of course. Mr Burton. Good to see you again, sir.'

'And, if you remember, I didn't run the morning after that night you had to help me up to my room and hold a bowl in front of me. I don't think I ever apologised for being sick on your shoes. But I apologise now.'

Ben held out his hand. Fisher grasped the outstretched hand and shook it vigorously. 'Apology accepted, Mr Burton. Part of the job – though not the most satisfying, I can tell you.'

Ben laughed. 'Mr Fisher, I was so grateful you didn't tell your father. I was terrified of him. We all were. How is he?'

'He's well. Retired ten years ago. Lives out at Linton. Misses this place, though. Worked here for nigh on forty years.' He sighed. 'They gave him a grand send-off.'

'Yeah, sounds like my uncle. He's thinking of retiring but I don't think he'll settle.'

Fisher nodded. 'It's a worry. Dad's lonely. Mum died last year so he's on his own. He's getting a bit slow on the old pins but mind as sharp as a needle. Lives in the past and loves to reminisce. I do my best for him but you know how it is.'

Ben thought about his unanswered question and smiled broadly. 'Could I go and see him? I'd love to talk over old times with him. I'm writing a sort of memoir and I need some information about this place. I think he might be just the person to help me. Do you think he'd be interested?'

'Mr Burton, he'd love it.'

Chapter 24

Friday 6th July 2012

Ben turned left at the lights and drove up Cherry Hinton High Street. Passing Giant's Grave reminded him of the last time he'd come this way. It had been a geography trip in primary school – or was it secondary – too many years ago to worry about. They'd had to walk in single file up Limekiln Road to visit the East Pit. He could picture it now. The quarry, closed for a year, had looked like a moonscape: sheer white cliffs with no vegetation, a flat floor and silence. No birds, no traffic noise, nothing to detract from the awe of the vast white bowl of empty space. With the rest of his class, he'd stood marvelling at the sheer size and blinding whiteness. And then they'd all started running and whooping and listening for echoes. He wondered why he'd never come back.

Yesterday, he'd had tea with Old Mr Fisher, and he'd eventually managed to get the conversation round to Stanley. At first Mr Fisher had been reticent but when Ben had suggested that any truth that came out couldn't hurt Stanley now, and that he was the soul of discretion, he'd told Ben a tale that was over thirty years old and as shocking today as it had been then.

He needed the last turning on the right before the level crossing. Mr Fisher had phoned Agnes Barrett while Ben was still with him and his endorsement and the fact that Ben was burying Stanley Murdock had clinched the agreement that she would see him.

The Victorian terrace had a down-at-heel look. There was rubbish in the small front gardens and a couple of wheelie bins lay on their sides. He parked further along the road and walked back to the door of number twelve. Before he could knock, the door was opened by a tall, erect woman. He knew that she was not much older than he was but, at first glance, he would have put her nearer seventy. Her face was striking, sculptured, and might have been beautiful but for the hard, lined look of the terminally unhappy. Her mouth was clamped into a forced smile of welcome. A welcome that was as grudging as it was undeserved. He would cause her grief, open old wounds. She had that weary look that he often saw on the faces of bereaved relatives and he had a good idea what she was grieving for.

She was looking down on him from the top step and he was reminded of his earlier meeting with Virginia Murdock when she had told him to use the tradesman's entrance. No tradesman's entrance here.

As he was ushered in, he shook hands and said, 'Mrs Barrett, it's very good of you to see me. Thank you. I hope I'm not disturbing you.'

'Well, young man. You probably will be, but time heals. Would you like a cup of tea? It's good strong Irish tea. Not the bilge-water they drink here.'

He smiled. 'Strong and dark, that's how I like it.'

'Ah, well. A good cup of tea can be a life saver. Tell me, Mr Burton, how is Mr Fisher?' She continued, 'I was glad to hear from him. I haven't kept in touch. He was good to me – and his poor dear wife – God rest her soul. I didn't know she'd gone.' She looked wistful and added in a low voice. 'They were the only ones. The only ones.'

He waited in silence while Agnes Barrett's eyes lost focus and he could see she was no longer in the present. The sound of the kettle bubbling brought her back and she warmed the pot and heaped three big spoons of tea into it.

As she made the tea, he expanded, 'He's well. I think he's a bit lonely now he's on his own. He's taken up bowls, plays regularly, says it keeps him in trim. But he likes reminiscing.' Ben thought about the hours he'd spent the day before, listening to Old Mr Fisher's tales of life at College. 'He was pleased to see me. I think he'd like to see you too.'

Agnes sighed. 'A good man and a good woman. He said you were a good man too. Otherwise, I wouldn't have seen you. She'll be missed. Not like him.'

For a moment Ben had lost the thread of her thought processes but what she said next put him straight.

'You can ask me what you like. Murdock was the last of them to go. Now he's dead, it doesn't matter any more. It was a shameful time for those who should have known better. I've lived a good life. Honest. Not like them. I've kept their filthy dirty secret all these years. Maybe it's time. But I don't want any of it written down. Understand? Don't want any of this in your memoir of that place.'

'Mrs Barrett, it won't be. Before Mr Fisher phoned you, he made me promise I wouldn't do anything to hurt you. If you want to end the conversation at any time, you just have to say. I'm really grateful that you agreed to see me, and as soon as you think I'm causing you too much pain, just send me away.'

'Go on then, ask away.'

Ben nodded but still felt reluctant to open the subject. Mr Fisher had told him as much detail as he knew, but only Agnes Barrett knew the full story. And, from what he could tell, it was a story that she had never previously shared.

Agnes frowned. The frown stayed as her face fell into repose. 'Carry the tea in and come and sit down.'

He followed her into the tiny sitting room and looked for somewhere to place the tray. Every surface was covered. There were ornaments and religious relics on every shelf, holy pictures covered the walls and clutter of every sort lay on the occasional tables. But there was not, Ben noted, a single photo of Agnes or her child. Agnes swept a pile of newspapers on to the floor and pointed for him to put the tray down. She then pointed him to the only empty chair and cleared another for herself. As she poured the jet-black tea, she said, 'I thought nowadays people could talk about this sort of thing. In my day it was hidden away, swept under the carpet, and it was always the woman who paid the price. Better these days. But it's still the women who have the burden. And it's still difficult to catch the bastards!'

This last was said with a ferocity that it shocked Ben. He could see that she was back in the past and she continued before he could ask anything. 'Murdock was the ring-leader. He'd tried it on before but I told him I wasn't that kind of girl. He wouldn't give up, so I said I'd report him. He didn't like that.' She looked into the distance and said quietly, 'Then he got what he wanted anyway.'

He asked gently, 'And your attackers were never brought to justice.'

'No. They all got away with it. It was brushed under the

carpet. All four went on to make names for themselves. One was a Cabinet Minister.'

It seemed strange to Ben, but it was almost as though Agnes were boasting. 'Yes, they all became rich or famous. I don't suppose any of them gave me a second thought. After all, I was a bedder – just a college servant.' She smoothed her skirt and looked at Ben. 'They were four young men from rich families, young men with prospects.' She took a noisy gulp of her tea. 'Yes, they thought they could get away with it. And they did.' She gestured to him to hand over his cup and topped it up with thick dark tea.

She sat down heavily. Ben waited and, after a pause, she continued, 'I reported them, but who would believe me? They all denied it but I could see there was something going on that I didn't know about. The College put me on a different staircase well away from them and I heard they were nearly sent down.' Here the anger took over again. 'Then I started to show, and they had to do something. At first, they wanted me to murder my baby. Kept pressing me but I wouldn't give in. I couldn't. They gave up on that one when it was too late to do anything. Then I was given two options; make it public and get nothing or keep their filthy secret and get a pension for life. I was seventeen. I had a baby on the way. What choice did I have?'

He'd had the names of the four attackers from old Mr Fisher, but he didn't want to know who 'they' were; those people who had let a gang-rape go unpunished. He simply knew that 'they' were not people he wanted to have anything to do with. 'And the four men? Did you ever hear from them afterwards?'

'That was one of the terms. I had to sign a contract. I wasn't to try to contact them or tell anyone who the father was.' She laughed. It was a hollow sound. 'Couldn't do that anyway, it could have been any of the four of them.'

'And now they're all dead. Will you make it public?'

'What, and risk losing my pension? Don't talk daft.'

It seemed a fair answer. And her choice.

'You never thought of moving? Making a life away from Cambridge?'

'Where would I go? I couldn't go home. Once I was pregnant, my family wanted nothing to do with me. Even though it wasn't my doing.' He could hear again the venom in her voice. 'My family was ashamed of me. And they've not been in contact to this day.'

'I'm sorry.' Then he asked gently the question he had come to find the answer to, 'And what of the child?'

Her face immediately closed in. Her hands shook so much that she had to put her cup down. She made the sign of the cross and took her rosary beads from her pocket. As she fingered the beads, her mouth moved in silent prayer. Then she spoke. 'The child's dead. So that's an end of it. No more questions. I think it's time you drank your tea and went.'

* * *

An immense sadness washed over him as he thanked Mrs Barrett and walked down the steps and away from her house. He decided not to drive yet, but to walk back down the High Street to see if he could lose the heaviness that Agnes Barrett and her crowded house had wrought. He was certain now that Stanley Murdock had led the gang rape of a seventeen-year-old college servant. This was the stuff of medieval history or Victorian propriety. It was all the more shocking as it had happened such a short time ago. A mere thirty-five years. And most shocking of all was that they had got away with it. Their only sanction had been that they were 'nearly sent down'. Ben found that he was shaking with anger at the iniquity of it all. He broke into a run. That way, the adrenaline would be dissipated. He ran on until he found himself back by Giants Grave. He crossed the road and ran up the hill to East Pit. There, he sat on a chalk boulder and thought about Agnes.

Abortion had been legal, but it would not have been an option for Agnes. Yes, she'd been paid off, but Agnes Barrett was still paying. She was living every day with the consequences of that rape.

Someone had organised for Agnes to be silenced. He wondered if the Cabinet Minister had ever felt remorse. Or the other two. He was sure that Stanley Murdock never had. Mr Fisher had provided their names and all four were now dead.

He had a sudden need to see his family, to hug his girls and his Uncle Mo. Then he had more searching to do. To see if that child was indeed dead. Or merely dead to Agnes. And there was the nagging doubt, unlikely as it was, that this woman might have systematically killed her four assailants. He'd already decided that he would strive to the best of his ability to ensure that Stanley's killer was never brought to justice. Doubly so if it was Agnes Barrett. She'd suffered enough.

As he left the East Pit, he looked around. In the intervening years, some vegetation had grown. But it still looked like a moonscape, beautiful in its way but desolate. It reminded him of Agnes Barrett.

Chapter 25

Saturday 7th July 2012

Ben's call to Chris had brought an immediate response with a time for a meeting. They sat in the Central Library café. Ben looked round the near-empty space. It was a perfect place for spies to meet, far from the mildly curious glances of the public or the more piercing gaze of those with reason to look. The only other inhabitants were a young couple, so entwined that they could only be seeing each other.

'First, I have a couple of questions for you.'

'Fire away,' said Chris.

'Turnbull. He's getting nowhere. Are they still going to bring in an SIO from the Met?'

'Been thinking about your call. Yeah, Met're trying to take over but it just won't happen. Trust me, Turnbull's here to stay. They don't know it yet, but they'll be winding down the operation soon. All leads gone cold. Competing priorities. All that shit. Next question?'

'What have forensics found?'

'Bugger all of use. No fingerprints. Some DNA – traces on his right palm – like he shook hands.' He gave Ben an appreciative look. 'Heh though, you're a dark horse. Saw you with that solicitor of his. Boy, is she fit! I'd solicit with her any day.' He grinned at Ben. 'Oops, sorry, shouldn't have said that.'

Ben ignored the comments. Josephine was a beautiful and intelligent woman. He just wished she… But he didn't quite know what he did wish.

Chris was still talking. 'Only one smudge not accounted for. Low level so difficult to analyse apparently. They're doing more stuff with it. Explained it all to me. No idea what they were on about. The gist is, they're worried about contamination so, no-go.'

'Anything on the ransom notes?'

'Clean as a whistle. Stanley's prints and DNA all over them. Nothing on the envelopes. All clean. They were careful. Too bloody careful. That it?'

'No. I've got three names for you.' He handed Chris a piece of paper. 'All dead. I want you to find out cause of death for each. They were all friends of Stanley's at Ethel's. Probably nothing but they've come up as a significant part of Stanley's past.'

Chris looked at the page. 'Holy shit! You don't come up with nonentities, do you? Care to tell me how they fit?'

'Not sure they do fit. If they do, you'll be the first to know. Actually, you'll be the only one to know. Can you do that for me, find out how they died?'

'Can do, but then I'll want to know why. So, what *can* you tell me?'

'Not much, but I'm getting somewhere. I've got to talk to Lucien again. He's the least forthcoming and I have a feeling he knows more than he's saying.'

'What gives with him?'

'He's cagey. The other two are like open books. Same with the cousin. Innocents abroad. You know how you get the feeling when it's all above board, and that other feeling when something's being hidden?'

Chris nodded. 'Know what you mean. Go on.'

'Lucien – could be he's just like that – short with everyone. He said something that I want to follow up on, something about his father being promiscuous. Lucien used the word "philandering". Does it have any relevance, do you think?'

Chris gave a low laugh. 'Not unless he fucked the wife or daughter of a UVF man. Might give us another motive a bit less volatile than the one we've got. Much better he was killed as an adulterer than his cover was blown. We've got one smudge of unaccounted DNA. Now, does that back up the affair-with-wife theory? Single perp avenging his honour. Could be. What we've got on file from those terrorist bastards doesn't match, but there's some we've never managed to get near to.'

'Worrying though, what Stanley might have said. Training or no, we all break at some point. Let's hope he lost consciousness before he could talk.'

Chris looked thoughtful. 'Yep. Still the same problem. What he said before he died. Anyway, give me some good news.'

'I'm ninety-nine per cent certain Virginia and Alistair know nothing about Stanley's double life. They were young, didn't see him often and they were too frightened to ask questions. Same goes for Michael. He was green as a cabbage. Stanley took him for a ride. He knows the UVF connection but has no idea Stanley was under cover. I've been invited back to the Murdocks', so I'll dig a bit deeper, especially with Lucien. I'll tell him it will speed up probate, that'll get him talking.'

'Pity they won't talk to my man in there.'

Ben gave a wry laugh. 'Look Chris, your man is crap at that job. He's put all their backs up and they can't wait to be rid of him.'

'Yeah, pity we can't tell them he might be saving their lives. Bummer of a job, innit?'

Chapter 26

The call to Lucien had not been well received. It was only when Ben had dangled the lure of hastened probate that the mood had changed. Yes, he would grudgingly grant him an audience at the Grantchester house. Ben had then phoned Virginia to arrange to see her afterwards, so she could tell him the rest of her story. He'd suggested that he should cook dinner for her and Alistair; a suggestion that she had accepted with alacrity. He'd arranged the time so he could arrive early for the meeting with Lucien to prepare the Bolognese sauce and put it on for long, slow cooking.

Things were moving forward but not quickly enough. He knew that killers usually struck close to home and the police would look at family first and then spread outwards. His suspicion was that this murder had its roots in the past – but that past had not been in Northern Ireland.

He rang that clanging bell and waited while he heard pittering footsteps crossing the marble hall. The door swung open and Virginia ushered him in. 'New shoes?' he said. 'Very smart… and they match the dress. Very nice.'

'Ten out of ten. You're getting better at compliments. God, looks like you've got enough food for an army. Want me to carry something?'

As she took one of the bags and led the way to the kitchen, he said, 'Want to talk to me while I prepare the veg?'

'Tell me what to do and I'll help.'

As they chopped onions and carrots, they chatted about this and that. After a while conversation flagged. Ben took the opportunity of the intimate surroundings to say, 'Can I ask you something that's been troubling me?'

'Fire away.'

'Usually, when it's a murder, it's the family who are first suspected. But you're not suspects. Why?'

'Oh, they had a good look at Lucien. At first, he was their favourite for it, even though he'd contacted the police and shown them the first ransom note. They kept going on about his posh pens. He collects old fountain pens. God knows why anyone collects anything.' She giggled. 'Except shoes and handbags.' He could see she was counting in her head. 'D'you know, since Father died, I've bought nine pairs of shoes and six handbags. He'll be turning in his grave. Sorry, what was the question?'

'Why you weren't suspects.'

'Oh, yes. Allie and I were off the hook straight away. We had a cast iron alibi.' She stopped chopping and looked directly at him. He could see that her hands were opening and closing convulsively so he carefully removed the knife from her grasp. She looked down at her hands. 'You see, it was on a Wednesday he was abducted. Wednesdays were our worst days.' She thought for a moment. 'Except it got us away from him. Every Wednesday he'd parcel the two of us off to a sort of retreat place near Ely. A taxi would come for us at two o'clock and take us there. We'd stay overnight and he'd collect us in the morning. Only that Thursday, he never arrived. It's a bloody awful place even if we'd been religious; in the middle of nowhere and they get you up like monks every three hours to pray, or at least pretend to in our case. So we were in the clear.'

Ben was mystified. 'But why every Wednesday?'

'Oh, that was when he got his tarts in. There were always clues – hairs in the shower, wafts of perfume hanging around, lipstick on a glass. He never tried to hide it. It was worse when mother was alive. She shouldn't have had to put up with the humiliation.'

Ben was incredulous. 'You mean he did it even before she died?'

'Oh yes, that's how much of a bastard he was. Her one and only insurrection was to become a Catholic. And that was down to Tommy, I think.'

'Tommy?'

It took a moment to bring her back to the present. 'Next-door neighbour in Moira. Used to come round to help Mother when Father was away. We were sworn to secrecy cos he was Catholic.' A look of sadness came over her face. 'We lost touch. He was a lovely man, kind and gentle.' Her face contorted. 'The opposite of that shite. He twisted her religion so he had even more control over her. Did it just to grind her face in the dirt. But she never said a word. And when she died, he just carried on with it. That's how much of a sadistic bastard he was.'

He desperately wanted to lighten her load. 'Been back to the retreat since he died?'

She looked sideways at him. 'You kidding?'

'And Lucien? When did they decide he was in the clear?'

'That was the ransom notes. He didn't have an alibi for the Wednesday but couldn't have delivered the notes. We had police in the house and another outside the door all that week. Each note came with the headline from the Cambridge Evening News to show when they were written. Lucien moved back in for that week, and we all waited in the house together for them to arrive. So eventually they reckoned he couldn't have done it. These god-awful policemen interviewed us all, on and on and on, trying to make us crack. That's why I was such a mess at the time. That and being able at last to mourn for my mother. It wasn't because *he'd* died. I was glad of that.'

He saw that she was tearful just at the memory so handed her a fresh handkerchief.

She wiped her eyes, smudging her mascara, then looked at the hankie. 'I've got two of these already. I've washed and ironed them. I'll get them for you later.' She went across to the mirror and wiped away her mascara. 'It was awful. The policemen – they were brutal – even though I had an alibi. I'd been battered all my life by *him* and then battered again by the police. No wonder I was a mess. Seeing the shrink, well, the counsellor. It helps. Like talking to you, that helps too.'

Virginia continued, 'I think they wanted to get Lucien for it. Kept asking over and over. Even if I'd known anything, I wouldn't have told them. They were just like Father and I'd been practising for years how to keep things from him.'

So much for the interrogation techniques of the real police and the undercover ones from MI5, thought Ben. 'Did they ask about the ransom notes?'

'God, yes. Kept banging on about, was it Father's writing, did we use that colour ink, how were they delivered.'

'Were the notes in your father's handwriting?'

'Yes, it was definitely his. And, before you ask, we never use purple ink.'

'And how *were* they delivered?'

'The first was posted in our letter box. It's on the front gate so no one saw it arrive. Then the police put someone outside the gate. The second came early morning. Policeman swore he saw no one but he must've been trying to save his skin. Third one came by post. Posted in Cambridge. Amazing it got here so quickly. The police wouldn't let us touch the second and third. Took them away. Lucien was under surveillance all that week, so I think they decided, unless he had an accomplice, he was in the clear. Then they got this hot lead about a gang so they pretty much left us alone. Just that god-awful policeman who snaffles the paper before we can read it and leaves it in a mess. Thank God we'll be rid of him soon.'

A link was being made in Ben's brain but it was just off-centre so he couldn't quite catch it.

'Then, when Father was dead, all the press arrived, and it was like a bear garden out there. At least I now know I never want to be a celebrity!'

Ben could see that the vegetable preparation was nearly done. He looked up at the wall clock. 'Nearly time Lucien was here. I'll fry the meat and put this lot on to slow-cook and then I'll give you the best spag bol you've ever eaten.'

'Great. Allie will be back soon. We've got some news, the two of us. I'll leave him to tell you.' There came a bellow from the hall. 'Ah,' she said. 'Lucien. I'll keep him out of your way. When you're ready, come through to the morning room.'

* * *

Lucien was in an ebullient mood. He met Ben in the hall and manoeuvred him into the morning room. He then put him completely off-balance by offering him a drink. Ben managed to ask for a beer. Lucien brushed that aside. 'Beer? Rubbish. This is a celebration. The old bugger. Need to drink to him.' As he was talking, Lucien was pouring two large glasses of whisky. He turned to Ben. 'Water or ice?'

'Ice, please.' This seemed to be the better option. Perhaps the coldness of the ice would dull the taste of the whisky.

Lucien picked up the ice-bucket from the side table. 'Won't be a mo, then I'll tell you our good news.' As he left the room he yelled, 'Allie, come here. I've got something to tell you.'

Lucien came back with the bucket of ice. 'Ginny, where's Allie?'

'He's out. Should be back any minute.'

'Can't wait for him. Ginny, listen to this. That old bastard has done us proud.' He put ice into the two whiskies and handed one to Ben. He held his glass aloft. 'To the crabby old bastard.'

Ben was becoming inured to toasting Stanley's memory. He held up his glass but said nothing. Lucien let out a whoop of a laugh. 'The cunning old bugger. I've just been to see that solicitor woman. She's been talking to his accountant and it's all above board.'

'What is?' said his sister.

'You remember when we got to eighteen he made us sign some papers? Said it was something to do with tax.'

'Vaguely. Is it important?'

'Is it important? Is it important! It means I can pay my debts. It means we don't have to wait for probate. It means we're free of him and anything else that comes will be a bonus.'

Virginia said in a commanding voice, one Ben had never heard before, 'Lucien, stop babbling! Start at the beginning and tell me what happened.'

Ben could see that they had forgotten his existence so he pressed himself further into the settee and stayed completely still.

'Sorry Ginny. Right, I went to the solicitor to see if I could get an advance. Bit strapped at the mo.'

Lucien began pacing the room waving his glass as he went. 'Anyway, she's been sorting his affairs with the accountant. Apparently he set up some sort of fund for each of us when we got to eighteen. We signed all the papers. Remember how he got us to sign things without telling us what they were. It's off-shore. Some island somewhere. The accountant says it's all legit. And he's been putting money in every year since. Ginny – we're millionaires – all of us – and we can get to the money now. Bastard wouldn't tell us

when he was alive. Made me beg, grovel every time, the bastard.'
He took a large gulp of whisky. 'Now he's dead, we can get the
money.' He downed the rest of his whisky in one then seemed to
remember Ben sitting silently in the corner. 'Want another? Drink
up man. You've hardly touched it.'

But it was Virginia who spoke. 'Lucien, will you do
something for me?'

'Anything. At this moment I can do anything.'

'I want you to phone Gamblers Anonymous? I've got the
number. Will you do that for me?'

Ben got ready to spring up in case Lucien became violent
but to his surprise Lucien sat down, put his glass on the floor and
his head in his hands. His voice was so low they could hardly hear
him. 'You had to spoil it, didn't you? You're just like him, always
rubbing my nose in it.' And he rose abruptly and left the room.
They heard the front door slam.

Virginia was looking wistfully into the distance. Ben went
and sat beside her and said, 'It's not your fault. He's a grown man.'

She smiled. 'Oh, that was a good response. Last time he
threw a vase of flowers at me. I was waiting to dodge the ice-
bucket. I think he's coming round to it. Hope so. But you're right.
It's his problem not mine. My counsellor says I'm not to take
responsibility for the actions of others. Only my own.' Virginia was
pulling on his hand. 'Come on, let's see how the dinner's doing.'

In the kitchen the scent of herbs and simmering tomatoes
filled the air. Virginia opened a bottle of Pouilly Fumé and showed
it to Ben. 'Want a glass of this or I can retrieve your full glass of
whisky if you want.'

Ben pointed to the bottle in her hand. 'Love one of those.'

On her way to the cupboard to get the glasses, Virginia
stopped in mid-pace. She swivelled round to face Ben. 'I'm rich.
And I'm going to celebrate with the best spag bol in the world.'

A tired voice came from the doorway. 'Those bloody trains.
Give me a drink someone. And food please, food.' Alistair dropped
his bag on the floor and collapsed into a chair. He looked up. 'Oh,
hello Ben. Have we got some news for you!'

* * *

165

So they all had a cast iron alibi – checked, no doubt, by both the police and MI5. The news that they were going to move to Brighton had come as a shock. He was not sure that Virginia needed what she described as a 'nose job'. They were in no hurry to move, even though they now had the means to do so. They had been insistent that he absolutely must come to visit when they were settled – and bring Katy and Maurice. The plans were necessarily slow because Virginia wanted to get a place at university there and her application was very late. Alistair had to find premises for his 'fashion house and emporium for the discerning male'. Ben couldn't wait to see that.

And what of Lucien? Of the three, he was the saddest case. He was still in the grip of his obsession, addiction, whatever you wanted to call it. Could he have engineered his father's death? There was a possibility that he had paid someone to keep his father hostage. But he'd had no money and no likelihood of any until probate was granted. He was a gambler, but his father had kept him in funds. At what price, Ben had an inkling. He could have had an accomplice, that gigantic man maybe, but why then had he involved the police? To cover his tracks? Possibly. He had to work out how the ransom notes, especially the middle one, had got through. He had to eliminate his remaining suspects. If he did that, he'd have to start on the list of mourners, which could only be a blackmail list. The more he learnt about Stanley Murdock, the more important it became that he should get to the killer before anyone else.

He called The Friary. As usual, it was answered on the second ring. 'Hi, it's Ben Burton.' He listened to the reply. 'Yes, I'm doing fine. But I'd like to come in to discuss something with Dr Clare. It's not for me, it's about someone else. Can I make a brief appointment with her, say, ten minutes?' He listened again. 'Perfect. I'll be there tomorrow at nine. Thanks.'

Chapter 27

Ben sat at his computer. He had two tasks, the first was difficult, the second abhorrent because in this second task lay the answer he suspected, but hoped he wouldn't find. His thoughts rested on Josephine. He'd been disappointed when she'd phoned to say she couldn't make it to dinner at Midsummer House. He'd been hoping that this would give them the opportunity to have the conversation that they needed to have. A stomach bug, she'd said, and she'd phone him mid-week to arrange something else. He knew she had a fear of being locked in and he got the feeling that her tidiness at home was close to obsession. Katy kept asking how things were going. Maurice kept giving him knowing looks.

He typed in OCD. As usual, pages of links appeared. He scanned through, rejecting Wikipedia for websites more focussed on remedies. As he read through these, he could see aspects of the Josephine he knew, and discovered further facets which might form part of her character. He'd certainly seen handwashing and cleaning, plus the perfect arrangement of her home and the ordering of her paperwork. If these were compulsions, surely they weren't serious? Lots of people were clean and tidy. It was as he moved on to the obsessions that he began to get worried. If, as he was now beginning to suspect, Josephine did suffer from OCD, then what were the underlying obsessions which led to her compulsive behaviour? As he read about the pattern of OCD, it made him want to offer her protection from her inner world; a protection that he knew he didn't have the power to give. He read about intrusive thoughts, repeatedly surfacing and the anxiety they caused for the sufferer and of the compulsions which brought only temporary relief from these thoughts. If she did indeed suffer from OCD, he wondered what Josephine's underlying obsessions might be.

An email pinged into his box. He knew he was stalling as he looked to see who it was from. He laughed and wondered how this man managed to get away with some of the things he did. It was from Chris@mylittleeye.me. It was short. 'Your three famous names – stroke from diabetes, lung cancer, heart attack then fell off his yacht in the West Indies.' Ben was relieved. That ruled out Agnes as a serial killer. Unlikely as it had seemed, he'd had to make sure. He knew that, from her mean little house in Cherry Hinton, she would not have been able to engineer those three deaths nor Stanley's. But he was certain that she had lied to him. Now he had to nail that lie.

He got on to the County Council website and eventually found his way to the page he wanted. He sat for a while looking at the sections to fill in. He filled in Birth. He knew the date but had to guess the year. He reached Surname and was about to type it in when Katy came up behind him. 'Hi, Dad. What you doing?'

'Hi Katy, didn't hear you coming.' He pointed to the screen. 'You know that couple that came in the other day. They need a birth certificate and don't have internet access so I said I'd do it for them.' Another lie.

'Aw, Dad. You're so sweet. I'm off out to meet Pam and Sarah.' She glanced at the wall-clock. 'Look at the time. Must rush. Byeeee.'

He turned his attention back to the screen and typed in the surname and first name. And there it was staring at him, the answer he'd been dreading. He'd need to see the certificate to make sure of the details but he knew he was on the right track. But, if she had found out, how had she done it? He was certain no one would have told her.

He idly picked up the Cambridge News. His mind made the leap to the sulky Family Liaison Officer sitting reading the paper and ignoring its owners. He had a question to ask Virginia.

Chapter 28

'I'm sorry sir, I can't help you.'

'But I've given you ID. I've told you why I want to see him. Surely I can meet him with you present. I just want to ask a few simple questions.'

'Look, I'm really sorry. But with child protection and all that, there is no way I can be involved in any meeting. Now, I've got other customers to serve, so, if you'll excuse me.'

His plan had misfired. He'd thought his cover story would suffice; that the fake ID and tale of being a football scout would be enough. He'd made sure to pick a time when there would be no one at the ground to verify his story. He could understand why the manager of the paper shop had refused to let him talk to the boy who delivered to the Murdock household, but it didn't make the failure any easier to bear. He hadn't thought it wise to approach the boy directly and now he'd burnt his boats with the paper shop. He would have to think up a new plan.

* * *

He hadn't wanted to involve Katy, especially after her caper at Lucien's, but he hadn't been able to see any other way. She, for her part, had been wildly enthusiastic and had taken the lead in planning her role. He'd felt a mixture of fear and admiration and he'd had to admit that the cover story she'd fabricated had been plausible. It remained to be seen whether the boy had felt the same.

'Hi, Dad,' she said as she slipped into the passenger seat. 'That was cool.'

'Any luck?'

'Yeah, it was sooo easy to get him talking. He swallowed the story about me being a poor student wanting to do a paper round. Told me what he got paid, what time he has to get up. Six o'clock.' She grimaced. 'No way could I do that!'

Ben surveyed his daughter in her faded jogging outfit. She

looked young, healthy and plausible as a student needing funds.

'Anyway,' she continued. 'When I said I thought he was underpaid, he said about extras at Christmas. Dead easy then to ask if there were extras any other time.'

'And?'

'And then I had to listen to him telling me about this old lady who pays him to bring her a bottle of sherry twice a week. Her family don't approve so they ration her.' She laughed. 'Old and fly. I want to be like that!'

Ben wondered briefly about the ethics of the sherry delivery but kept quiet. 'So?'

'Oh, yeah. I just asked, like, low key, any other ways of getting extras? So then he told me about this woman who gave him twenty pounds to deliver a note with the paper. Said it was a surprise birthday card. I asked where to and he told me. The Murdocks.'

'Hang on. He definitely said a woman? Could he describe her? Did you ask?'

'Ha ha, that's where I was just a bit brill. I said, 'Weren't you scared, with her being a stranger and all?' and he said, 'Nah, I could tell she was all right.' And I said, 'How can you tell? She could have been a murderer or something.' And this is the best bit cos I didn't even have to ask. Remember, Dad, he's a fourteen-year-old boy. This is so typical. He said, "I could tell cos she had this sexy bum. And a real sexy smile."'

'Is that it?'

'No… but this is a bit nuts. He said she sort of backed off when he came nearer, like she was scared of him. That doesn't make sense to me.'

But it did to Ben.

Chapter 29

Wednesday 11th July 2012

He was dreading this meeting. He needed answers but he didn't want to ask the questions that would lead – where, exactly? Where would those answers take them? Josephine had lied about her mother. Agnes was alive and well and living in Cherry Hinton. Her mother had equally lied about her child being dead. It seemed certain that they were dead to each other. But did those lies lead incontrovertibly to Josephine being Stanley's killer? No, they didn't. He had not an iota of proof, only the leaps of fancy that Katy might have made.

He walked alongside Parker's Piece feeling the late afternoon sun on his back. The change in the weather was welcome. Josephine had phoned following her cancellation of their Midsummer House date, and he was picking her up from work to go for a drink. When he arrived, he could feel his heart pounding. He didn't want to hang around inside so marched up and down, breathing deeply and reminding himself of his yoga breaths. Then he turned resolutely and entered the building. It was the same young receptionist who had given him Josephine's birth date. He gave her his most dazzling smile. 'I'm early. Say, have you got a minute?' She nodded and returned his smile. 'It's just that I wanted to take Josephine away for a few days – a surprise – you know.' She nodded again. 'And I don't know how much holiday she has left. Can you tell me? I think she took some time off recently. D'you think you could check?'

'There's a rota. I'll have a look.' She took out a well-thumbed file. 'Oh, yes. Here it is. She was away for ten days in May. Caused a bit of a stir at the time. Short notice. Not at all like her. I asked her if she'd had a good holiday and she said something about a relative being ill.' She smiled up at him. 'She's got plenty holiday left. Taking her somewhere nice?'

Before he could answer, Pam tapped him on the shoulder. 'Hi, Mr Burton. Look,' and she pointed to her shoulder. 'See the stripes? Sergeant now.'

'Brilliant! Congratulations. Can I still call you Pam, or should I be more formal and call you Sergeant Pam?'

'Pam will do. Sorry, I'm on duty so I'd better get on.' She turned to the receptionist. 'I'm here to see Ms Finlay. I don't have an appointment but it's police business.'

Ben was immediately concerned, but surely they wouldn't send a lone sergeant to make an arrest. 'Nothing serious, I hope.'

Before Pam could reply, the receptionist turned to Ben. 'Can you show the Sergeant through to Miss Finlay's office.'

He pretended to doff his cap to Pam. 'Walk this way.'

He knocked on Josephine's door which, as usual, was ajar. 'Come in.' He held the door open for Pam. Then he looked round the door and said to Josephine, 'Shall I wait outside?'

He saw the colour drain from Josephine's face as she sat down abruptly. But it was Pam who answered, 'Don't go. I think this might be of interest to both of you and it's not sensitive.'

Ben went in and pulled the door to behind him. He knew not to close it properly or Josephine would have to open it again. She was sitting by her low table. With a shaking hand, she indicated that they should come and join her. Ben looked, with interest, at the neat row of files that she was working on. She quickly tidied them away. Josephine smiled and Ben noticed that it only reached her mouth. 'Some of Stanley's paperwork. There's a lot of it.' She turned to Pam. 'Now, what can I do for you?'

'Well, actually. I've come to give you some news. We've NFA'd the Stanley Murdock case.'

At their perplexed looks, she started again. 'Sorry. You get so used to the jargon. NFA – no further action – it basically means we've mothballed it. No useful evidence, all avenues investigated and exhausted. The word came from on high this morning. Other stuff to concentrate on. I've been told to tell you that all the beneficiaries are in the clear so you can get on with whatever you have to do.'

Josephine smiled again and this time it did reach her eyes. Some colour returned to her cheeks. 'Well, that *is* good news. Very good news. I'm sure the Murdock family will be delighted.'

Ben joined in. 'Thanks, Pam. Tell me again what the

172

terminology is. Josephine, you've got a pen in your hand, will you write it down for me. Thanks. NFA – no further action. I'll have to remember to use it when Sarah's around. Bit of street cred never goes amiss with your offspring.'

Pam stood up. 'Well, that's all I came for. I'm off duty now.'

As Josephine handed the note to Ben, he stood too. 'Thanks Pam. Can you pass on the message that we hope they eventually find this London gang, but we won't be holding our breath. On second thoughts, you'd better leave out the last bit.' He moved towards the door and Pam followed.

As they reached Reception, Pam said, 'We're all going to the pub tonight. Like as if we'd solved it. Might cheer us up. Sarah'll be there, Katy too. Want to come?'

'Sorry, I'm busy tonight.'

'Oh, well. Another time. Anyway, we'll be at the Prince Regent if you change your mind.'

When he got back to Josephine's office, everything was tidy. She was sitting demurely behind her desk. She shrugged. 'That's that then. I can tie up the loose ends and leave probate to take its course.'

But Ben's thoughts had moved on. He took her written note from his pocket. He looked down at it. 'NFA. I'll have to remember that. You do such neat writing, not a bit like mine. And the ink's a lovely colour – unusual. Would you call it turquoise or green? It suits you, anyway. D'you always use that colour?'

Josephine tidied an already tidy pile of papers. 'Yes,' she replied. 'Always. It's my favourite colour. I never use anything else.' After a moment of silence, she looked up from the tidy pile. 'D'you know Ben. I've got a bit of a headache. I think I'll just go home if that's all right with you. Sorry to put you off again but I think it might be left over from that bug.' She turned away from him so that he couldn't see her face. He was surprised when she half turned and said, 'I was thinking. I've got a bungalow at Hunstanton. It looks out over the sea. Why don't I meet you there this weekend?'

'That would be great. We need to talk.'

'Yes, we do. I'll email you details. Goodnight then. Sorry,

I'm tired and I'll need to lock up.'

Ben left the building with a heavy heart. He needed some company; happy, light-hearted company. Maybe he wouldn't get that, but his two girls would be there. He headed across Parker's Piece to the Prince Regent.

He could hear sounds of heavy drinkers long before he got to the pub. He was sure the police sorrow-drowning would go on long into the night. He quickened his pace. He would think later. Now he needed the company of uncomplicated people leading uncomplicated lives. Or at least lives less complicated than Josephine's. As he neared the pub he could see Sarah, Katy and Pam on the edge of a large group that had spilled out on to the grass. He waved to them and they waved back. They looked so young and carefree and his heart leapt at the sight of them.

Pam beamed. 'Hi, Mr Burton. Glad you could come. There's a tab at the bar. What can I get you?'

'For a start, you can stop making me feel like an old man. Call me Ben, and I could murder a pint.' He looked at the rest of the gathering and laughed. 'Probably not the best word to use in present company.'

As Pam went inside to get his drink, he gave each of his daughters a hug. 'I'm so glad to see you two.' He turned to Sarah. 'How's it going at work?'

'A bit too quiet really. Now it's the vac there's been no more women assaulted on Midsummer Common so we're waiting for the new term. And Dad, don't be alarmed, they've decided to go ahead with the decoy thing. I'm going to volunteer. But don't worry, it will be perfectly safe. It's the middle of Cambridge for God's sake.'

He knew that Sarah was sort of asking permission, keen not to add to his worries. He grinned at her. 'Of course you will.' He waved his arm at the collection of semi-drunk officers. 'They'll be sober, I assume?'

She smiled back at him. 'You bet!'

His grin became even wider as he realised that he wasn't having any adverse physical reaction to the news. His heart was beating normally, his hands were not shaking, there was no pain in his scar. He'd have to tell Dr Clare.

Sarah continued, 'You've come at the right time. Pam was just about to tell Katy the inside story of the murder but the big news is that Turnbully's taking early retirement. That's all we know at the moment.'

As Ben looked up to see Pam approaching, he caught the eye of a tall woman who was talking to a group of men who were so obviously policemen that it made Ben smile. The woman smiled back. Ben recognised the man standing next to her as Pam's replacement at the Murdock house, Chris's man.

The woman was excusing herself and coming towards them. She walked with confidence and ease. She reached them at the same time as Pam. Pam held back to let the new woman approach ahead of her. The woman held out her hand to Ben. 'Mr Burton, I believe. Sorry, that sounds a bit Livingstonian. I'm very pleased to meet you. Lavinia Wainright. Friends call me Vin. I'll be joining the Force here soon and I hope we'll meet again. I've heard good things about you.' She turned to Sarah. 'And I hope to be working closely with your daughter. I hear she's doing well.' Sarah beamed and Katy eased herself forward so she was in the centre of the group..

Ben took Lavinia's outstretched hand and put his other arm round Katy. 'Pleased to meet you too. And this is my younger daughter, Katy. She works with me and is also doing well.' Ben could see that Pam was hovering with his drink. 'And Pam has saved my life by bringing me a pint.' He noticed that Lavinia was still holding his hand and didn't seem inclined to let go. Her grip was firm and curiously reassuring. His thoughts turned to Josephine who found touch so unpleasant that she avoided handshakes whenever possible. He closed off those thoughts as Lavinia released his hand.

Lavinia smiled at Katy and then looked across at Sarah. 'I can see the resemblance. Katy, I'm pleased to meet you.' She put a hand lightly on Ben's arm. 'I'll leave you in peace now. Enjoy your evening.'

Sarah waited until Lavinia was out of earshot. 'What was all that about? How come she knows about you, Dad? I never said.' She turned to Pam, 'Did you mention my dad?'

Pam was busy trying to untangle her shoulder bag and hand a drink to Ben at the same time. She slopped some of Ben's beer as she passed it over. 'Sorry, Mr Burton… oops, sorry, Ben. No, I didn't say anything.'

Katy asked, 'Heh, you two. Let us in on it. Who is she?'

Pam answered. 'She's our new boss, a Chief Inspector. They've got rid of Turnbully. Early retirement they said.'

Katy was looking speculative. 'See, I think there's more to her than meets the eye. She's got that look about her. Sort of cool and clever. But then, I think there's more to my dad than meets the eye.'

Ben changed the subject. 'So we're celebrating Pam's promotion.' He held up his glass. 'Well done, Pam.' And they ceremoniously drank a toast. He continued, 'What gives with the murder investigation – no result and it's shoved under the carpet?'

Pam replied, 'Yeah, strange so early. I haven't been on homicide long but it feels wrong. True, we were getting precisely nowhere. Everyone near-to checks out. No leads, no usable DNA. Whoever it was, they were bloody clever. Mind you, Turnbully was useless. But it still seems too early.' She looked across again at Lavinia who was now chatting to a coterie of male colleagues. 'Word came from above that the case is closed. So it's back to the boring stuff. I'd love to know how they did it though.'

Katy responded. 'Me too. But heh, your new boss has deffo got class. What's the word on her?'

Sarah pointed to Pam. 'She knows more than me. Sergeants get more news than we do.' And she poked her tongue out at her friend.

Pam moved closer. 'Seconded from the Met. Not sure how long for. Can't think why she decided to come here. Bit of a come-down from London. See that guy she's talking to… don't look! He took over Family Liaison from me. Arsehole of the first order. Gives me the creeps.'

Ben laughed. 'If it's any consolation, the Murdocks couldn't stand him either. Virginia kept making cutting remarks about him and said how much better you were.'

'Yeah,' said Sarah. 'You're much better than that chauvinist git. D'you know he had the cheek to come on to me. Pulled rank – you know the type.' Sarah looked at their glasses then pointed to one of her colleagues who was beginning to sway. 'Drink up, we're lagging. Katy, come with me. Same again? Pam, wait till we get back before any more gossip. And that's an order!'

'Yes Ma'am. Practising for promotion already? Go on then, and don't stop to pick up any stray men on the way back.'

'This lot. You must be joking!'

Chapter 30

Friday 13th July 2012

'Tell me again why we're looking at these.' Katy picked up the photocopies of the ransom notes and waved them in the air. 'They weren't even on Dad's list. Bloody cheek. He swans off on a dirty weekend and expects me, a girl in her prime, to sit at home doing the dusting.' She grinned at Maurice. 'Good, isn't it. Fingers crossed, eh?'

Maurice smiled back. 'He deserves a break. Why are we looking at these? Because I got em from my mates. Had to bribe them by paying for an extra round. Showed them to your dad a while ago and now they've wound up the case, I thought we'd have a look. Anyways, maybe they might be more interesting than hanging that picture your dad has had on his list for at least six months. Am I right?'

'Oh, Uncle Mo, you've no idea how much more interesting.'

'Your dad gave me strict instructions to look after you. Telling me where everything was kept. As if I didn't know. Made sure I had the address.' Maurice shrugged and shook his head. 'Come on, would I want to gate-crash their week-end? Spent half an hour telling me this, that and the other. Then another half hour telling me how to look after you. I was waiting for him to tell me to wrap you in that bubble wrap and not let you out of my sight.'

'Yeah, I know it's hard for him but I thought he was getting better at letting go. I'd find it difficult if I'd brought me up on my own.' She looked across at Maurice. 'You know what I mean. He's been great, but I thought he was coming to terms with the idea that we're grown-ups now. I know it's a big deal for him but it was as if he didn't want to go. Kept reminding us of more and more things. I told him to turn off his phone and forget about us for the weekend.'

'I bet he won't turn his phone off. Now, this is for your education.' Maurice spread the three ransom notes on the table. 'They are the last words of a dying man. Obviously not your usual dying words. But, if you're going to spend your time dealing with the dead, they might help you gain some insight.' He grinned at

Katy. 'Who am I kidding? It's really because I miss the excitement. Let's look at em one last time. Then we'll have dinner. Read them out to me.'

'Right. First one, "Please help me. They say they're going to kill me. Do not go to the police. More instructions will come." Not much there. Uncle Mo, you ever seen ransom notes before?'

'No, lassie, I was only uniform, remember, petty crimes and the like. Did a stint at driving and that's as far as I got – or wanted to.'

'So you don't know what's normal?' She didn't wait for a reply. 'Cos I think they're a bit odd, specially the next one. "They want diamonds. I put all the jewellery in the ice-bucket. Await further instructions." That doesn't give us much either. And it doesn't make sense. Why would Stanley put jewels in an ice-bucket when he had a perfectly good safe? OK, last one. Blimey, the writing's gone downhill, like he's aged twenty years. "I'm sorry for what I've done. Please forgive me." Wowie! That sure doesn't sound like the Stanley we know about. Look at the writing. It's gone all wobbly. He must have been in a bad way. I almost feel sorry for him, but I can't forget what he did to Virginia and her baby.'

'Hold on now, Katy. We don't *know* he did anything. We're only guessing.'

'Well, I *know* he did something bad. And he had all that funny money. And he had a gun. And he had that list of people with notes about them. Why would he keep all that? Huh? Because he was blackmailing them, that's why.'

'You don't know that. The police think it was a London gang kidnapped him for the money. I don't rate Turnbull but they must have had something concrete to go on. They'd be getting intelligence that we don't know about. Must of.'

'Maybe. OK, let's have another look at what a dying man writes.' Katy spread the three notes on the table and looked closely at each in turn. 'Old-fashioned writing. Funny, I didn't expect that from him. Uncle Mo, I'm still not sure what I'm supposed to get from this.'

'To be honest, I'm really trying to relive my youth – solving crimes. Mine was all small; this un's a big deal. Let's put these notes away. I shouldn't have bothered you with them.'

'Hang on. I expect your mates will have pored over them. Did they get anything?'

'Nah, said the same as you. Looked at the last one and said "Poor sod". That was all.'

'Funny writing though. It's that old-fashioned, joined-up, posh writing. What d'you call it?'

'Copperplate?'

Katy peered at it again. 'We learnt stuff a bit like this at primary school, all loopy-loopy and we couldn't leave any spaces in the words. Bloody ridiculous, I always thought.'

'Language, Katy.'

'See, though.' She pointed to one of the notes, 'For all he was so good at it, he left spaces.' She flicked the note with her fingers. 'Look. The i in diamonds is all alone. Same for the c in bucket and the second i in instructions. That spells ici – that's French.'

Maurice picked up the last note. 'Here it's the t in what, the o in done and the r in forgive.'

Katy grabbed the ransom notes. She looked at first one, then the others. She wrote down the three oddities in the lettering in the right order: sol ici tor. 'Shit, shit, shit, shit, shit. Phone Dad. Now!'

Maurice looked perplexed. Katy scrabbled in her bag, searching for her phone. 'Quick Mo, we've got to warn him. Where the fuck is my phone?'

Maurice silently handed her his phone. She found her dad's entry and pressed dial. 'Oh, sodding shit, for once in his life he's done what he was told. It's gone straight to voicemail.' She twitched as the automated voice rolled slowly through its message. 'Dad, it's me. Phone me. Don't go to Josephine's. She killed Stanley. Please pick this up… *please.*'

Maurice's eyebrows reached full height. 'Katy, what's got into you? That's ridiculous.'

'No, it isn't. No time to argue. I'll tell you on the way. We need her address. Mo, get a map book from Dad's study. I'll take my phone. The address, the map, your car keys, your phone, my phone. Anything else? God, yes, the ransom notes.'

She scooped everything into her bag, grabbed her coat on

the way out and called behind her, 'Mo, come on, we've got to get there before she kills him too.'

* * *

Getting out of Cambridge was the usual mess. The Friday rush was in full throttle, unlike the cars, which just crawled along. Once they were on the A10 the traffic eased and Maurice drove faster than he had since he'd left the Force.

'How long till we get there?'

'Same as I told you two minutes ago. It'll take about an hour and a half if we don't get held up again. Now you just sit still and I'll get us there as quick as I can. Try your dad's phone again.'

Katy's fingers trembled on the keys. 'I can't do it. My fingers won't work.'

'Deep breaths and try to relax. Do it with me. In, out, in, out. Now try again. Take it slowly.'

She jabbed at the phone. 'Still voicemail. D'you think we should call the police?'

'No. We'll look right fools when the police turn up and their weekend is interrupted. Watch out you idiot!' Maurice swerved to avoid an oncoming car. He shouted at the retreating tail lights. 'Bloody fool. Want to get yourself killed?'

Katy started to cry. Her tears rolled silently down her cheeks and into her mouth. 'My dad might be killed. Why not call the police? Mo – I can't lose them both. I *can't.*'

'You won't. We'll keep your dad safe. Course we will.'

'So we should call the police?'

'No, I don't think we should involve the police yet. You think you've found something. It's a flim-flam of a clue and probably won't stand up to examination. I think we need to go look for ourselves. I bet we'll get there and it'll all be tickety-boo and we'll look right bloody fools. We'll probably find your dad and Josephine having a cosy dinner. Now tell me again where we leave the A10.'

Chapter 31

Friday 13th July 2012

Ben took a long breath, let it out slowly, then took another. He stood on the pavement and looked again at the card on which he'd written the address of her holiday home; 79, Cliff Parade, Hunstanton. This '60s bungalow was not what he'd been expecting. The front garden was a jumble of flowers of every colour. The house had the look of one maintained with the minimum of effort. It was so different from Josephine's pristine flat that he had to look again at the number on the door. He checked with his phone to make sure it was the right street and immediately switched it off again. He saw that he had several missed calls, but that could wait. The last thing he wanted was to be interrupted. He had to do this alone.

Having checked that it was the right number in the right road, he stood away from the house and looked out over the grassy stretch to the sea beyond and below. From this perspective, the stripy cliffs were hidden beneath the edge of the bank. A flimsy and broken wire fence had one notice saying, 'Keep Out' and another advertising the Samaritans. These were the only clues to the danger beyond.

And, once again, he could be facing danger. He turned abruptly, and although the door was slightly open, he rang the bell. Josephine ushered him in. It was the first time he'd seen her looking other than serene. Disapproving sometimes but never agitated. Whereas before, she'd always seemed so in control of her limbs, now she appeared not to be able to keep her arms and legs still. She led him past two closed doors and into a tidy kitchen. It was unlike her Cambridge flat in that utensils were on show, but Ben could still see a regimentation that was absent in his house. Josephine paced back and forth filling the kettle, rattling the teacups in their saucers, her hands making dry washing movements all the while. At last, she turned to him looking anguished. 'I have a confession to make.'

He smiled softly and took her two hands in his. He held

them gently and stilled their movement. 'You've no need to tell me. I know what you did.'

Now she looked perplexed. 'You know? You can't know. You don't know how wicked I've been.'

'Not so very wicked. Stanley Murdock was an evil man. He did terrible things that you have no idea about. He killed innocent people. He was an abusive father. He was blackmailing some poor souls who had taken a wrong turn. What you did was not so terrible.'

'But he shouldn't have died. I killed him and he shouldn't have died. I didn't mean him to die.' Silent tears started to roll down her cheeks. She withdrew her hands from his and brushed her tears away. 'No, that's not true. Some of the time I did want him to die and I wanted to be the one to make it happen. And sometimes, I didn't know what I wanted.' She accepted the clean white handkerchief that Ben held out to her. She sat down abruptly. 'How long have you known?'

Ben gave a sad smile. 'Since your birthday. That's when I first suspected. D'you remember, I said, 'Close your eyes and hold out your hands?' and I saw that one of your little fingers was longer than the other. Then I had to make sure, so I started to check up on you. I found out about the paper delivery. And when you lied about the ink colour, and you realised that I knew you'd lied. Then I was sure it was you.'

She looked dejected, like so many of the grieving people he'd comforted. None before had killed the person they were grieving for. Not that he knew, anyway.

'But you don't know the half of it. I'm wicked. So very wicked.' And she started to cry in earnest. She whispered, 'I'm evil.'

'What, because you thought you had to kill me too? That you invited me here to have a nasty accident or to die in my bed? Because I was the only one who could find you out.'

'Oh God. I'm so sorry. I planned it but, as soon as I saw you, I knew I couldn't do it. But I can't go to prison. I just can't.'

Ben felt a surge of relief now that he knew he was in no immediate danger. 'Of course you can't. Sit down while I make us some tea. Then we'll decide what's to be done for the best.'

As he turned to make the tea, she moved like lightening. She grabbed a thin-bladed kitchen knife. It was long and sharp. The edge glistened in the shaft of sunlight streaming in through the window. Ben's eyes caught the reflection. He spun round. She waved the knife towards him. He looked around for a cloth, anything to grab the knife. Nothing. He'd have to chance it. He was still holding the teapot. That might do to deflect the blade. As he moved, she pounced. But she didn't attack him. Instead, she hurled herself out of the kitchen, through the hall and flung open the front door. She ran across the road and over the grass towards the cliffs.

Ben could see her running figure through to the open door. He dropped the teapot and ran after her. She had a good twenty metres start. He shouted, 'Josephine!' but the wind whisked his words away. He ran as he'd never run before. He narrowly missed a car which hooted wildly. He noticed the driver give a V sign. Ben ignored him. The sun was in his eyes but he could see the movement of her running figure. She was fast but he was gaining. She was making for a gap in the fence. She clambered through the gap, nearly tripping as she went. He followed. He needed her to live. He was gaining, his long legs having less difficulty with the undergrowth.

She was standing at the very edge of the cliff. One more step and she'd be over. She turned towards him and waved the knife in a wide arc, nearly unbalanced herself. 'Don't you come near me. D'you hear? I *will* kill you if you try to stop me.'

As she regained her balance, he held up both hands with palms towards her. He spoke quietly and slowly. 'OK. I won't come any closer. But, please, let me talk to you from here? I've got something I must tell you.'

She nodded but still held the knife in front of her at arm's length. She was breathing in quick, sharp breaths. 'Two seconds only. I mean it. I don't want to live any more.'

'Two things.' As he spoke, he still held his hands aloft but began inching towards Josephine and the edge of the cliff. 'Firstly, I want to thank you from the bottom of my heart. Stanley Murdock murdered my wife, and you avenged her death. You did me a very great service. If you hadn't caused his death, I might have.'

He watched Josephine as this information began to sink in.

She faltered and edged backwards, a step closer to the brink. Her eyes were wild. Ben could see both fear and desperation. Before she could say anything, he continued, 'Listen, Josephine. I can promise you that you will not go to prison. Do you hear me? You will *not* go to prison.' He held out his hand to her. 'We can sort this out. Take my hand. It will be OK.' He smiled at her. 'Let's go and have that cup of tea.'

He was nearly within grabbing distance. Just an arm's length away. Josephine's shoulders suddenly slumped. She took one step towards him, now holding the knife by her side. As she moved, the ground started to give way. Ben lunged and grasped her arm. The knife grazed his arm as she let it go. Time stopped as he watched it tumble in slow motion, into the surf below. Then he was flat on his front, holding on to Josephine with one hand. It was his injured arm and the pain was excruciating. He felt his grip loosening as the pain was gradually overcoming him. He grimaced and concentrated on just one thought. I must not let go. I must *not* let go. 'Grab my other hand,' he gasped.

She obeyed and slowly, with every sinew stretched, he dragged her to safety. Bleeding and shaken, they sat together away from the edge. He held her in his arms as she wept uncontrollably.

Suddenly, over the low horizon, a black and white spaniel appeared followed by two strangers. 'Thumper, heel, I say. Good God, are you two all right?'

As the dog tried to lick them, Ben smiled at its owners. 'We're fine. She just went too near the edge. We shouldn't have come through the fence.' He forced a laugh. 'Won't make that mistake again.'

As the man put the dog on its lead, the woman asked, 'Can we do anything to help? Call an ambulance?'

The man added, 'Your arm's bleeding. I should drive you to the hospital.'

Ben looked down at the growing patch of blood on his sleeve. 'Thank you, but no. We live just over there.' He pointed to the bungalows. 'We'll go back and I'll see if it needs attention. I think it's just a scratch, looks worse than it is.'

The man helped them both up and insisted on accompanying them as they shambled along, just managing the short walk to the front door. It was wide open. 'God,' said Ben. 'What a day. We even left the front door open. Thank you so much for your help. We'll be fine now.'

The woman looked concerned. 'You sure?'

'Absolutely,' said Ben. 'We'll be fine.'

The man still looked reluctant to leave, so Ben added, 'Look, you don't have to worry. There's a doctor lives next door so we can easily get help if we need it. Thanks again. They should mend that fence.'

The woman looked relieved. 'So glad it wasn't worse. I'll get on to the Council first thing about replacing that fence. It's a magnet for suicides.' She glanced at Josephine. 'And accidents, of course.' And then, she took the dog's lead, put her hand through the man's arm and hurried them both away.

* * *

Ben picked up the teapot, wiped the spilt tea from the floor, collected all the sharp knives, locked them in Josephine's desk drawer and pocketed the key. Then he retrieved his first aid kit from the car and patched up his arm, He sat opposite the silent and immobile Josephine. 'I'll make you that tea and run you a bath. You're in no danger now. You won't have to go to prison. Do you understand that? You won't go to prison.' As she nodded, he added, 'Promise you won't do anything silly.'

She looked across at him with baleful eyes. 'No, I won't try to kill myself again. But I can't go to prison.'

'You won't. That's a promise. You won't go to prison. After your bath, you can tell me all about it.' He felt as though he were talking to a child, so vulnerable did she seem. 'We'll need some help to get you back to Cambridge. I'll phone Mo. He can make some excuse to Katy. It'll take him about an hour and a half to get here, so there's plenty of time.'

'I'd like that. He's kind. You both are. Kinder than I deserve.'

He turned his phone on and his first call was to Chris. It went to voice-mail so he left a message. 'Found the culprit. No Northern Ireland connection… repeat *no* Northern Ireland

186

connection. Will need your help. Phone me.'

His call to Maurice was answered at the first ring by Katy. 'Dad! Oh, thank God. She killed him! Josephine killed him! Get out now!'

To which he calmly replied. 'Slow down, Katy. Listen. Don't worry. I know she killed him. I'm in no danger. Understand? No danger. Can I speak to Mo?'

'He's driving. We're on our way to you now. How long, Uncle Mo? Mo says should be with you in about half an hour. Are you sure you're OK?' He could hear her turn to Maurice and say 'He's OK!'

And he heard Maurice's reply, 'So, can I slow down now?'

* * *

Ben ran a bath for Josephine and made sure she didn't lock the door – as if she would. He looked round her bedroom. It could have been a hotel room. Every surface was empty. He rummaged in cupboards where each item of clothing was perfectly aligned and again felt an immense sadness at the orderliness of this exterior world, and its counterpart that he imagined to be the inside of Josephine's head. He put out some clean clothes for her. While she was in the bath, he phoned The Friary confirming Josephine's admission the next day. He hovered outside the bathroom door to ensure the splashing sounds continued. As soon as he heard the water draining away, he felt he could relax, for now.

He sat her down at the kitchen table and gave her a cup of sweet tea. As she sipped it, Ben sat down opposite her. 'Anything you want to tell me before Mo and Katy arrive?'

She sighed. 'You deserve an explanation. You can tell them whatever you want.' She took another sip of tea and then drew in a long, deep breath. She looked down into her cup. Ben could hear a robin singing. He turned slowly to see it sitting on a branch just by the open window. Its song was the only sound, an embodiment of the normality beyond their small world. He waited. Slowly, she started, almost as though she were talking to herself. 'You see, I thought he was my father. So, when he phoned and asked me if I wanted to go for a drink, I said yes. I thought I'd be able to talk to him; to tell him. But in the pub, he wasn't like my father. He was so uncouth, boasting about how he'd spent his life making money and doing people down. I didn't like it.'

Ben asked quietly. 'Was this the Wednesday?'

'Yes. He said he'd been let down. A meeting cancelled.'

'And can you remember what time he phoned?'

She glanced at him then looked away again. 'It was just after three. Is that important?'

To Ben it was. It meant that Stanley's usual Wednesday lady had stood him up. 'So what happened next?'

'We met in the pub he'd suggested. It was one I'd never been to before, but they obviously knew him there. It was a disaster from the start. He wasn't kind like I expected him to be. I didn't get a chance to tell him that I thought he might be my father. Then, after the first drink, he sidled closer, and I realised he was coming on to me. I was horrified. I said I had to go to the Ladies. I didn't know what to do. He was an important client for the firm.' She stopped and took a shuddering breath. She focused her eyes on the far wall. 'On my way back, I looked across to the bar. We were drinking red wine. He hadn't even asked me what I wanted. He'd bought two more and was emptying something into one of them. I watched him go back to where we were sitting. He put the drink that he'd doctored in front of my place. I hurried back and dropped my scarf near his feet. As he bent to pick it up, I swapped the drinks. It was spur of the moment. I didn't even think about it. It was that easy.'

She stayed silent for a good while, looking into her empty cup. The robin continued its soaring trills. Ben half listened as he remained still and silent. Eventually she looked up. 'He started to go woozy so I said I'd help him to get home. I got him into my car and he started talking. Telling me things I didn't want to hear. Things he'd done. Dreadful things. About killing people, making people suffer, taking their money. And then he passed out.'

She paused and took a great shuddering breath. She had begun to shake again. Ben picked up his jacket and wrapped it round her. The shaking subsided and she stroked the jacket sleeve as she continued, 'That's when I got angry. I knew what he would have done if it was me who was out cold. How dare he!' Her eyes flashed. 'I was livid and I could only think of the terrible things he'd said. I knew about a place in the fens that was empty, waiting for probate. So I drove him out there. I don't know what I was thinking. Maybe I thought I'd teach him a lesson and then let him go. Leave him there and let him find his own way home.' She paused and looked into the distance. 'It was so dirty there. I thought he should sit in the dirt. It was where he belonged.'

'So why didn't you let him go?'

'I don't know. It was as if I was on a roller-coaster and I couldn't get off. I thought of the awful things he'd done and I didn't want him to get away with them. I found a chair and some rope and tied him up. When he woke up, he was livid. Said I'd go to prison. He'd make sure of it. So I couldn't let him go, could I?'

She stopped with a shuddering sigh and tears started to roll silently down her cheeks. For the first time since starting, she looked at Ben. He could see utter hopelessness in her eyes. He asked gently, 'Did you tell him you thought he might be your father?'

'No. I didn't want to tell him anything about myself. I didn't want to give anything of myself to that man. This was the man who was going to drug and rape me. He couldn't be my father!'

'I understand that. Of course.' They were silent for a second, then Ben asked, 'Did he tell you about his time in Northern Ireland?'

'Said he was a spy. Boasted about it. Threatened me. Said he had powerful friends who would silence me. After the other things he'd said and the threats he'd made, I believed him.'

He held her chin and turned her face gently towards him. 'Josephine, I'm going to tell you something very, very important. This is so important that both our lives might depend on it. Yours and mine. Do you understand?'

She drew her eyebrows into a frown. 'What could be that important?'

'This. Stanley Murdock *was* a spy. You know that and I know that. You must tell no one. I must tell no one. Otherwise, our lives could be in danger. Do you understand? You must keep this hidden for the rest of your life. Can you do that?'

She spoke so low that he could hardly hear. 'D'you mean

you might be killed if I tell anyone?'

'It's possible.' Ben hoped this would satisfy her.

She smiled a wan smile. 'Then I'll take it to my grave.'

And he believed she would. Something was still niggling at him. He asked, although he thought he already knew the answer. 'There was no trace of your DNA at the scene. How did you manage that?'

'I never even thought about DNA. That place was filthy. I couldn't possibly touch anything there. I always wear latex gloves and a mask and plastic overshoes when I'm doing dirty jobs, even at home. I suppose that helped. I carry some in the car with me in case I need them.'

'And what about the ransom notes? I can't understand why you got him to write them.'

She thought for a moment. 'It was so I could tell him what to do, on my terms. Write what I tell you. He protested but he did it. He put me right with the second one. Who would think of keeping jewellery in an ice bucket? He said it was the last place a thief would look. I thought the police would get involved, and I had to try to stop that, so I delivered the first one. And once I'd sent one it became a way of keeping control. Can you understand that?'

Ben couldn't. He was still trying to puzzle out why she would have put herself in danger by delivering notes to the Murdocks' door, when his phone and the doorbell rang in unison. As he picked up, he said to Chris, 'Hold on, got to get the door.' He heard Chris shout, 'Bugger that. Tell me what's happening,' which he ignored. He opened the door. Katy flung herself at him and burst into tears. Then she punched his bad arm. He flinched but she didn't notice. 'How could you do that to me?' She turned and pointed to Maurice. 'To us? We were sooo scared!'

Maurice shook his head slowly. 'Katy was worried. I thought she'd got it all wrong, stopped her phoning the police. But she ain't, has she.' Josephine was visible, still sitting at the kitchen table. Maurice nodded his head towards the kitchen. 'True then? She did do it?'

'An accident. She didn't mean to kill him. Be gentle with her. She's very fragile.'

But Katy was already on her way to Josephine. She leant

over and hugged the bowed figure. Josephine burst into tears afresh. 'Please don't be kind to me. I can't bear it.'

Katy looked at Josephine and took charge. 'You look exhausted. You need a good sleep. Do you have any sleeping pills?'

Josephine nodded towards her handbag. Katy took out three packs of pills. She held them out to Ben and whispered, 'Diazepam, enough to kill an elephant. You keep them and I'll give her one.' Ben watched as Katy carefully removed one pill and gave it to Josephine with a glass of water. She took her hand and led her to the corridor. They heard her say, 'Show me your bedroom and I'll stay with you till you go to sleep. I'll stroke your hair. Dad used to do that for me. Whenever I was upset, he'd sit with me till I went to sleep. You'll see, it'll help.'

With that, Josephine again dissolved into tears. Ben suspected that no one had ever lulled Josephine to sleep, no loving father to ease her fears. And, having met Agnes Barrett with all her problems, he suspected that she'd never had a loving mother either. He'd thought Josephine was a complicated woman. Now he realised just how complex her personality was. He heard a disembodied voice coming from his phone. 'Ben, what the fuck is happening? Are you OK? Answer me, for fuck's sake?'

He held the phone to his ear. 'Hi Chris. Yes, I'm fine. Yes, I've got the culprit. No, there's no danger to anyone. You can relax. His cover wasn't blown. Understand that? His cover wasn't blown. Stop! I'll answer all your questions tomorrow. Listen, this is what you must do. Meet me at The Friary first thing. Say about eight? You'll need to be able to pay for someone to stay there for a while. Got that? Yeah, you're paying. See you tomorrow.' And he finished the call.

Maurice had obviously been listening. 'You going to tell them at The Friary it's an emergency? Maybe they won't have space? Thought of that?'

'No problem, Mo. I booked a place a few days ago.'

Maurice looked first perplexed, then annoyed, then amused. 'You sly old bugger. You knew this was going to happen, didn't you?'

'To be honest, Mo, I didn't know what she was going to do. But I knew she needed help. Either she was going to try to kill me or herself – or both. I didn't know which.'

'Why, in heaven's name, didn't you tell us. I could've been back-up. Not too old yet, you know.'

'I know. I thought of it. Believe me, I thought about it. But if anything had happened to me, the girls would have needed you so I couldn't put you in danger too.'

'Blimey, what a thought! Would've been hell for all of us. Good God.' Maurice sat down abruptly. 'Lucky it turned out all right then. Don't tell the girls, eh? Katy'll be all right in with her, won't she?'

'Yes. I've promised her she won't go to prison. That was why she killed Stanley. She's got this phobia about being locked in and he threatened her with prison.' He pointed to his phone, still in his hand. 'I'm positive Chris and his lot need to keep this out of court, so I could promise her that much. It will be difficult at first at The Friary. They won't let her wander. But they'll manage her anxieties.'

'You sure you can promise no prison? And this Chris? How come he's paying?'

'Mo, the less you know about Chris the better.'

'Ah, yes. MI summat. Yeah, I don't want to know about them buggers. Had to deal with them once in the Force. They're trouble, you know. You keep away from them, Ben. They ain't nothing but trouble.'

Ben said, 'Let's just say they'll be picking up the tab cos she did them a favour. And, Mo, you can be sure that I'll be keeping my distance.'

Maurice nudged his arm. 'S'like Shipman.'

'What?'

Maurice looked triumphant. 'You know, that doctor, biggest serial killer ever. And who raised the alarm? An undertaker. That's who. Otherwise, he might still be at it.'

'Thank you, Mo. I'm sure that's the only similarity. But just in case, I'd better go and see if Katy's all right.'

Ben quietly opened the door to Josephine's bedroom and tiptoed in. Josephine was on the far side of the big double bed. She was curled up like a small child, fast asleep and breathing deeply. Katy was lying against a bank of pillows on the near side, playing a game on her phone. She put her finger to her lips and motioned Ben to step back into the corridor. She followed quietly and pulled the door to. 'She's fine. I'll stay with her.' Then she poked her father in the chest and hissed at him, 'But you – I'm still sooo cross with you. Why didn't you tell us? You could have been killed.' She stopped and looked at him. She poked him in the chest again and her voice wobbled. 'And you wouldn't even have said goodbye.'

He folded her in his arms and she clung on tightly. He stroked her hair and kissed the top of her head. 'I'm sorry, love, but I couldn't put you or Mo in any danger. And anyway,' he lied, 'I knew it would be all right. I just thought she might try to take her own life.' He kissed her hair again and gently eased her away. 'But how did you know?'

She immediately brightened. 'Oh, that was easy. Obviously, Stanley had been forced to write the notes. He'd used them to put in a message in code. I deciphered it and made Uncle Mo drive me here. He didn't believe me, but he came anyway. Drove like a maniac.'

Ben smiled down at his daughter. 'Katy, you never cease to amaze me. How did you decipher the code?'

She removed three crumpled bits of paper from her pocket. 'See the writing. All joined up. In each note there are three odd letters, not joined when they should be. The ones in the first note spell s o l. The next i c i. See, I got that one first and thought it was French. That put me off for a bit. The last one spells t o r. Once you get the pattern it's easy.'

'Your mother would have been so proud of you.'

Katy looked quizzically at her father. 'Dad, you never talk about Mum. And Sarah and I never liked to ask because it all seemed so painful to you. Can we get together some time and talk about what she was like?'

Ben suddenly realised that all the time he'd been protecting his two girls, they too had been protecting him. 'Of course, my darling. We'll do that soon. I've got a whole photo album. We could start with that.' He looked doubtful for a moment. 'All I've got to do is find it. Now you'd better go back in with Josephine and I'll see you in the morning. Is that OK?'

She nodded and reached up to kiss his cheek. 'I'm so glad

you're my dad. Goodnight.' And she slipped back into the darkness of the bedroom.

* * *

After a disturbed night, where only Josephine had slept well, they drove to The Friary in two cars, leaving the third in the driveway. They arrived at 7.30 to be met outside the main entrance by Dr Clare. 'Early shift?' enquired Ben.

'Oh no. When you described this client's problem, I really wanted to help her so I volunteered to be here to meet you.' She pointed behind her towards the front doors. 'Your colleague is already here. He's explained to us the status of our client. But, with the type of people we deal with here, confidentiality is the watchword anyway. We've dealt with cases like this before – military, etc. – so we know the drill. Funnily enough, he's organised the finances but couldn't remember the name of the client.' She looked sideways at Ben but said no more.

Ben turned to help Josephine out of the car. Although he'd already explained to her what was going to happen, he was none too sure that she'd taken it in. 'Josephine, come and meet Dr Clare. She'll be looking after you.'

Josephine spoke quietly, her voice still weary even after a full night's sleep. 'I remember. You told me. I'm to be looked after until I'm well again.' She turned to Dr Clare. 'Thank you. I need a rest, a long rest. I've had a difficult time recently.'

They entered the lobby and Chris leapt out of a very low chair and came to greet them. Ben told Chris that he would be of most use if he went back to Hunstanton with Maurice to collect the car that they'd left there. To Ben's surprise, Chris didn't demur. Maurice and Katy gave Josephine a hug and wished her a speedy recovery. Ben smiled inwardly. It could have been a scene from any posh hospital where someone was being admitted for a minor op. As they waved, they called that they'd come to see her soon.

Ben and Josephine were ushered into a small room and offered coffee. Ben took it as a good sign that Josephine asked whether it was possible to have green tea. While the coffee and tea were on their way, Dr Clare took some details and outlined the process of diagnosis and treatment. She suggested that she and Ben should talk separately and would that be all right with Josephine. Josephine nodded. When it came to saying goodbye Josephine said in a voice stronger than he had heard since her attempted suicide. 'Just say goodbye. Don't touch me. Just say goodbye and go.'

Chapter 32

Ben and Chris sat with pints in front of them in a quiet corner of the Regal. Chris was adamant. 'I'm going to have to talk to her.'

'All I'm saying is, not yet. Stanley told her nothing about Northern Ireland. It's not what she was interested in. She thought he was her father. Then he came on to her and tried to drug her. Think about it. You believe you've found your long-lost father and he tries to date-rape you? How would you feel?' Ben raised his hands. 'Don't answer that!' But he left a short space for Chris to accommodate the prospect. 'She kept her cool at first, switched drinks. Then she panicked. She honestly didn't know that he'd die quickly if she didn't give him water. And she's not robust mentally. Plus, she's in shock so I don't think the people at The Friary will let you see her.'

'Hah! Too bloody clever, you are. That's more or less what they said.'

Ben wondered if this young man had an ounce of sensitivity in his soul and decided that he hadn't. 'Anyway, do you want me to tell you what I've found out? And how I came to catch your killer for you?' Ben held his empty glass aloft. 'Your round again, I think.'

Chris laughed as he eased himself out of his seat. 'You've become a pushy git all of a sudden.' He added in a low whisper, 'But seriously, thanks, mate. We owe you. You got the Service out of deep shit. You won't know how deep. But we need to know what he said to her.' He pointed to Ben's glass. 'Same again?'

As he waited, Ben rehearsed once more what he was going to tell Chris and what he definitely was not. It needed to be enough to satisfy him and his bosses without opening avenues that should remain closed.

When Chris came back with two more pints, Ben said, 'A few questions and then we need to talk about Michael.'

'Fire away.'

'What I don't understand is why you involved Dobson. Did

you think he could persuade me any better than you could? Cos if you did, you were so wrong.' He could see Chris shaking his head so he added, 'So, why not come straight to me?'

'Easy one, that. Don't take this wrong but I was pretty sure I'd be able to get your conscience on board. But I need people like Dobson. See, he thinks he tipped the balance and that makes him feel good. Costs me nothing except a bit of arse-licking.'

That seemed plausible to Ben. He could see that Chris would use people's weaknesses for his own ends. He shuddered inwardly. In his youth, espionage had been his game but he was definitely no longer part of it – nor did he want to be. But before he left it behind, he had to get what he wanted from it. 'OK, now to Michael. What can you do for him?'

Chris cleared his throat. 'We knew Stanley was the guilty one.' Chris looked sheepish. 'But we had to protect Stanley.' He held up his hand to stop Ben's repost. 'We can help Michael. We can doctor his records to add the suspicion that he was innocent. This will cast doubt on any paramilitary connection as well. No one will want to revisit this, so it'll make him very low level for surveillance.' Chris made a note on his phone. 'That'll be done and if Michael doesn't break the law, and – this is important – doesn't rock any of our boats, he's as good as a free man. Can't do better than that.'

Ben looked disgusted. 'And I suppose Stanley thought he could abduct and rape Josephine and "be protected". How much can these people get away with?'

Chris held up his hands in a gesture of surrender. 'Cards on table. Stanley had become a nightmare. He was stepping way out of line. We had orders from on high. Stanley Murdock was to be kept happy. She did us a favour, you know. And for that, I'll make sure she's looked after. I've put it though in a devious way so the Service will help her without them ever knowing what they're paying for.'

Ben was beginning to see a fuller picture of Stanley's life. He pointed an accusing finger at Chris. 'He'd done it before, hadn't he? How many other women has he raped?'

Chris put a hand on Ben's arm. 'Look, Ben. We kept him in check as best we could. But he knew too much. Big stuff. And he was clever. We didn't know what he'd spill and where. That's why I told you to bury all his papers. Bigwigs said, better in the ground than anywhere else. As for his sexual appetite, we had to accommodate him; keep him on-side. We made sure he got prostitutes and we made sure they were all right.'

Ben could stomach no more. He moved on. 'And Michael? He'll inherit the violin?'

'No probs. It's his. We've put it all in the hands of a tame solicitor.' He grinned. 'Thought of raiding the offices of Marriott, Henson and Finlay but decided it was a bit OTT. A quiet word about suspicion of money laundering got us all Stanley's papers. Another word about possible complicity got us Marriott's agreement to confidentiality. We left him to tell the staff that Josephine has suffered a breakdown and is in good hands but is not to be contacted. Now tell me what I need to know.'

'OK. Let's get the Murdocks out of the way first. They know nothing.' He pointed towards Chris. 'You any idea why they left Ulster so abruptly?'

'Yeah. We knew our Stanley was into something on his own account. Couldn't trust him over there. Had to bring him back.'

Ben took a deep breath. He was moving on to very sensitive territory – sensitive for him – and painful. 'It was the Barracks bombing, wasn't it?' And he pointed to the scar on his temple.

Chris looked perplexed. 'What? Say again?'

'Stanley was involved in the bomb that killed my wife. Dobson told me.'

'Ah, Shit! That bastard is so twisted one day he'll fuck himself.' Chris looked round after his outburst but no one was in earshot. 'Listen. Dobson lied to you. He lied.' Chris paused for a moment while Ben digested this information. Then he continued, 'Stanley Murdock was a dirty bastard but we know who set that bomb, and it wasn't him. Dobson must've thought you needed an incentive to help us. So he gave you one.'

This abrupt change in his understanding stopped Ben in his tracks. He sat in silence for a moment then said quietly but with fierce intensity, 'You know who planted that bomb? Who are they? Where are they? Give me names.'

'Hang on, Ben. They're all dead. Fell out and killed each

other. Internecine war. We didn't have to do a thing.' He looked almost sympathetic. 'So, perhaps you can put a lid on that one now.'

'No. I need answers. You're telling me it wasn't Stanley. Tell me why I should believe you.'

'Hell, it's me or Dobson. Which one do you believe? Think of it. You know Dobson. Would you trust him?'

Ben's world was re-orienting again. He took a sip of beer to give himself time to think. Then he peered into his glass for a long time. If Chris was to be believed, then the terrorists who had changed his life for ever were dead. He realised that Chris had been waiting patiently for him to assimilate all this.

Ben took a deep breath. 'I want names. Then I can let it rest.'

'Sorry, no can do.'

Ben looked straight into Chris's eyes. 'You owe me big time. I need this. Do you understand?'

'OK. I can give you something. But if it gets out, I'll be in big trouble. This is all I'm going to say. Find out which of the Shankill butchers didn't die in their beds. Then you'll have your bombers. Now I've told you more than I should. So what else have you got for me?'

'Hang on! They're Protestant.'

'Yep... funny old world, ain't it?'

Ben couldn't see anything funny but, looking at Chris's closed face, he knew that this was all he was going to get. It might be just enough to give him closure – if he could summon up enough belief in the Services to trust Chris. 'Back to the Murdocks. I'm sure that they have no idea about their father's double life. They know he was in some sort of murky business in Belfast, criminal, paramilitary. That sort of thing. He didn't want them to ask questions and he made sure they didn't.

'Now, Josephine. I'm sure she's Stanley's daughter and that she knows nothing of Stanley's Service connection. To cut a long story short, I went to see a retired College head porter who told me Josephine's mother had been gang raped by four young men led by Murdock. You knew about that, I suppose?'

'Bloody hell, no. That never came up in his vetting.'

'If you didn't know about it, then it seems he started "being protected" long before your lot got their hands on him.' Ben looked at Chris and grimaced. 'No-one was ever charged with the assault, the girl was pregnant, she was paid off and Josephine was the result. Josephine's mother never told her anything about her father. For one thing, she didn't know which one it was. Could've been any of them. That's when I asked you to find out about their deaths.'

'Christ Almighty. I wondered about that. What a haul.' Chris counted on his fingers, 'One Cabinet Minister, one Senior Civil Servant and one merchant wanker. Who'd have thought it?' He laughed, then looked across at Ben's disapproving expression.

'Now, here's a question for you. Was her DNA taken to eliminate her from enquiries?'

Chris grinned. 'You'd think so, wouldn't you? But no, Turnbull seems to have overlooked her. Mind you, everyone thought she hadn't seen Stanley for six weeks, so I suppose it's not a hanging offence.'

'Have you got a sample from her now?'

Chris laughed a long, hearty laugh, took a draught of his beer, then looked round to make sure he hadn't raised any interest. 'Isn't DNA a blast? Yeah, we got one from her office when we cleared it. Hairbrush. She matched. Stanley was her father.' Chris looked round again and lowered his voice still further. Ben had to lean in to hear him. 'But this is the real blast. The only other match was Lucien! The other two were, let's say, misbegotten. By the same father.' He grinned. 'While the cat's away in Belfast! Stanley's quiet wife wasn't so downtrodden after all. No one will find out, of course. The samples'll be destroyed and no one will ever know.'

'Good God. So Margaret got one over on Stanley?'

'Two over.'

'What about Josephine and the two Murdocks? Will they be told?'

Chris was dismissive. 'Nah. Don't think it will do them any good. Best leave well alone. Sleeping dogs, eh?'

Ben suspected that it wasn't Josephine, or Virginia and Alistair, that Chris was protecting but the Service. Sleeping dogs would suit them just fine.

Chris continued, 'And that's not the end of it. There's another oddity. Michael Murdock says he's Stanley's brother's son, right? Well, he ain't. Not a blood relative anyway. Best we keep quiet about that one too.' Ben didn't have time to assimilate this disclosure as Chris leaned towards him. 'You were close to her. How d'you feel about her now?'

'Me? I feel achingly sorry for her. She'd already killed someone by the time I met her. I know she used me to get close to the investigation and I truly don't know if she had any feelings for me at all. Anyway, water under the bridge. Look, Chris, I'm very grateful that there are people like you working to keep us safe, but I'm not like you. So, if there's nothing else, I've got a family to feed and a couple of funerals to arrange.'

'No. Well. Thanks. My boss says to thank you. She's mightily impressed. And we think there is something in you that is just like us. The offer's still on the table to join us full-time.' He added wistfully, 'Any chance?'

It took Ben only a second to feel again the immense relief that he wouldn't have to lie any more. He grinned widely and said, 'Join you? No chance!'

But Chris wasn't about to give up completely. 'Well, if you ever change your mind, just email me. The phone number's dead after we wind up this op. Tell me 'Rosemary wants to talk', and I'll get straight back to you.'

* * *

Ben walked out of the Regal with a light tread. He strode out into the sunshine, meaning to turn right and head for home but found that his feet were directing him left towards Ethel's. He decided not to stop them. He darted across the road weaving in and out of the phalanx of cyclists careening down St Andrew's Street. He needed to have it out with Dobson now. For some reason that he couldn't fathom, he'd believed Dobson. Maybe it was because he still hadn't appreciated quite how devious that man could be. In the cold light of day, that degree of trust seemed ludicrous. He needed satisfaction, retribution. He needed something but he didn't know what. He arrived at St Etheldreda's and marched under the archway ignoring the porters lodge with its signing-in book. Traffic noise had dimmed to a bumble-bee buzz. Exotic ducks waddled across the grass. Tourists exclaimed over the Wren chapel and took photos of themselves, the ducks, the yellow stonework. The sun was at that oblique angle that softened the colours to yellow-orange. For a moment, Ben was captivated. He sighed and turned towards Dobson's staircase.

He took the stairs three at a time and marched into Dobson's outer office. Before his secretary could utter a word, he had crossed the room and flung open the door. With Mrs Jones close behind, Ben marched into the inner sanctum. A look of alarm crossed Dobson's face. It was quickly replaced by that obsequious smile. He gestured to a chair. 'Welcome, Benedict. What an unexpected pleasure. Do have a seat. A glass of sherry, perhaps? Mrs Jones, there is no problem. You may return to your desk.'

Ben laughed. It was a laugh without a hint of irony, a laugh of pure joy. He looked at Dobson and decided that this man was not worth any outpouring of emotion. As Mrs Jones quietly closed the door behind her, Ben spoke. 'You lying toe-rag. I thank all the deities in the firmament that I am not like you. And I'll make sure that we never meet again.'

He turned on his heel and was about to leave when Dobson responded. The words brought Ben to an abrupt halt. 'Benedict, please. I didn't lie. I need his killer to be found because I know I'll be next. You were my only hope.' Dobson stopped speaking until Ben was motionless then continued, 'I'm sorry. I hope you can forgive me.'

Ben turned to see Dobson diminished. He looked small and old. His usual proud back was hunched. The lines on his face had turned into ravines and there was supplication in his eyes.

Ben looked again at his erstwhile professor and realised that, besides a thorough dislike of this man, the undergraduate Ben had also been in awe of him. That sense of awe was now replaced by loathing and a need to escape his presence. Ben turned away with the words, 'Forgive you? No. Whether you lied or not, you had no thought for anyone but your loathsome self. You don't deserve forgiveness.' As he reached the door, he heard muffled footsteps retreating beyond. He opened the door to see Mrs Jones sliding behind her desk. He grinned at her and in return she held up her thumb and said in a low voice. 'Good for you! I've been waiting years for someone to stand up to him. Thank you.'

Ben walked home slowly, relieved that he had attacked Dobson verbally and not physically. He began practising what he would have to say in order to gain a second meeting with Agnes Barrett. He had promised Dr Clare that he would try to get Agnes to talk to her. And, for his part, he knew that Agnes deserved to know what had happened, or at least some of it. He phoned her as soon as he got home and, yes, she would see him. To his surprise, she sounded eager.

* * *

He followed the same route to Cherry Hinton but this time it brought back no memories. As he rounded the last corner, he could see Agnes standing at her threshold, waiting for him. He parked the car and walked back to her. She chided him, 'You took your time.'

Her next words astounded him for he had not given her any reason for his visit. 'Is she all right?' At his look of incomprehension she repeated, 'Is she all right? Josephine?'

He replied immediately, 'She's in hospital. She's in good hands. She's not in any danger.'

'Oh, thank God, thank God. I was so worried. Come in, come in off the doorstep. I'll make you some tea.'

He followed her into the kitchen wondering how she had known that anything was amiss. 'Mrs Barrett, she's in a clinic for people with mental issues. I'm afraid she's had a sort of a breakdown.'

Her next answer also surprised him. 'Of course she has. I wondered when it would come. But she's not hurt herself?'

'No, she's not hurt herself.'

'Thank God.' She took her rosary from her pocket and kissed the crucifix. 'I'll get us some tea and then you can tell me the whole story.'

Ben watched as she busied herself in the small kitchen, 'Can I ask you something? Something that's been bothering me.'

'Ask away. It's time.'

'Did she know how she was conceived? Did you ever tell her about the rape?'

'Never. I couldn't tell her the truth and I wouldn't tell her lies. So I didn't tell her anything. Maybe that was my mistake. I don't know.' She put all the tea things on a tray and handed it to him. 'Take this into the front room.'

The front room looked much bigger than on his last visit. Every bit of clutter had been cleared away. There were still statues and holy pictures in abundance, but the shelves and surfaces were clear. He could put down the tea tray and sit in the chair without hindrance. Agnes smiled. 'Cleared up after your visit. Knew it was time. Once you start to rake over old coals, sure, the ashes start flying.'

He looked at the grate which had no coals and no ashes, just a small gas fire. He said, 'It's serious. She didn't hurt herself but...' he paused, looking for the right words. 'It's complicated. Do you want me to tell you what happened?'

'Don't think you have to spare my feelings. I've been waiting for years for that knock on the door. Tell me what happened.'

He sat back and put down his cup. 'She met Stanley Murdock.' At Agnes's gasp, he paused. He waited while Agnes, with shaking hands, put down her cup. Then he continued. 'He became her client. She saw that he had one long little finger just like hers and she decided that he was her father. I don't believe that she ever knew about the circumstances of her conception. No one at the College would have told her and I know that she never went to see Mr Fisher.'

Agnes looked to be about to speak but Ben held up his hand. 'There's more, I'm afraid.' Agnes nodded, and he continued, 'Stanley Murdock tried to drug her. He was going to rape her. So she killed him. I'm so sorry to have to tell you this.'

Agnes looked aghast, then angry, then a look of supreme sadness settled on her features. 'The poor girl. The poor, poor wee girl.' Her expression changed and she looked at Ben with a challenge in her eyes. 'But I'm proud of her. She did what I should have done all those years ago. That shock you?'

'No, but I have no idea what an attack like that would do to me. I don't know how I'd react.'

Agnes suddenly looked tired. 'How is she now? Oh, dear God, will there be a trial? Will they let me see her?'

'You can rest easy, there certainly will not be a trial. That we can be sure of. Whether you'll be able to see her... I don't know. But she's in good hands.' This was now getting to be even more delicate. 'When I came to see you before, you told me she was dead, and she told me you were dead. Have you thought that she might not want to see you?'

'We parted because of that divil. Maybe he'll bring us back together.'

'Can you tell me?'

'She was always asking after him. I thought it would get better when she got older, but it got worse. She wouldn't let it go. On and on and on. In the end I got so angry, I said I was never going to tell her and she'd just have to live with it. She packed her bags and left and she's never been back since.'

'But you've heard from her?'

'Not a word.'

'Then how did you know she was in trouble?'

Agnes took sip of her tea then carefully replaced her cup in the saucer. 'It's like this. Every day, I go to work. I get the bus and go in early, so I can sit on a bench on Parker's Piece. I watch her walk from her flat to her work. I always sit in a different place so she won't notice me. And she never has.' She paused for a moment. 'Or if she has, she's ignored me.'

She sighed, 'If the weather's not too bad I go back at lunchtime. I take my sandwiches and a flask if it's cold. I see her nearly every day. It eases me to see her. And she was looking so well.' Agnes smoothed her skirt, then continued, 'A few weeks ago, things changed. I know she had a holiday in May. She has a few holidays every year. I know that from my watching. After that last holiday she started to look sort of strained, troubled. As the days went on, I could see she'd lost weight. It was too quick. A mother sees these things. Then, she wasn't there on Friday and she wasn't there today and I knew something had happened.' She paused, as if trying to find the right words. 'She's always had problems.' She pointed to her head. 'Up there.' She got out her rosary beads and rolled them between her fingers. 'I didn't help – I know that now. But I didn't know any better.' Agnes wiped away a tear with the back of her hand – the first Ben had seen from her. She took out her handkerchief, wiped her eyes and blew her nose.

Ben asked quietly, 'Couldn't you have got help? I'm sure the Social Services would have helped you.'

Agnes sniffed and sat up straight in her chair. She looked Ben in the eye. 'Tsk. Why would I want to involve them? They'd only have wanted to take her away from me. I didn't ask for any help and none was given.'

He said gently, 'You can help her now. Do you think you could tell her doctor what you've told me? And more, if you can.'

Agnes brushed down her skirt again. She looked straight at Ben. 'Of course I will. I'll do anything. Anything at all. You see, I love her so very much.'

* * *

Later that day, Ben whistled as he worked. He was alone in the house and was relishing the peace. He was trying a new recipe and had invited all the family to come and share it. His visit to Agnes had been more successful than he could have hoped. He'd organised to drive her to The Friary to see Dr Clare and afterwards to take her to tea with Mr Fisher. He'd told her that he would take her to The Friary whenever she wanted to go. He'd reassured her again that Josephine was in a safe environment – and hoped it was so. He didn't add that he thought she was in as safe a place as she could be in the circumstances.

There were still some loose ends. Most urgent was what to tell Sarah. He wanted to move as far as possible from the deceits of the last few weeks, but some things would have to be kept secret. Tonight they would discuss it. Sarah must be told what Katy knew and no more. So Katy should tell her. She'd like that. He and Maurice could keep their counsel on the 'Chris' side of things. He'd have to find out if Maurice really did want to retire. And try to persuade him not to. He would be so bored playing bowls. Perhaps he could be persuaded to join a dance class and find a lady to jive with. And he could be given the job of helping to induct both Katy and Michael. That should keep him busy, and happy. Ben knew he'd been neglecting his studies and his assignment was overdue. He'd never missed a deadline and had had the foresight to ask for an extension. It was due next week, and he hadn't even started it. The motivations of prisoners. What was he going to write? He had no idea.

At some point he would have to extricate himself from Josephine's life. He didn't want to precipitate another crisis so he'd ask Dr Clare. And he'd be going to see Dr Clare on his own account. He could tell her that he thought he'd reached a turning point and was beginning to grieve for his wife. He'd tell her what Alistair's counsellor had said about ghosts only staying if you feed them and that he needed help to stop feeding his. He'd tell her that he wanted to start her new therapy.

Then, there was the little matter of the illicit papers he'd kept that should have been buried with Stanley: the blackmail list, the threatening note and the mysterious key. What to do with those?

The doorbell rang and he called up the stairs for Katy to come down. As soon as Sarah was through the front door, he broached the subject that needed airing. 'Sarah, we've got some things that we need to tell you, but you must promise that you won't tell another living soul.'

Before he could go any further, Sarah butted in, 'Oh, I know. Kate told me this afternoon.' She turned to her sister, 'Hi, Kate.' Then she continued, 'And I promised I wouldn't breathe a word, didn't I?' Katy nodded but Sarah didn't see because she was looking at her father. She continued, 'Bloody Hell – sorry, Dad – no swearing, I know. But he tried to date-rape his own daughter! Bloody Nora! What a … I can't think of a word bad enough.' She pointed a thumb towards Katy, 'We think that evil bugger deserved it and she definitely shouldn't be dobbed in.'

He looked reprovingly at his younger daughter and Katy had the grace to look just a little ashamed. 'Sorry Dad. I bumped into Sarah in town and I just couldn't leave her out of it. And she has promised that she won't even tell Pam. But, if you tell her she can, she knows Pam will keep the secret too.'

'I think, perhaps, it's best not to. The fewer people who know the better.'

The two girls nodded sagely. Then Katy added, 'I told her how I worked out the code in the ransom notes. She was well impressed. And I told her how you worked it out from the ink and the long fingers. She thinks we're both magnif.' She turned to her sister. 'That's right, isn't it?' Katy didn't wait for an answer. 'But I didn't tell her about Mum. Not until you were here too.' Before Ben could respond, she said, 'This is the worst bit of all. He planted the bomb that killed Mum. So that's the best reason for him to be dead.'

Sarah's face contorted. Tears welled in her eyes and slipped down her cheeks. She wiped them away with her sleeve, leaving a trail of mascara on her face and sleeve. After a pause, she hissed, 'That fucking bastard! Well, that's the best reason ever to look after his killer.' She turned and gave her father a faltering smile. 'Dad, you OK? We know it's hard for you to think about Mum.'

He had to decide whether or not to put his daughters straight. He was sure that Stanley Murdock had participated in bombings and maimings – and Dobson had told him the Murdock was involved that that particular bombing – but Chris had told him it was not Stanley's work. He wasn't sure he trusted either of them. Easier for the girls, he thought, if they could close it off now, so he would keep Chris's rebuttal to himself. Instead, he said, 'Yeah, I'm OK. I've found those photo albums – the pictures of your mum. We could look at them together after dinner.'

At that moment, the doorbell rang. 'That'll be Mo. Katy, can you let him in? He can tell you lots of stories about your mother.'

Katy was dismissive. 'Oh, he's already told us loads. Since we were little. We want to hear them from you.'

'Of course you do,' said Ben.

Addendum
Josephine's diary

24th May 2012
So that's it. He's dead. His end was gentle, quiet – peaceful even. He just stopped breathing, slipped away. Nothing more. He bowed his head and he was gone.

How could I have let that happen? Dear God, no. He didn't deserve to go like that. That was so wrong. He should have died with ear-splitting yells. He should have left this earth screaming for mercy, squealing like the pig he was. He should have suffered to his very last breath, full of remorse for the things he'd done. Then justice would have been done.

In the beginning, when he could talk, he asked me to let him go – tried to bargain with me. But he was always defiant, always controlled; his training, I suppose. Early on, he told me about his training. He never pleaded, never cried out. And even when he couldn't speak, I could see in his eyes that there was no remorse.

I misjudged it. I should have given him water. And now he's dead. It's finished. And what of tomorrow and tomorrow and tomorrow? Now, maybe, I can begin to live.

6th June 2012
Was he my father? I think so. But maybe not. Whichever – I know he wasn't my <u>real</u> father.

Patricide, parricide? Which is correct? Not to worry – both work for me. Whichever one you choose, I did it. I killed him. Who would kill their father? Me, of course, and Oedipus. Lizzie Borden did it and got away with it. Richard Dadd was mad so he doesn't count. Bamber did it for money. I'm not like any of them. My motive? Sweet revenge. And they're right. It is best served cold.

Did I do it for me or was it for her? She suffered. I know she did. Never uttered a word against him. I did it for me; for the times he looked through me as if I wasn't there. I made him suffer. Like he made us suffer. He would have got away with it all, but I got him. I made him pay.

Friday 8th June 2012

Control – his life was all about control. But in the end I controlled him. In that last week he couldn't sleep, couldn't move without permission. That felt good.

I made him write those notes. I dictated every word. When he tried to write something different, I made him start again. He soon learned who was in charge. But he was defiant – I'll give him that.

I was full of rage. That one last thing tipped me over the edge. Why did he have to say that? If only – but what's the point of 'if only'? As the hate dissipates, what's left? A vacuum – I feel empty, sucked dry. I continue my life, but I live like an automaton. No-one seems to notice that I'm a different person. It's all a charade. Maybe one day normal life will return.

Wednesday 13th June 2012
He's gone. The earth has swallowed him. Dust to dust – and all that. Everyone wanting to see the back of him. I've done them all a good turn!

And Ben was perfect. Wish I'd had a strong man to comfort me all those years. I suppose I did have my <u>real</u> father – but that doesn't count. Just got to keep my nerve – keep strong. Just like my <u>real</u> father would want. Got to make him proud.

Friday 29th June 2012
It's getting so difficult – trying to hide my true self. He has such a gentle manner. So quiet and reassuring. Just the sort of father any child would want. Why couldn't I have had a father like that? I suppose it's because of the job he's in, he has to have empathy, dealing with grief all day, every day. He cares – he really cares about people.

He doesn't say much but you get the feeling that you can rely on him. A port in the storm – a stalwart. Is that the right word? If I'd had a stalwart behind me, someone to love me, maybe I wouldn't have done what I did.

When this is all over, when I move away, I can start a new life. I'll start afresh. Maybe, if I'm lucky, I'll even find someone to share my world. Someone like Ben. Someone like my <u>real</u> father.

He deserved to die. Oh yes, he deserved it. But a steadying influence, someone who cared for me, might just have made the difference between human retribution and waiting for the divine.

Too late now – it's done. I've just got to make sure I'm never found out.

9ᵗʰ July 2012
I thought I'd be free of him when he was dead. But he won't go away. His face keeps coming back. Laughing, always laughing. Looking at me as I pass by shop windows, behind me in the bathroom mirror. I turn round and he's not there. I was sure it would all be better when he'd gone but it's worse. Far, far worse.

I can't sleep. I mustn't go to sleep in case he's there – waiting. Now I'm not sure I'll ever be free. My world's beginning to disintegrate. I dread the knock at the door and I open it to see two big policemen waiting to arrest me. I made three mistakes today. I never make mistakes. I must regain control. And yet nobody notices – how can they not see what I have become?

Wednesday 11ᵗʰ July 2012
I don't know what to do. He won't talk to me. I talk to him and he doesn't answer. I ask him questions and he is silent. Maybe he's jealous. That's it – he's getting his own back because I know I need someone else in my life.

Do I have to choose? That would be so hard because I've been with him for so long. And do I know that he'll come back? He might think I'll leave him again. What can I do? My <u>real</u> father is ignoring me.

Friday 13ᵗʰ July 2012
My last ever diary entry. I'll have to tell you. Because I can't live with the lie. And anyway, I know you suspect – that's why you asked about the ink. You're a good man – an honest man. You'll have to turn me in. What a weight to put on you. But we can't go on. You've already lied for me to that policewoman. All that talk about a London gang when you already knew it was me. That is my worst crime – turning such an honest man into a liar. You're such a gentle person, too good – too good for me anyway. In my heart, I know

you'll eventually have to choose duty and honesty over lies –
because you're truthful and honourable. And I know it will break
your heart. Mine too.

I've been in a courtroom before. I know what the verdict will
be. I can't put you through that and I can't go to prison.

My brain keeps telling me what I must do. I haven't the
strength left to fight it. I've talked to my real *father and he was very*
stern – he's never been like that before. He says it has to be him or
you. It's an impossible choice so, I'm taking the only way out I can
think of. I thought of just killing myself but that won't solve the
problem for you. So I'm going to have to kill you first.

I can't think of any other way. It will punish me and save
you from losing another love. You've been through it once – I can't
make you go through that again. I'll have to be brave. The only
courageous thing I've done in my life was to kill that man. I'm not
sorry for that. Just for all the hurt I've caused to you – the man who
loves me.

You can't imagine how I cherish those five words. The Man
Who Loves Me.

I love you. Forgive me, please.

Monday 16th July 2012
They told me I should continue my diary; it will help with my
recovery. But I'll show it to no-one – especially not Dr Clare. I
swear she can already see into my soul.

I saw a priest yesterday, made my confession. Bless me
Father for I have sinned – not the father I've been talking to – not
my real *father.*

He asked about my real *father. I told him it started and*
ended with him. He was always there just because he wasn't. He
was everywhere because he was nowhere. My mother never
mentioned him and when I did, she'd shut down. I used to wish she'd
react, hit me or something. But she just retreated from me, back into
her shell. When I wouldn't stop she'd lock me in the cupboard under
the stairs. I'd scream and scream. She stopped when the neighbours
complained. So then, I decided for myself how he would be. I was
certain that he was out there somewhere, just waiting to make
himself known to me.

Then I met Stanley and I knew he was my father. I just knew. He was tall and handsome. He had a family and he had the long little finger. But I didn't take it on trust. I investigated his past and found that he was at St Etheldreda's when my mother was a bedder there. So I knew he was my father but came to realise that he wasn't my real *father. He was an evil man and he was killing my* real *father.*

At first I didn't mean for him to die. I just wanted to hurt him like he'd hurt me; to make him feel abandoned. I listened to him for six days and every day I hated him just that little bit more. He'd done despicable things. He deserved to die.

He said he was going make sure I went to prison. I couldn't allow that. And then he lied to me. He said he'd make sure I went free. He said, "I'll look after you. Keep you safe. Tell everyone that you're my daughter. Now will you let me go?" So then, I couldn't, could I? He couldn't be my real *father because he was lying to me. My real father is honest so, if he was lying, he couldn't be my* real *father – that proved it.*

I wanted to make him feel neglected like he'd neglected us, so I didn't give him food or water. How could I know he'd go so quickly? It took just seven days – a week of my life to end his. Did I want him to die? Yes. Do I regret that he died. No – because killing him rescued my real *father.*

It was only after he died that my life began to fall apart. If only I'd met Ben first – but I couldn't, could I? I met him because that man was dead. I needed to make sure I wasn't found out. I used him. I had to get Stanley buried and forgotten; to get it all done and dusted and move on with my life.

Then came disaster. For the first time in my miserable existence I found someone to love, someone who loved me. Ben is all the things I want in a man: he's tall and handsome and kind and honest and reliable. His daughters adore him – why wouldn't they?

I tried to jump off that cliff because I needed to atone for my wickedness – for hurting those two good men. My real *father and Ben. I don't know if I'll try again. I get these thoughts coming into my brain and I have to fight against them.*

I hurt him. I destroyed him. And for that I will never forgive myself. I compromised his sense of duty – his honesty. I destroyed

213

what I admired and loved in him. That was my crime. I killed to save my <u>real</u> father and in doing that I destroyed the only other man I've ever loved.

Ben's love was the best and worst thing that ever happened to me. I'd do anything to return him to the way he was. I just hope he can forgive me and that my <u>real</u> Ben will recover. I need to be punished. My act of contrition will be that I'll never see him again. That will be so very hard. But I'll have the memory of him to cherish. He will always be The Man Who Loved Me.

Book 2 - Bury the Lies

He removes evidence from a murder scene. He has people he needs to protect. When he is targeted and his family threatened, he decides to become the bait to catch the killer.

November 2012

Ben Burton receives an anguished message from Professor Dobson at St Etheldreda's College. He discovers Dobson's body in his ransacked rooms. Ben believes that Dobson was a blackmailer and removes a list of names. Then he calls the police.

DCI Vin Wainright and her team arrive. Ben is sleeping with Vin and she is his alibi for the time of the murder. He has not told her that he and Dobson both worked for MI5. He contacts Chris, his handler. Chris organises for Ben's firm to bury Dobson as cover for investigating his death.

Ben's world is rocked when he finds clues about his wife's death among Dobson's effects.

Then a nun is murdered…

Book 3 - Bury the Past

Only by returning to Northern Ireland and finding the truth about his wife's death can he gain peace of mind. But, in finding his own peace, he uncovers a plot which could destroy the fragile peace in Northern Ireland.

February 2013

Ben Burton is recovering from a complete breakdown caused by finding evidence of his wife's double life. He discovers an old photo from their time in Northern Ireland but can't remember who took it. He finds a coded message. 'Find Moira then find Kevin's cousin. You'll know him when you see him.' He sets out to crack the code.

He uncovers evidence that Stanley Murdock and Jeremiah Knatchbull, a mid-ranking MI5 officer led a plot to commit genocide in Northern Ireland and that plot is still ongoing. Knatchbull has now risen to second tier MI5.

Ben must seek him out and outwit this powerful adversary …

Printed in Great Britain
by Amazon

16222740R00123